SPINES

Printed in the United States of America

First Printing, 2018

Published by ZoomDoom Stories
ISBN-13: 978-0692156353
ISBN-10: 0692156356

www.SpinesPodcast.com

SPINES

JAMIE KILLEN

Chapter 1
Grove, Mosaic, Trumpet

Grove. Mosaic. Trumpet. If you recognize that combination of words, these messages are for you. And if those words stop you dead and make you look around for a place to hide, I think that means you're on my side. If those three words just make you feel confused, on the other hand, it means you're lucky enough not to be a part of this. In that case, I'd recommend not listening any further. It's gonna get a little rough from here on out.

Two months ago I woke up in an attic, terrified and covered in blood and with very few memories of my life before that day. But, as soon as I woke up, I knew those three words were important. If you recognized them, you might be able to help me fill in some of the blanks.

And if you're that extra-special person I'm talking to, you know who you are. I'd really like to hear from you.

I found Carson today. Carson. The first of eight names on my list, the eight people from the attic whose names I remember. Carson, Aisha, Claire, Jose, Bilal, Natalie, Lexi, Sage. That doesn't include you, the one whose name I don't remember.

I hadn't really planned on looking for Carson first, but once I found the street art it just seemed to make sense. I was walking down a street with lots of bars and clubs, lots of college kids making out and getting in fights and throwing up in alleys. *Did I do those things back when I was in college?*

I was wondering. Did I even go to college? Maybe you know the answer to that one, extra special guy whose name I don't remember. Maybe that's where we met.

I was still pondering that one when I found the street art. It stood on the sidewalk next to the streetcar stop. On one side of the stop was some fancy wrought-iron trashcan. And on the other side of the stop was the art, or the sculpture, or whatever Carson would call it.

Imagine a tree. Not a realistic one, but a jagged, impressionistic metal sculpture in the shape of a tree. It's maybe ten or twelve feet tall, the trunk six inches in diameter, the branches spindly and leafless. Now imagine that, instead of being a rusty brown or a shiny painted color, the surface of the tree is the light pinkish beige of pale skin. Got it? Ok, now imagine touching the sculpture. It should be about the same temperature as the night air. And it should be the rigid texture of iron or plastic or maybe ceramic. What it shouldn't do is breath. It shouldn't feel soft and yielding and warm to the touch. It shouldn't sweat, or have pores or body hair.

But, of course, this one does. And that's when I know it has to be Carson.

Hang on, back up. I said before I have a list of names. But I don't know if that's really accurate. There isn't a piece of paper in my back pocket. I don't have the names written down anywhere. I don't need to. I've had them in my head ever since that day in the attic. I've never been in danger of losing them, not one. So, not so much a list as a chorus.

Remember the day in the attic, mystery guy? Sometimes I wonder if that's why I can't find you, or why you can't find me. I wonder if maybe your psyche had a different breaking point than mine, if maybe you blocked out different things than I did. Maybe you don't have the same chorus I do, or maybe you have more. Maybe you know more about them than I do. Maybe you remember more than just some names and hobbies and anecdotes and food preferences. Maybe you remember my name, even though I can't remember yours.

But, for whatever reason, I did remember Carson's name, and seeing that sculpture on the street made me remember a couple other things about him. Enough to look for more of his work.

Thing is, when I found this sculpture, and when I found the other things later, there were people all over the place. Those college kids I told you about, and people going in and out of a tattoo parlor, and the people eating out on the balcony of the restaurant across the street. So many of them must have looked right at Carson's work and then turned away. Maybe they just assumed it was another pretentious street sculpture, maybe something made out of foam rubber. Or maybe they suspected what it was and couldn't let themselves think about that any longer. I don't know. It's becoming pretty clear that I don't think much like other people. But then, how could I, given what I've been through?

I found three more of Carson's pieces that night, all in the downtown area. One was disguised as a decorative archway leading into a beer garden. Like the tree, that one was warm and pulsing with blood, but unlike the tree it also had long bones jutting out and forming sharp corners. It shuddered a little when I touched it, and as I passed beneath the arch I looked up to see two green eyes blinking down at me. How oblivious must the people working at this beer garden be if they don't notice this thing? Or maybe it's supposed to be here. Maybe Carson made it on commission.

The second piece was a slowly shifting mural, droplets of blood chasing each other across white painted bricks. It looked like a sunset when I first got there, but by the time I left it was more like a cityscape. You'd need to sit there and watch for a while to notice the droplets moving. But the smell. . . Jesus. I can't believe anyone could walk by that wall without realizing how wrong something was.

The last one was a curtain. It hung across an alleyway like drapes in front of a window. The skin was stretched so thin it was translucent. I could see fluid moving through capillaries, and past that just the outlines of trashcans and a fire escape crawling down the side of one of the buildings.

I turned away from the curtain and found a homeless man staring at me. He had a duffel bag over his shoulder and he was pushing a shopping cart full of junk. His beard was scraggly and he didn't smell very good. I think my sense of smell is better than it used to be. I'm not sure how it was before, but it seems like the people around me don't smell the things I do.

"I used to sleep there," the homeless man said. "But not anymore." And he walked away, shaking, while everyone else around us ignored the curtain of human flesh.

I was just about to walk away, too, when I heard a sound. I looked at the curtain a little more carefully, and I found a pair of lips stretched across a section three feet wide, almost too distorted to see clearly. But they were there, and they moved a little. I leaned closer, and the softest voice whispered to me and told me where to find Carson.

A memory from before the attic: My car is broken down by the side of the highway. It's hot, brutally hot, so hot it's hard to even stand up straight. The tow truck is coming, but I don't know if I'm going to last that long in this heat. I start to get dizzy. My sunglasses slide off my face and crack on the pavement. And then I fall, too. But I never hit the ground. I open my eyes and I'm just floating in the air, right next to my car, about four feet off the ground. A silver Hyundai drives by. The woman behind the wheel doesn't see me. She's too busy playing with her phone. But the kid in the back seat, a kid maybe eight years old, he sees me. He stares at me with big wide eyes as I float above the earth, and then the silver car whizzes by and it's gone.

I found Carson in his studio. I'm sure that's what he'd call it, although I'd probably call it a smelly ratshit-stained hellhole with a pottery wheel. I smelled it before I saw him. There weren't any lights on near the front of the warehouse, just some streetlights shining through the windows. I tried to be quiet as I picked my way through the dark, but I started to hear a loud whirring sound, and I realized no one would hear me coming over that racket. First came that sound, and then the smell. Sour, meaty, like some terrible combination of BO and rotting hamburger. And after the smell, I finally saw the one room with lighting, fluorescent light spilling into the hallway.

The sound, of course, was Carson's pottery wheel. He sat with his foot on the pedal, working on an uneven lump with his hands as it spun on the grinding old wheel. I watched him for a minute before he noticed me. He was naked, way too thin. The kind of thin that makes you wonder if someone has some fatal disease, collarbones standing way out from his skin, ribs you could count. He looked like he hadn't showered or shaved in a few days, and I think at least part of the smell was him. But not most of it.

I don't really want to talk about this part, but, oh, man. . . Here we go. Carson was spattered with dark red fluid, his wrists and forearms soaked in it. As I watched, he reached down to a trashbag on the floor. He pulled out a human foot. Then he added it to the fleshy, bloody lump on the wheel.

Now, I'm sure you can picture what would happen if you put a human foot on a spinning pottery wheel. Big old mess, right? It would probably just fly off the wheel, splashing blood everywhere as it went. But that's not what happened here. No, under Carson's hands, that foot, with its bones and nails and hair, it just melded in with the rest of the stuff on the wheel. Just like clay absorbing into a bigger lump of clay. I'm sure there's a technical term for that, but, fuck it, I'm not a potter.

I must have made some sound, because Carson looked up. "Oh. What are you doing here?" he asked.

That hurt a little, I'll admit. I thought he'd be happy to see me, or at least concerned. We must have been friends, once, for me to know so much about him. But he just looked at me like I was the last person on Earth he wanted to talk to. Or maybe the second last. But I'll be getting to that later.

I said, "I found your artwork downtown. I didn't know where anyone else went, so I came here."

"But what do you want?" he asked, like I was wasting his time. And for a minute I couldn't answer, because I hadn't really thought that far. And because, if he was asking that question, it meant our history wasn't what I thought it was, and maybe I didn't know what any of this was really about.

After the attic, I didn't look for any of them. Not even you, mystery guy. I was terrified and naked and running away from the fire. They all scattered in their panic, and I lost track of everyone. So at first all I could think about was finding clothes and a place to hide and food. And then I just waited. I thought, my friends and my lover wouldn't leave me. Not after what happened in the attic, and the fire, and everything else. They'll come back. They'll find me. So I waited near the house where the attic had been. I watched the fire crews and the police and the people who came to gawk. I stayed after everyone left. I got food and water and clothes when I needed and then I went back as fast as I could to watch the burnt-out house. But no one ever came.

Not even you, mystery guy. I really need to think of something better to call you until I remember your real name.

"What do you want?" Carson asked again. So I said, "I want to know how we knew each other before the attic. I want to know who I am."

Carson said nothing for a moment, just stared at me with his mouth open. Then he laughed and laughed and laughed like I'd said the funniest thing ever. "Before the attic?" he said when he was finished laughing. "Who you were *before* the attic?" and that set him off again, laughing and laughing. Finally, he asked, "What are you calling yourself these days?"

"Wren," I told him. "With a w, like a cactus wren."

"Brave little bird who isn't afraid of the spines. Not a bad choice," he said. Then, "Tell me, Wren, what do you think you are?"

What, not *who*. I didn't like that, but I just shrugged and told him I didn't know. The whole time we'd been talking, all through the talking and the laughing, he hadn't stopped shaping the lump on the wheel. Now he'd formed it into a tall, narrow cone. Days later, as I say these words, the smell is still in my hair. No shampoo in the world can get rid of it.

Then Carson said, "Think about this. How'd you get in here?"

"Through the door."

"No you didn't," he said. "Go look. The door's still locked. The security system is still on. You didn't trip it. So how did you get in here?"

I didn't remember. He was right, though. I hadn't come through the front door, I hadn't broken a window, so how was I here? But before I could spend too much time thinking about that one, Carson said something else: "How about this?" he said. "What about these three words? Grove. Mosaic. Trumpet."

And those three words just scared the shit out of me. I don't know why. But I knew I wasn't the only one. I knew those words were important to people, certain people. It was like hearing a line from a popular song or a quote from a famous book. They weren't just three words. They had a heaviness to them, a heaviness that came with hidden meaning. Carson could see from my face how much they scared me, and he just laughed. "Don't even ask," he said. "I'm not telling. And I'm not repeating them."

"I thought we must have been friends," I said. "But I don't think I'd be friends with somebody who makes sculptures out of corpses."

"Corpses?" Carson said. "I'd never mess around with corpses. Not at all." And then he gestured with his chin. "Come see."

I was scared of him, but I circled around to get a better look at the trashbag near his feet. What was in there wasn't a person anymore, not really, and I'm not sure it counted as alive, but it was moving and blinking and breathing, so I guess he was telling the truth about not playing with corpses. I threw up, then. He laughed at me while I puked in the corner. When I was done, I asked him, "Why would you do this?"

He glared at me, and I don't think anyone's ever hated me as much as he did. If so, I'm glad I don't remember it. "You don't get to judge me," he said. "Not you. Not being what you are. You don't *ever* get to judge me."

"But I don't even know what I did," I told him. "Tell me."

"No," Carson said. "If that's the only revenge I get, not helping you, then I'll take it." Then he started reaching for the bag again, reaching for another lump of flesh for the pile.

I told him to stop. He ignored me, kept rooting around in the bag.

I told him again to stop it. Still he ignored me, pulling out a hand with a wedding ring still on one finger. He took off the ring and started to add the hand to the lump on the wheel.

And then I made him stop. I'm not. . . I'm not ready to talk about how, yet, not how I stopped him or exactly what happened. But I stopped him. There won't ever be another one of those sculptures, not ever again.

Carson said just one thing before I stopped him. Just one curious thing. He said, "At least it was you. At least it wasn't the other one."

And I knew, even without asking, that he was talking about you, mystery guy, the one I love. That almost made me hesitate, almost made me wait and see if I could get him to tell me about you. But he had that person's hand, and the wheel was spinning, and it had to stop. So it did.

I hadn't planned on searching for anyone before I found Carson. I was still waiting before I found that street art, still wandering the city and hoping one of you would find me. But I see now that isn't going to work. I see now that the only answers I get will be ones I find myself.

And so, I'm putting this out in the world, hoping someone recognizes those words and tells me what they mean. Hoping someone can tell me how I got into that attic, and what happened. And, most of all, hoping I find you. Until then, goodnight.

Chapter 2
The Always Storm

There's a point at which you get so dusty no amount of bathing can get rid of it. It gets caked on, gets in your eyes, your teeth. Little grains hang onto your scalp even after you shampoo two or three times. That's how dusty I am right now. That's how dusty I got before I finally found Lexi. It didn't go the way I hoped.

If this had happened before the digital age, I guess I'd be doing this as a personal ad in the paper. Missed Connection: In the candlelit attic surrounded by 8 people I think might have been our friends once upon a time. I was the blood-drenched brunette, you were the cute guy with black fingernails and a coyote skull in one hand. I think we had a moment, but I lost track of you after the fire started and I stabbed the Skull Man with his own obsidian dagger. Let's meet for coffee, and maybe we can help each other remember our names.

But no one reads newspapers anymore. And these messages aren't just for you, mystery guy. They're for you, but also for our friends, and for anyone else who recognizes these things I talk about. And it's already paying off. After that first message, I got a lot of email. Like, a LOT a lot. And most of it was crackpot bullshit. Like, *hey, you and I were abducted by the same aliens*, or *you're possessed by the Devil*. Stuff like that. But there were a couple real ones. I can't talk about some of them, not yet. But here's one I think is important to share. It says, "Dear Wren: The Seekers won't stop until they get their Trumpet. If you can, kill them all."

The Seekers. Some others mentioned them. And I might have written these messages off as more crackpot garbage, except that one email just said the words "Seekers of Dodona." When I looked up Dodona, guess what I found? Bingo. A grove. A sacred grove in Greece. So. The Seekers of Dodona. Sounds like a shitty roleplaying game. But maybe that's my first big lead. So, dear listeners: The Seekers of Dodona. Whatya got for me?

I was working on finding some of the others when I heard about the dust storms moving along the edges of the city. If you live in this town, then you know what I mean. If you don't, you probably haven't heard anything. It hasn't been in the paper, or on the TV, or the radio. It's like there's just something about the dust people don't want to think about too much. But these weren't just regular dust devils, not just regular windy days carrying a lot of dirt in the air. No, these were big, dark storms, so thick with dust they blotted out the sun. Cars had to pull off to the side of the road, and a lot of them crashed anyway. People who got caught in them had to go to the hospital because they couldn't breathe. It was like those pea soup fogs that hit Victorian London, the ones that just suffocated people by the thousands.

In case you're wondering, I think I might have been a little bit of a history geek before I forgot everything. Stuff like that just keeps rising to the surface.

But worse than anything that happened when the dust storms hit was what happened after they were over. After the storms had blown away, things were just different. People whispered about it; I listened while waiting in line in coffee shops, in the aisles at the grocery store, wandering down the streets at night. No one really wanted to say too much, but they couldn't help noticing that the places hit by the storms were never quite the same. Not in a way people could really pin down. Plants would die, and people would be sick and tired, but more than that, it was like every place the dust storms happened just felt worse. Older, more run down, more broken. At that point, I didn't know it was Lexi, but I did think it was probably one of my old friends. I don't know why I thought that, but I did.

So I went to find myself a dust storm.

A memory from before the attic: I'm sick. I'm in bed and sweating and half-delirious with fever. I can't get comfortable, and I keep sneezing and coughing, and my throat hurts. I'm thinking about getting up and making tea or something, but I just don't have the energy. So I lay in bed and feel miserable and try and fail to sleep. At some point, though, I notice a pain in my chest different from the other flu symptoms I seem to be having. It's a sharp, jagged pain, climbing slowly up my chest, getting closer to my throat every time I cough. Finally, I spit something up. It's hard and angular, and it nearly cracks my tooth. Shaking, I turn on the light on the bedside table. There, in my hand, is a deep green gem. An emerald. Then I wipe my forehead, where I've been sweating with fever, and my fingertips shimmer with tiny particles of diamond.

Finding a dust storm is harder than you might think. They don't talk about them on the weather report, and you can't just see the clouds coming like with rain. But at this point the dust storms were happening ever other day or so, so I figured if I drove around enough I was sure to find one.

On my third day of searching, I got lucky. I was driving around the edge of town, making my second pass across the city, when I finally saw the heavy, black-brown wall of dust on the horizon. All of the other cars on the road were headed away from it, frantically trying to get home before it caught up with them. I was the only car heading straight for it.

It didn't take long for us to meet, this dust storm and I. I couldn't believe how hard the winds were, how much it made my car swerve around the road. I lost visibility right away, and I slammed on the brakes. Even with the doors shut and the windows rolled up, dust was still getting into the car, somehow. I sat there for a minute, doing nothing, because I realized I hadn't really bothered to come up with a plan beyond finding the dust storm. So I just sat there and stared at the dust flying by and tried to see if there was anything weird or different about it.

At first, it was just dust. Thick, brown, boring. I couldn't even see one foot past my bumper, so I couldn't tell what was going on out on the street. Then I noticed something weird about how the dust right in front of my windshield looked. There was some kind of shape in it, some texture that stood out from the surrounding cloud. It was a little darker from the rest, a kind of blobby shape about two feet across. I also thought I caught just a hint of spindly little legs sticking out from the sides, like a tick. And then, just as the car rocked with a particularly strong gust of wind, two yellow lights blinked from the middle of the shape. Eyes.

A second after I saw the eyes, the shape darted up and out of sight, to the roof of my car. There was a tapping sound, and even though the wind roared all around me, so loud I could barely think straight, I knew that tapping wasn't just the sound of the storm.

I didn't move until the storm passed. Even after the air had mostly cleared, I waited until I saw other people walking outside, other cars on the streets. Then I got out and checked the roof of my car. There, right in the middle of the roof, the blue paint job had been worn away to the metal in a big, messy circle. Like when you see cars that are thirty years old, where the paint is peeling away from sun damage. Except this car didn't even have a scratch on it yesterday. Not that I really give a shit about how my car looks, but it did make me wonder about what kind of thing can do years of damage in a few minutes.

The first expedition into the dust storms was obviously a failure, so I decided to make a second attempt. This time, when I found a storm, I didn't stay in one spot. As much as it scared me, and as much as it seemed like a dumb idea, I kept crawling along the road at about 2 miles per hour, headlights on and a flashlight beam pointed out the window. I almost bumped into parked cars a couple of times, but I managed to drive through the storm for a while without any big crashes or disasters. I saw those weird blobby shapes with the yellow eyes three times. One of them settled on the hood of my car, which now has another spot where the paint is worn through. Another just darted around the window, like it was looking for a place to get in. The third was attached to a stop sign, which I could barely see through the storm. I went back later and found that that stop sign was now so faded you can barely tell what it used to be.

I saw something else, though, aside from those shapes. I was on a wide, four lane road, one I'd picked because I thought it would be easier to avoid hitting something. I knew there was a concrete median in the center of the road, because I kept bumping into it. I was inching along, trying to spot one of those shapes, when I saw something bigger out ahead of me, where only the median should have been. At first, I thought it was just another one of the creatures, with its two glowing yellow eyes. But then I realized that this shape was actually a lot bigger and a lot farther away. It came into focus as I got closer.

A house. A cottage, to be exact. A little cottage with lights burning in the two front windows, like little eyes. I stopped the car and watched. There was no way a cottage should have been where this one was, but it was definitely there, right on the median. It was only about ten feet away, but between my car and the front door was roaring wind and dust blowing so fast it could sand your skin off.

I tried to do the thing I did before. You know, when I somehow got into Carson's studio without opening a door or going through a window. I imagined myself just closing my eyes in the car and opening them in the cottage. Then I imagined flying through the air and through the front wall like a ghost. None of it worked. I guess it's something I can only do when I'm not thinking about it.

Then the dust storm started to clear. I turned to look through the back window, and when I turned back the cottage was gone. The dust gradually thinned, and soon the air was clear again. There was nothing there that shouldn't have been there, just an empty concrete median on a dusty road.

Ok, so, zero for two. I decided to give it one more try. This time, though, I got myself some goggles and a mask. I looked pretty stupid in all that gear, but it sure beat getting sand in my eyeballs. Just like the other times, I drove around for a couple of days until I found a storm. Just like the other times, I spotted those vague shapes attaching themselves to cars and signs and buildings. And, just like the last time, I found the cottage.

It wasn't in the same spot, though. I found it at the end of a cul de sac, where an empty lot had been before. Other than that, though, it was the same as the last time, a tiny ramshackle wooden house with light flickering in the windows.

I got my mask and goggles on and, before I could think better of it, I went out into the storm.

Even bracing myself, I wasn't prepared for how hard those winds hit. I thought they were going to blow me off my feet, but I managed to stay upright. It wasn't very far to the front door of the cottage, but it took a long time. By the time I reached for the doorknob, the parts of my skin exposed to the air felt raw, like they'd been sandblasted. I didn't bother knocking. I just went in.

The moment I shut the door behind me, the noise stopped. I mean, all of it, like it was completely still outside. I took my goggles off and looked around. A fire burned in the fireplace, and there were lanterns in the windowsills. The ceilings were low, with exposed wood beams. The floor was made up of rough wooden boards, not the fancy polished hardwood people pay extra for. But, of course, the thing that really caught my attention was Lexi.

She sat at the small kitchen table, her palms pressed to the surface. Sweat poured down her face. Her hair was so damp it was flattened against her scalp, even though it wasn't that warm in the cottage. She panted and groaned like she was in pain. I said her name and she looked up.

"Not you," she said, tears pouring from her eyes. I found out with Carson how bad it feels to realize someone hates you. I found out from Lexi that finding out someone fears you is much, much worse.

I didn't want to scare her anymore than I already had, so I stayed by the door. "I'm not here to hurt you," I said.

She didn't say anything. She just bent over and groaned again, like she had a bad stomach cramp. "What's wrong?" I asked. "What can I do to help?"

"Nothing," she snapped. "I'm fine. I've done this enough times before."

I let her pant and writhe for a while before I spoke again. "I thought maybe you were trapped out here. In the storms."

"Trapped?" she said. "Of course I'm not trapped. This is where I need to be. This is where my babies need to be."

I looked around, but I didn't see any babies, and the cottage was only one room. "Lexi," I said at last, "can you tell me anything about how we got to the attic? Or how we knew each other before?"

"Before?" she asked. "That doesn't make sense. Before is an illusion.

There is only now, always already now."

Ooookay, then, I thought. I tried again, asking her about the attic, but she didn't want to talk about it.

"Oh, can't you see I'm busy?" she said, and then she let out a howl and pressed her hands to her stomach. "It's coming," she said.

Then Lexi opened her mouth wide. She made some gagging sounds, and I thought she was going to be sick, but nothing came up. As I watched, her neck expanded. It got wider, far too wide, wider than her head. She twitched her jaw, and it unhinged, falling open even wider. At this point, her open mouth was bigger than most people's faces, a giant gaping black hole.

After a few seconds, something crawled out. A blobby, nonspecific shape, translucent. Like a jellyfish. And, of course, two of those winking yellow eyes. It pulled itself out of Lexi's mouth and flopped onto the kitchen table, laying there for a moment like it was catching its breath. Lexi sat back, her neck shrinking back to a regular size, her jaw snapping back into place. She stared down at the little shape with a happy, tired smile. "My newest baby," she said.

At that moment, it jumped into the air. It didn't have any wings or anything, and I'm not sure how it stayed off the ground. But it glided straight toward me, fixing itself to my arm. I screamed and started to shake it off. It felt moist, unpleasant, but not like a solid. More like a puff of air from a humidifier. "Don't worry," Lexi said. "It needs to feed off time, and you don't have any."

Sure enough, it let go and floated away, like it wasn't interested. It flew over to one of the windows and passed through the glass like it was air.

Once I calmed down, I asked Lexi, "What do you mean, I don't have time?"

But she ignored the question. "The forward progression of time is an illusion," she said. "Look." She took off the watch on her wrist and smashed it against the table, little gears and bits of glass flying everywhere. Then she stared at the wrecked watch, frowning like she was concentrating. Slowly, the pieces moved back together, and the watch reassembled itself. "There," she said, once it started ticking again, like I should have understood the point she was trying to make.

I asked her how she did that.

She looked up at me. "Wait, when did you get here? And when did my baby leave?"

"Lexi, please," I begged, "please, can you tell me anything? Is there anything you know about me, my life before two months ago?"

I could tell she was annoyed. "I told you, that question doesn't make sense." She sighed. "Fine. I'll tell you this, but it's not my fault if you don't understand." Then she said, "A mosaic has two ages. Its time began at the moment it was assembled, but it also began whenever each of its tiles did."

If you're wondering what that means, so am I. I've got no idea. I asked her more questions, of course, but she either wouldn't answer, or she just babbled something else incomprehensible about time. Finally, I gave up. I told her I'd leave and stop bothering her as soon as the storm passed.

"What do you mean?" she said. "The dust storm never passes. It always is. My babies need it to hide in."

"No," I said. "The storms only happen every few days."

Lexi shook her head. "The city meets the storm every few days. But the storm is always."

So I put on my goggles and my mask and I went back out into the roaring dark. My car was gone, so I walked and walked until my skin was rubbed raw by the sand in the air, and I finally got through the storm and back to the city. Two days had passed since I opened the front door of the cottage. My car got towed while I was gone, of course.

And so, to anyone who's listening, if you see the dust storm coming, take shelter. Because that storm is forever and always, and it hides creatures within it, and at the center of it is their mother, who would do anything for them.

Chapter 3
Three Coins in the Sinkhole

I failed at finding Claire today. I was close, but you were faster, mystery guy. Except, you aren't mystery guy anymore, are you? At least, not as much as before. So. Why didn't you wait for me, Zachary?

I've been wondering about my age lately. I look in the mirror and I'm just not sure. Medium height, medium build. Short dark brown bob that I think might be kinda young and hip, but who knows, I could also be a really hip soccer mom. My face seems to be of someone in their twenties, but then again maybe I'm eighteen and I've just had a rough life. That's plausible. Or maybe I'm forty and I just used to be a vegan who exercised a lot and always used sunscreen. I'm pretty sure I was never a vegan, though. I like burgers way too much to have ever sworn off them. For right now I'm calling myself twenty-five and hoping that's not wildly misrepresenting myself in either direction.

Two important emails today. One had the subject line "Sweating Diamonds". It said, "That memory of making gems was mine, you fucking bitch. That was mine." It was signed, Sage. I tried to email her back, but she hasn't responded. Sage, if you're listening, I'm sorry if I took something that was yours. I didn't mean to, and I don't know how it happened. That other email I'll tell you about at the end. For now, though, let's talk about Claire.

I woke up to the same news as everyone else, the story about the sinkhole. You all saw the picture; a giant, circular pit where a stripmall once stood. The coverage focused on how lucky everyone was that no one was in any of the businesses at the time, that no one had been pulled into the earth along with the brick and mortar and merchandise. Turns out they were wrong about that part, although it's easy to understand why they missed her.

The other stuff you might have heard about the pit wasn't on the news. Still, you might have heard something. Like the one about how if you sneak past the caution tape and sit right next to the edge, and if you drop a coin inside, someone will whisper something about your future. That's the one I heard, anyway, from people on the street. So I went to see if it was true.

A memory from before the attic: I'm at work. I don't even know for sure what kind of work I do, but I sit at a desk and feel bored and depressed. There's something I'm supposed to be working on, something with spreadsheets, but I know it's bullshit and I hate the people I'm supposed to be doing it for anyway so why bother? I tell myself I'll doze in my chair for just a few minutes, and then I'll be energized and I'll get back to work. I know it's probably not true, but it's the deal I make with myself anyway. So I close my eyes, and I think about a much nicer place. It's an old library, a place I think I visited when I was a kid. There are multiple floors, and a spiral staircase leading up the center of the building. It's quiet, and the smells of the books are comforting and make me happy. In this memory, I feel the office chair disappear under me, and there's a whoosh of air around my face, and when I open my eyes I really am in that library from my childhood.

The really weird part about this memory, aside from, you know, all of it, is that I'm pretty sure I remember myself as a man in this one. At least, from the clothes and the heaviness of the build, it certainly feels like I was a man. I'm not trans, I'm pretty sure, so I don't think I ever lived as a man. So why do I remember it that way? If anyone out there has any ideas, I'd sure like to hear them.

I've given up on trying to just regain my memories. I've tried everything: drugs, meditation, wandering around and waiting for something to remind me of something else. Little pieces back every once in a while, but I'm starting to realize I won't just wake up with restored memories one day. That said, there are ways of figuring things out about my life before. For example, I listened to news broadcasts in as many languages as I could find, and it turns out I'm fluent in English, Spanish, and Urdu, and semi-fluent in Tagalog and Greek. That seems like an unlikely combination, right? Maybe I was, I don't know, in the CIA or something. No, wait, shit, that's the Bourne Identity, isn't it? No way that could really happen. Right?

Well, at least now I can add, "has seen the Bourne Identity" to my list of things I know about myself. What a pathetic list.

Of course, I went to the sinkhole. I'd seen pictures of it on the news, but I was still surprised at how big it was. It was just a huge, empty pit, maybe fifty feet across. It was surrounded by chainlink fence by then, but I just waited until the security people went home and then hopped over. I sat as close to the edge as I dared, and I peered into the hole, and I listened. It was perfectly quiet, nothing at all moving down there. So I flipped a quarter into the pit. It disappeared into the dark, and I never heard it hit the bottom.

I waited, but nothing happened. I was just about to give up when I heard a whisper coming up out of the dark. It said, "You'll see the Skull Man one more time, before the end."

And that sentence scared me so bad I fled. I don't mean I ran. I mean, I panicked and blinked and found myself in a parking lot way down the street, out of sight of the pit. I'm still not sure how I do that, and I still can't do it on command. I couldn't make myself go back to the pit that night. Not with the thought of the Skull Man at the back of my mind.

I don't know his real name, just like I didn't know yours, Zachary. All I know is that the Skull Man was the one who brought us all to the attic. I don't remember him capturing us or taking us there, but I know it was him. When I woke up on that day, he was standing over us with a skull mask and a knife in one hand, and we were covered in blood. So the memory of him scares the shit out of me. But not as much as the thought that I'll see him again before the end. Because, thing is, I was pretty sure I killed him.

So that makes me wonder if I should be taking that message literally. Maybe I'll be seeing a picture of him before the end? Or maybe I'll see his ghost? And before the end of what? Try as I might, I don't think there's any interpretation of that message that isn't bad news for me.

I finally got up the nerve to go back to the sinkhole the next night. I tossed another quarter into the hole and waited for it to speak. Like the last time, it took a while. But then, sure enough, I heard the whisper. This time, it said, "You'll have to kill again, if you decide not to die."

That was almost as bad as the first one. I still don't want to talk about what happened with Carson. But. . . I do know I want to avoid killing again, if I can help it. If this pit is to be believed, maybe I can't.

I didn't flee from the message this time, though. Instead, I flipped a third and final coin into the pit. These things always come in threes, don't they?

And, sure enough, up came the whisper. "You'll find his name in the place that was mine." That one made my heart pound like none of the others, because I knew it was about you. But I didn't know where she meant, the place that was hers. So I left and did some research on the places that had been pulled into the pit, the businesses that had made up that crappy little strip mall. I didn't know what I was looking for at that point, just something that seemed familiar. But the businesses all seemed boring and unimportant: a Laundromat, a donut shop, a thrift store. If I'd ever been to any of them, none of them rang a bell.

Finally, it occurred to me to look for the people who had worked in all those places. I didn't recognize any of the names I found for the first business, or the second. But then I checked the owner of the Laundromat, and I saw the name "Claire". And I knew right away that she was my Claire, our Claire, from the attic. I found her home address and checked there. Not that lucky, of course. There was mail piled up on the front mat, flyers stuck to the door, no one answering when I knocked.

So, of course, I did the thing I'd been dreading. I went back to the pit.

I tried to think of smarter ways to get down into the sinkhole, but in the end I kept circling back around to my first dumb, simple idea: I made a rope ladder, tied it to a concrete pillar on the edge of the parking lot, and climbed down. Turns out I'm really, really afraid of heights. Or maybe it's not so much a fear of heights as a fear of climbing alone down into a mystery oracle pit. Either way, it wasn't my idea of a good time.

I didn't think the rope ladder was going to reach the bottom, but it did. I noticed as I climbed down that the pit wasn't completely dark. I mean, you couldn't make out much, but there was some kind of phosphorescent green moss on the walls, glowing so faintly you didn't really notice it until you were climbing down.

I saw more once I got to the bottom. How would you imagine the bottom of a sinkhole? Dust and rubble? Buildings collapsed and buried in mud? That's what I pictured. Instead, the ground was smooth and dry. But, even weirder, the old buildings from the strip mall still stood. They stretched out in a row, just like they did when they were up on the surface. None of them even looked damaged.

My plan had been to go straight for the Laundromat, or whatever was left of it, but then I saw all the other buildings. As I moved my flashlight to where the strip mall's farthest left business would have been, I saw another structure. This one was painted white clapboard, in a style you don't see much of in this town. I was positive that one hadn't been in that stripmall before the sinkhole appeared, so I went to check it out.

Up close, I could see it was one of those old houses that someone decided to convert into a business. On the front porch was a little plaque for an orthodontist practice. But I didn't look too carefully at that one, because I was distracted by the entire street full of old buildings stretching out into the dark. Turns out the sinkhole wasn't so much a hole as the entrance to a very, very big cave system. Two rows of houses and buildings, facing each other like on a regular street, just stretched out into the distance. I walked along that makeshift little street for half an hour, and I never reached the end.

None of the buildings went together, and I could tell they'd come from a lot of different places. There were tall glass office towers like you'd see in LA or Chicago, quaint little B and B's that only could have come from Vermont, a double-wide trailer, a garden shed. Finally, I saw something I think must have been a wigwam, a circular wood-and-mud structure with a hand-carved front door. I'm no expert, but it sure looked authentic to me.

I didn't check inside any of them. Because, while I didn't hear another sound the whole time I was walking, I was sure the place wasn't abandoned. Not really. I kept almost but not quite seeing motion through windows, feeling the pressure of being watched from a distance, but I never quite got a look at anything. I think whoever or whatever lives in all those buildings was content to stay out of my way as long as I kept to myself out on the street, but it didn't seem smart to push my luck by going inside.

So, once I realized I could walk forever without reaching the end of this cavern, I turned around and went back to Claire's Laundromat.

It was just a Laundromat, like any other. If you ignored the fact that it was sitting at the bottom of a cavern, there was nothing at all special about it. The lights even still worked. I called out and took my time checking the whole place, certain I was about to run right into Claire.

But she wasn't there. At least, if she was there, she managed to keep herself hidden from me. As soon as I gave up on finding Claire, I found your note, Zachary. You know the one I mean. The one taped to the door of one of the dryers, the one I almost missed because I assumed it was just an "Out of Order" sign. You know what it said, but for those listening at home, here it is: "Dear Wren: You don't need to keep doing this. You're safe. Please just try to live a life. I love you." And it's signed, Zachary. So now I have a name I can put to my memories of that face. Zachary.

I tried one more coin, once I'd climbed out of the sinkhole. I thought maybe she would tell me something useful about where to find you or where to go next. But there was nothing. Just as I thought: fortunes come in threes. Or maybe she'd give someone else a fourth prediction. Because, it makes me wonder, Zachary, why did you go down there? Did you go to see Claire? And, if so, did you manage to meet her when I couldn't? Did you try to get her to discourage me from looking further, the way you did in your note?

But, oh, Zachary, the things you must have forgotten about me. I'm not gonna stop. Especially now. Because, here's the other email I got today: The subject line says, "Let's meet". And the rest of the message is a time and a location, which I'm not going to name here. It's signed Bilal.

So, if this is who he says he is, I might finally get my answers about the attic, and everything that came before. At least I hope that's what he has to tell me.

See you soon, Bilal. And you too, Zachary. Whether you like it or not.

Chapter 4
What Happened in the Attic

So, you know that message I got from Bilal, last time? Turns out, big surprise, it wasn't from him after all. No, turns out it was from three guys in ski masks and bullet-proof vests, carrying really big guns. Oh, those poor stupid guys. They had no idea what they were dealing with.

Right after my first message, after I mentioned Bilal's name, stuff started showing up in the place I've been living. The first time it was three willow leaves on the doorstep. There aren't any willows around here, so I knew someone had to have left them there. The second one was a frog in my living room. That probably sounds gross, but he's actually really cute, with little gold speckles. I got him a little pool to play in, and some crickets, and named him Akira. He's not in a cage. I figure he'll stay as long as he wants, or as long as Bilal wants. I don't really know how I knew these messages were from Bilal. I just felt sure of it, the same way I felt sure about Carson and the sculptures. It's like there are memories I don't quite have, like they're just below the surface, but they still nudge me in the right direction.

That said, those submerged memories aren't perfect. I misinterpreted the messages at first. I thought they were warnings, or calls for help. They're not. But more about that later.

I guess people have noticed how much I avoid talking about that day in the attic. You would too, if you were there, believe me. But, I guess if it brings me more answers I should probably tell you what happened.

As you know by now, everything before the attic is hazy, cluttered, doesn't make sense. I don't remember how any of us got there, so I guess I have to skip that part. The part of the attic I can remember clearly and, I guess, the very first part of my life I can remember clearly, goes like this:

I woke up with my chest hurting. Imagine trying to breathe in an icicle, a stabbing, freezing pain going right into your lungs, and that might be a tiny fraction of what I was feeling. I couldn't move. I just lay on my back, gasping, wishing I'd pass out again. And even though the air going into my lungs felt achingly, horribly cold, everything else around me felt warm. At first, all I could see was a bare wood ceiling. I thought it was moving at first, but that was just the flicker of candlelight.

I wish the first thing I saw when I sat up had been your face, Zachary, but it wasn't. It was the Skull Man.

The man who stood over me was tall, and shirtless, and he wore what might have been a horse's skull as a mask. Something long and heavy-looking. But horns had been added to the skull, I think rams' horns. I could see the place where they were glued on. It was a little cheap-looking, to be honest. So was his loincloth.

Seriously. A goddamn loincloth, like he was an extra from the set of *Exodus* or something. It almost would have been funny, except that he was also pointing a black glass knife at me. Obsidian, I think. I looked down at myself, and that's when I realized the warm liquid I'd been floating in was a kiddie pool full of blood. That's right, a kiddie pool, blue with little cartoon fish on the sides. That also might have been kinda funny except for the blood, and the fact that I held little dry animal skulls in my hand, maybe birds or cats. I dropped them, and they sank into the red. Then I looked around and saw the eight, my friends, and all of them were naked and tied up, arranged in a circle around the pool. All had one arm tied to a little sluice, and all bled from deep cuts in their wrists. I saw all of them and I knew their names and things about them, and more than anything I wanted to help them.

But then, oh then. Then I saw you, Zachary. Sitting across from me in the pool, crosslegged, also holding a skull. You stared at me and I stared at you, and yours was the only name I didn't know. But I knew we loved each other. We were meant for each other. I knew that, the same way I knew the sky was blue and gravity keeps us on the ground and leaves grow on trees.

I didn't have a whole lot of time to bask in that love, though, because the skull man grabbed my arm. He was chanting something, but it was hard to understand his voice through that hollow mask. I did catch one phrase, though: "Binding of the mosaics." Binding of the mosaics. I've spent so much time trying to figure out what that meant. Not at the time, though. At the time, I was screaming.

I didn't think. I grabbed the wrist holding the knife and I shoved it back up into his chest. I don't know which of us was more surprised by how strong I was, me or him. Probably him.

And then, as the Skull Man fell, you, Zachary, you opened your mouth and you made that sound. I still don't know the word for it. Not a shriek, because that's a human sound. More like tearing metal, the wing of a jet ripping off midair. And that sound, somehow. . . Well, I know you remember this part, but for the folks listening at home, that sound tore off all the ropes tying our friends and holding them in place. They all got up and ran for the door, even though they all bled so much they must have been so dizzy and sick. One of them, I think Aisha, kicked over some of the candles as she ran, and the flame touched something else, and pretty soon the whole place was burning. You'd think it was soaked in gasoline, the way it went up.

The Skull Man was still alive when I ran out of the attic. I remember, Zachary, you were hauling me by my wrist, but I looked back and I saw him twitching and trying to pull himself toward the pool full of blood. Then he was out of sight and we were tumbling down wooden stairs. That's the first time I understood we were in an attic, and beneath us was a house, and outside was the world. I don't remember much about getting out of the house, but I know I tripped and fell on the pavement outside. It knocked the wind out of me, and you let go of my hand. I don't know where you went. The others were already gone.

When I could breathe again, I looked up and saw the flames coming out the top of the house, smoke pouring out through the windows. If you weren't there, you're probably picturing the house wrong. The listeners at home are probably picturing some spooky Gothic ruin, something that looks like it would be haunted. But it wasn't like that. It was just another McMansion, boring, white and pink, badly constructed. Even before it caught fire and collapsed in on itself, I wouldn't have liked it.

People started to gather in the yard across the street. Some part of me knew I shouldn't be seen, that I shouldn't be there when the police arrived. I still have that feeling, that thing holding me back from just walking into a police station and asking for help, even though it would probably be easier than what I'm doing now. Somehow I just know that would be a bad, bad idea. So I ran. I got back on my feet and ran until I found a dark alley between two houses. I crouched there and I tried to catch my breath. And that's when I saw a little cactus growing outside the alley, and standing on it was a cactus wren. I saw it, and I knew what it was, but I also realized I didn't know how I knew. I didn't remember learning about birds. But I saw the little bird standing on those spines without getting hurt, and the way it stared back at me without fear, and I guess that's the moment I decided I'd be Wren until I figured out my real name.

And that, dear listeners, is the story of what happened in the attic.

So, about those guys who pretended to be Bilal. I went to the address in the email. It looked like a normal house, nothing sinister. As soon as I reached the gate, though, these guys in black ski masks and military-looking clothes pulled up in a van. Not a black van, since that's probably what you're picturing. No, it was an old white van with a carpet-cleaning logo on the side. I bet there's no such thing as a real carpet-cleaning company. I bet every time you see one of those they're just a cover for some shady organization like this one.

One of the men yelled at me to get in the van. I told him to fuck off.

He said: "Get in the van on your own or we'll shoot you in the leg and take you anyway."

"Ok, then shoot me," I said. And he did. I have to admit, that came as a surprise. I thought he was bluffing. But he really did shoot me right in the leg. Turns out getting shot really hurts.

So I stopped them, the way I stopped Carson. I avoided talking about it before, but I guess this is the best way to warn off any other guys with guns who want to come after me, so here it goes: I reached out, and I felt the water in their bodies. And then I just separated it out from the rest. I don't know how I do it, but in the moment it feels really simple. I just find the water, and I grab it. Picture a human-shaped lawn sprinkler, water flying out in all directions, raining all over the pavement. That's what it looks like. It's pretty instantaneous, so at least I don't think they feel any pain. Once the water jumps out of their bodies, all that's left are these dry little husks, like mummies. The human body is something like 60% water, so picture a shrunken little body a little less than half the size of a grown man. That's what's left. Just a little mummy, twisted and hidden in clothes that are now way too big for it. And these big ridiculous guns lying beside them.

I feel bad. I do. After I did that to Carson, I swore I'd never do it again. But, to be fair, that guy did fucking shoot me. Oh, speaking of that: Here's another thing you might want to think about if you're another guy who wants to come after me with a gun. I found the bullethole in my leg, going almost all the way through my calf muscle. Then I did something I didn't know I could do: I just kneaded the flesh like bread dough, like clay, until the muscles pushed the bullet out and knitted themselves back together. That part still makes me sick to think about, because it's the same thing Carson could do, and that makes me remember about how he used it. But there wasn't time to think about that then, because there had been a gunshot and I knew the police would be here sooner or later. So I fixed my leg, and then I searched the dead men's pockets as fast as I could. There was nothing there. If this was a movie, there'd be a nice distinctive amulet or something, something I could use. Instead, just Kleenex and extra bullets.

Still, even without finding anything, I think I know who these guys are. These guys are working for the Seekers.

Back to Bilal. Around the same time I started getting his messages, I also started hearing things about a place that started showing up around the city. Now if you're wondering how a place can "show up" anywhere, I'm with you. I didn't get it either, at first. But I've been paying street kids to keep an eye out for certain things, things that might be related to my list. And several of them started telling me about the same thing. They said: "Folks say you can't be looking for it. You only find it when you're not thinking about it." Apparently, most people find it for the first time while playing Pokemon Go. That makes me wonder how many others just passed right by it, or through it without realizing it was there because it didn't contain a goddamn Pikachu.

Here's the way they described it. "It's a spot next to a little stream. There's a grassy, soft hill that leads down to the water. It smells really nice, like honeysuckle. And at the very edge of the stream there's a willow tree with branches that touch the ground and the water, like a curtain. While you're there, you can see the water and the grass go all the way out to the horizon, without anyone else in sight. But if you try to go deeper into the place, past the stream, you wind up back in the city. Just not always in the same part of the city as where you started."

The way these kids describe it, the place with the willow tree shows up in alleys, strip-mall parking lots, a highway underpass. One girl even claimed she found it in the fitting room at the Gap. I think visiting this place gives them bragging rights. They compete with each other; one kid says he's been there three times, and another will chime in claiming he's been there four.

I asked all these kids what they liked about the place. I mean, these are skatepunks, teenagers, kids who can't look up from their phones for three seconds. What the hell would they like about a cute little stream and a willow tree? None of them really gave me a clear answer. They all just said, "I don't know. It's just cool," but they couldn't really say why.

Naturally, I set out to find it. But you already see the problem with that, right? You can't find it while you're thinking about it. It made for an infuriating couple of days. I tried listening to music, playing games on my phone, getting drunk and wandering around. Nothing worked. I just couldn't stop thinking about it.

Still, every once in a while, I'd wake up in the morning and find a few willow leaves on my pillow, and the smell of clover and honeysuckle in the air. And Akira stayed in my living room, just hanging out in the little gravel-and-water filled bowl I got for him. So I thought, Bilal must want me to find him. Maybe he's stuck there, the only one who can't leave. Maybe I can rescue him, I thought. So I kept looking.

A memory from before the attic: I'm kissing someone. It's a man, but not Zachary. A man whose name I don't remember. He starts grabbing my boobs under my shirt, and the really weird part of this memory is that those boobs are way, way bigger than the ones I have now. I don't think I ever had a breast reduction, but it's pretty hard to explain otherwise. Anyway, he's grabbing at me, and I'm annoyed because I've already told him I don't want him to do that. But he ignores me and does it anyway. So I pull away, and instead of asking him, I tell him: STOP. And he does. He stops and steps away, his eyes wide. And in that moment, I realize I can tell him to do anything, and he will. So I ask him to punch himself right in the nose. And he does it. Blood pours from his nostrils, and I feel guilty and sorry, but deep down there's also this nasty little thrill at what I've done.

Just like the kids said, I found him when I least expected it. I was at a gas station, filling up my car, and the pump stopped working. I was cursing and struggling with it, trying to get it to start pumping again. And as soon as I got it working, I looked up, and there it was, right at the edge of the gas station parking lot.

It was just the way the kids described it. A warm summer day on the edge of a stream far away from this city. Willow branches trailing in the water. A perfect scene.

So I went, of course. I wandered along the stream and listened as the sounds of the city faded. I parted the curtain of willow branches, half-expecting to find Bilal sitting there. But it was just me. It felt so calm, so peaceful, that it was hard to stay focused. I just wanted to recline on the grass and watch the frogs and the bees having their lazy day, take a nap under the willow tree. But I had a mission, so I made myself focus enough to search for him. I peered into the water, and poked through the reeds and cattails along the streambed, and stared out at the hills rolling away into the distance. I called out Bilal's name. Nothing.

Except, that's not really true. I didn't see anything, sure, and I didn't really hear him. But I kept getting the feeling that he was standing right behind me, that he was watching me. Not in a creepy way, just like he was there but I was missing him somehow. Still, every time I turned around, it was just me.

Finally, I gave up and sat on the edge of the stream, right next to the willow. And then, just as I stopped looking for him, one of those branches reached up and caressed my cheek. It could almost have been the wind doing it, except the breeze wasn't strong enough to make the branch move like that. I looked up at the tree, and around at the landscape. A voice, one almost hidden under the wind, whispered something in my ear. I'm not going to repeat what it said. It's too personal. But I finally understood. Bilal wasn't hiding here. He wasn't crouched behind some reeds or perched up in the tree. But he was here. He was all of it. The tree and the smell of honeysuckle and the sound of the stream bubbling as the water went by.

Bilal had a perfect memory of a perfect day. And I think, after the attic, he decided to just be that perfect memory, and nothing else. I have no idea how he stepped out of this world, out of his body, but I'd never try to drag him back from where he went. I'd never be that cruel. So instead I just sat with him for a while, saying nothing. Then I got up and went back to my car, sitting next to a faulty pump at an ugly gas station.

I think I understand now. I thought those messages were warnings, or maybe asking me for help. They're not. They're something else. Of all the people on my list, all these old friends I've been trying to find, Bilal is unique. Of all of them, only he forgives me.

Chapter 5
Just Say No

You know those news reports they do every now and then, where someone claims there's a new deadly drug craze among teenagers? Like, "Are American Teenagers Eating Caterpillars to Get High? Tune in to find out." And it always turns out to be bullshit. Like the whole vodka-soaked tampon thing. I can't even remember my name and even I know that wasn't ever a thing.

So most of those stories are crap. That said, I did actually uncover a new teenage drug craze this week. And that dangerous new drug is called Natalie.

A couple of people have asked me how I live if I wandered naked from a burning house with no memory, no money, and no ID just a few months ago. It's a good question. And I don't totally understand myself how I've managed, but here's a story that explains the basics. Three days after the attic, I was standing near the front of a grocery store. I'd eaten out of dumpsters until then, stolen some clothes out of an outdoor laundry room, stuff like that. I was getting pretty tired of stale donuts and pizza crust, so I was thinking about shoplifting. And as I looked at the store, this guy walked by. Without even thinking about it, I just opened my mouth and said, "Please buy me some groceries." But I didn't just say it. It was like I found an extra set of vocal cords, ones that made the air vibrate in a way only I could feel. I'd demonstrate, dear listeners, but I don't know what would happen if I did this in a broadcast.

Anyway, I asked. And the guy just said, "Yeah, ok," like it was a totally normal thing to do. And I followed him into the store and filled a cart and he paid for it and went away without a word. Now, I know what you're thinking. Maybe he was just a nice guy who bought some food for a homeless girl because she asked. I know that's what I thought. At least, until I tried the same thing with clothes, and a $300 laptop, and an apartment. I ask in that special way, and people give me what I want. I know, I know. It's not very ethical. But, I promise, I only use it for necessities, and only on people who look like they can afford it. Dude, let's see you lose your memory and escape a ritual sacrifice and see if you feel all judgy then, ok?

This is the email that pointed me toward Natalie. It said, "I don't know anything about your Seekers or your dumbass trumpet, but it seems like your friends are responsible for all the freaky shit happening in this town lately. So go over to 10th Street and see if you can stop whatever's happening there. I think whatever it is took my boyfriend." I guess I've made myself the go-to freaky shit specialist. Good to know.

I went to 10th Street. It's not a nice part of town. Shady businesses, pawn shops, lots of graffiti. But it has a skate park, which I assumed was the thing that drew in all the teenagers. I don't remember being a teenager, but I'm pretty sure I never liked them. All that posturing and drama and pretend tough-guy stuff gets on my nerves. Although, to be fair, these particular teenagers were pretty damn tough.

It took me a long time to notice anything amiss. I found a place to sit next to the skate park, and I watched the teenagers come and go. They moved around in little cliques or packs or whatever, five girls in a group, four boys in a group, the occasional young couple in love. For most of the day, they just looked like every other group of teenagers at any other hangout. Nothing special.

Then it started to get dark, and I noticed that most of the kids were in an awful hurry to leave. And that seemed weird, because I always thought after sunset was the time to hang out. These kids, though, they checked their watches and their phones and looked at the horizon and got out of there. I thought, well, maybe there's a really strict city curfew or the cops bother people at a certain time, or something.

But then, a new group of kids showed up, and I understood pretty quickly why the others were so eager to stay out of their way.

A memory from before the attic: I'm cooking. It's not going well. Whatever it is, it's burning while something in another saucepan has the wrong consistency. I'm starting to freak out about it. I look out the window, and I see my dog, whose name is Perky, digging up a rose bush. I yell, but he doesn't stop. The thing on the stove pops and sizzles and I smell smoke. Right then, the doorbell rings. And then, somehow, I'm seeing three different images side by side at the same time. One is still the mess on the stove. One is opening the door to sign for a package. And the third is running outside to pull Perky away from the rose bush. Then all three of those images collapse into one, and I'm back at the stove again.

Like I said before, I'm not a fan of posturing and fake tough-guy stuff. And there was a little of that coming from this new group who showed up at the skate park after dusk, but I actually got the sense that they'd really been through some rough patches.

The first thing I really noticed was the body art. Plenty of tattoos and piercings, sure, but some of them went way past that. A couple of them had what looked like little horn implants up near their hairline. Others had knobby ridges standing out from their knuckles, right where you'd punch somebody. A couple of them growled and bared their teeth at me, I guess trying to scare me away from their hangout. Their teeth seemed way too sharp and pointy, like they'd filed them down. Just the thought of that makes me cringe.

They didn't manage to scare me off, so I just kept watching as they gathered in the skate park. I noticed pretty quick that their motions were weird. None of them just sat around, like people do. They didn't seem like they were there to hang out. Instead, most of them walked around the edge of the park, like they were on patrol or something. Others went to the middle of a flat concrete area and stripped down to pants and sports bras or undershirts, then started punching the air like they were warming up for a boxing match.

I noticed the kids nearest me were twitchy. They kept biting their nails with those sharp teeth, bouncing up and down on the balls of their feet, checking their phones every few seconds. After a while, one of them came up to me. "Hey, lady," he said, "you should go."

I told him it was a public park, and that I had every right to be there.

"Nuh-uh," he replied. "This is the queen's turf. She doesn't like strangers hanging around when she holds court. You should get out of here, or there'll be trouble."

I told him I was going to stay. Just then, a black SUV bumped over the curb and drove right toward the middle of the skate park. "Don't say I didn't warn you," the kid said, and then he and everyone else in sight fell to their knees and bowed their heads.

A man and a woman in matching suits got out of the SUV. Both went to the back and opened the door. The man held out his elbow, and a small, pale hand took his arm. Natalie stepped out of the car, and every kid in the park pressed their foreheads to the dirt, like she was a goddamn Empress.

I want to talk about another email I got the other day. I get these every now and then, little bits and pieces about the Seekers. Hard to say how much is true. But this one is by someone who says they want to meet. Someone who says they want to help me. I'm pretty skeptical of that, as I'm sure you can imagine. But they said something interesting. It said, "The real Seekers wouldn't do the kind of thing you described happening in the attic. But one of their apostates might."

Apostate: someone who leaves a religion, someone who rejects all they once held sacred. I could very easily imagine that word applying to the Skull Man. Then again, if that's what he was after he lost his faith, I'm not sure I want to know what the faithful are like.

I don't know much about clothes, but even I could tell Natalie was wearing something incredibly expensive, some kind of glamorous designer gown that looked completely out of place in a grungy skate park. She took her time wandering from one cluster of kids to another. Sometimes she leaned down to touch their heads or their arms, and those ones would kind of just melt into a dazed puddle the second her skin came into contact with theirs. Some of the others would look up to peek at those ones, and I've never seen such jealousy.

It didn't take her long to spot me. I wasn't making any effort to hide, after all. I just sat on my bench beneath a tree. For just a second, she looked scared. Like really, truly frightened of me. Then she smiled. "You must be Wren."

I stood and said hello. She said, "I guess you're here to take more."

"Take more what?" I asked. And she laughed.

"You'll never get to me," she said. "Never again."

"I just want to talk," I said, but she wasn't listening. She turned to all the bowing kids scattered out around the park.

"Stand!" she barked, like a drill sergeant. They jumped to their feet, even the ones she'd touched who staggered a bit and seemed a little woozy. "Let's show our guest what we're made of," she said.

A bunch of the kids closed in around me. They kept their distance, but they also made sure I couldn't make a run for the park's exit. And that's when I realized my big mistake; I knew I could defend myself against anybody, the way I had when I got lured into that trap. But what about people I wasn't willing to kill, like a bunch of enthralled kids? As far as I knew, I didn't have any nonlethal weapons. So I just stayed put and waited to see what happened.

One of Natalie's, I don't know, bodyguards or retainers or whatever, pulled a chair out of the back of the SUV. It wasn't a very portable-looking chair, big and padded and plushy. He struggled to carry it, but he finally set it down along the edge of the skating area, in a spot where the concrete curves up into a bowl shape. I assume it's for people to practice skating up a wall or some other bone-shattering trick. But, for now, it was the spot where Natalie held court. She sat in the chair while her other retainer poured her a drink from a flask.

Then Natalie clicked her fingers, and the kids who had been warming up like they were getting ready for a boxing match crawled toward her. She reached out toward the first one, and he just started licking her hand. Then one of the others went to her other hand and did the same thing. I got grossed out just watching it, but the way she looked at them was affectionate, almost maternal. After a moment, though, both of the kids slumped over on the ground. One of them moaned like he was in pain. Then he sat up, and I saw how he'd started to change.

Those nubby little horns I'd seen some of the kids wearing? Turns out those weren't implants. The skin on the kid's forehead shifted and rippled, and then the horns grew up and arched out from his skull. The rest of his face changed, too, his eyes retreating behind a dense new shelf of bone in his brow. He held up his hands, and I saw thick bony ridges like plate armor encasing his hands.

While all this was happening, the other fighters crawled forward for their turn at Natalie's skin. Some licked her hands, others her bare feet. All of them changed just like the first two. Soon ten of them stood there, heavy, strong, roaring and spoiling for a fight. "Tournament!" someone shouted, and the crowd echoed it. The fighters turned to face each other, squaring off like they were ready to start swinging.

But then Natalie held up a hand, and everything stopped. "No," she said. "Not a regular tournament. This one is our warriors versus the Wren." She pointed at me. "Kill her."

They ran at me, looking a little like rhinos with their tusks and scaly grey plates. I froze; I lifted my hand to pull the water out of them, but some of those kids must have been only 14 or 15. I didn't know if I could live with that. And I wanted to jump away, take one of those shortcuts I've taken before, but I'd never been able to do that at will. So I froze, and waited, and hoped something would come along to save me.

Then I felt something slide, and I realized they were taking a long time to get to me. Way too long. Almost like they were moving in slow motion. And I felt a hum in the air, the same way things had felt in Lexi's cottage.

I didn't know how I'd done it, but I knew it wouldn't last forever. I already felt it slipping away from me. So I ran through their lines as fast as I could, so I stood behind them. But all Natalie's other followers still stood in a ring around the pit, and I couldn't slip through. I lost my grip, and time sped up again, and the fighters stopped and looked around, obviously confused at how I'd managed to disappear in front of them. Then they realized I was behind them and charged again.

Again, just by instinct, I slowed everything and got out of their way. And then again. And again. Every time they got too close, I slowed them and got away. It made me feel tired, more tired and sicker with every pass.

Finally, I knew I didn't have many left in me. So I slowed them, and then I ran to Natalie. I got behind her and wrapped my arm around her throat before time sped up again. This time, they didn't charge. They stopped, and even under all their plates and horns I saw they were scared.

"Tell them to let me go," I said.

Natalie turned a little, so she whispered in my ear. "I'd rather die than keep sharing this world with you," she whispered. And then, louder, "Don't stop. Take her."

And then I proved Claire right again.

Everyone in the park wailed as the husk of Natalie's body dropped to the ground. They seemed to forget I was even there, way too focused on her corpse to care about how she died. They all gathered around her, crouching and sobbing and swaying back and forth. Then one of the fighters said, "We'll keep her with us always." And he sank his teeth into the dried flesh of her arm. From there, it was a feeding frenzy. They fought for bits of her dried muscle and skin, to crunch into her powdery bones, to swallow strands of her hair. The ones who managed to get pieces of her fell to the ground, writhing as they changed. This time, though, it wasn't just new horns and armor. This time, when they stood, it was as something I'd never seen before. Something scaly, grey, something with teeth, something that runs on all fours and keeps to the shadows. Not all of them got a bite. Not all of them changed. But enough of them did. They ran off into the bushes at the edge of the skate park, roaring into the night. I didn't stay long enough to see what they did next.

So, another one from the attic, another failure. My record's pretty spotty at this point. So I've made a decision. I'm going to go meet with this informant, this person who supposedly has inside knowledge of the Seekers. I know that's not really the safe move. But it's the only option I see right now. So, if this ends up being my last message, I guess you know I walked into another trap, this time one I couldn't get out of. If I'm not dead, though, you'll hear from me again next week.

Chapter 6
The Full Realization of Human Potential

I got your message, Zachary. Jose passed it along, just like he promised. You know I love you, Zachary, but even so, here's my response: Fuck you.

I know what Grove means. I mean, not exactly. But I have an informant, now. Turns out this invitation to meet was actually the real deal. She told me what she knows, and that was a whole lot more than I had before. I'm calling her Winry, because I was watching *Fullmetal Alchemist* when I got her email. And she told me what little she knows about who's been looking for me, and what they want.

Before I get into the stuff about the Seekers and the Grove, though, let me tell you about what happened with Jose.

Finding Jose was a lot simpler than with any of the others, because he just sent me an email and asked me to meet him. And, this time, unlike when I got that email from Bilal, it actually was him. Sort of.

Of course, given the trap I'd walked into with Bilal, I staked out the place for a while before I went in. At first, I thought I had the wrong address. I assumed it would be a house, or maybe a café. Instead, it was a strip club. After I spent all afternoon watching the place, I decided it was worth the risk to go in. So in I went.

Of course, the first person I encountered was the bouncer. He was, in almost all respects, really bouncer-ish: Tall, muscular, surly, with his black hair in a buzz cut. The only thing that really caught my attention about the guy was his eyes. They were green, with thick dark lashes most women would kill for, but I'm pretty sure he wasn't wearing mascara. He didn't say a word, just waving me on through. As I walked, though, I thought I heard him say something behind me. I thought he said, "I hear San Diego is nice this time of year."

"What?" I asked, turning back.

He stared at me, totally blank. He might as well have been a statue. So I kept going.

It actually wasn't too bad, as strip clubs go. I mean, sure, it was dim and a little bit grimy, but at least they really seemed to enforce their no-smoking policy. There weren't a whole lot of patrons in there at that point, just a few guys scattered around at the tables near the stage. None of them looked the way I remembered Jose, although I'll admit my memory of his face was pretty hazy. I went to the bar and sat there until I got the bartender's attention. He was a short, wiry little guy with a pencil mustache and a Hawaiian shirt. The kind of guy who gets whacked for being a rat in gangster movies. As he came up to me, though, I couldn't help but notice his eyes. They were the same beautiful green, the same thick lashes as the bouncer. Maybe they were brothers, I thought, although they didn't really look anything alike aside from that one feature.

"Do you know where I can find Jose?" I asked.

He cupped a hand around his ear. "Joey?" he asked, even though it was quiet enough he should have been able to hear me the first time.

"Jose," I corrected him.

"Oh. Because Joey's my name," he said. "You sure you ain't looking for me, little bird?"

"The guy I'm looking for is named Jose," I said, starting to get nervous.

"Can't help you there, little bird," he said. "You'll have to talk to one of the girls. Of course, they don't talk for free, you know?"

I asked him where the girls were.

He pointed at the empty stage. "Take a seat. Jojo's up next. She might be able to help."

I started toward a spot next to the stage, but he told me it was a one-drink minimum, so I got a beer I had no intention of drinking and took it to a table where I could wait for Jojo to start her routine. As I carried my drink away from the bar, he called out, "There are cities other than this one, and lovers you have yet to meet."

That one stopped me dead. I went back and asked him what the hell that meant. He shrugged. "Exactly what I said. Now hurry up before you miss Jojo's number."

A memory from before the attic: I'm working in a store. I'm not sure what kind. I stand behind the counter and take people's money and put it in a clunky old cash register. A man steps forward and hands me some money. A crumpled five dollar bill. As the money passes from his hand to mine, I see something. It's not really a vision, or even an image. It's more like a story written in the contours of his face. It's a story of two deaths. One is of this man bleeding and gasping, his torso crushed and his legs shattered in the moment his car collides with a tree. It's something that happens not too long from now. The other death comes when his hair is much thinner than it is today, thinner and full of white strands. In this death, he's watching TV. When it goes to commercial, he rises from his patched old armchair, and then crumples to the floor of his living room as pain grips his chest. I see these two stories radiate out from this moment in this store, and I see my place in it. I see the two chains of events that will spin out from this moment, this point at which I can give him his change as a dollar bill and two quarters or a dollar bill and five dimes. I see the microscopic shifts that begin with the way he spends that change, the shifts that become bigger over the next days and weeks. So I reach into the cash register and find five dimes instead of two quarters, and I grant this stranger a long life.

The music started up just as I sat down next to the stage. Jojo came out and danced, getting less and less clothed as the show went on. I'll admit, she was beautiful, and it was quite a show, even though I was nervous and focused on finding Jose. Don't worry, Zachary. Sure, I was tempted, but I don't know if we have an open relationship or not so I'm playing it safe.

Anyway, Jojo danced, and some of the men watching slipped dollar bills into her G-string, and then it was my turn. I was a little more focused on her navel ring at first, but then I got a good look at her face for the first time. You guessed it: Bright green eyes, thick black lashes, the exact same pair for the third time that afternoon.

"I hear you're looking for Jose," she said as she danced, just loud enough for me to hear.

"Yeah," I said. "Can you tell me where to find him?"

"Mm, I don't know," she said. "Have you thought about why you want to find him? Whether the truth is really worth it, no matter what it is? Because you have other choices, you know. You can go anywhere you want. "

She went off to dance in front of another customer, leaving me to think over that one. On the surface, it's pretty obvious why I'd like to find Jose, just like I wanted to find all the others. Except that, I haven't really gotten the result I wanted from any of the others. Most of them have either refused to tell me anything, been unable to speak, or have tried to kill me. Why should Jose be any different?

And then there's the whole "is the truth worth it?" question. It's not the first time I've thought about this. The truth about me and my history might be really terrible. I might be a serial killer, or a Nazi, or something. So is the truth necessarily going to be worth it?

After a minute, I made my decision and waved some cash and called Jojo back over. "I made up my mind," I said. "I want to see Jose."

She sighed like I'd disappointed her, even though I'd just stuffed a truly generous amount of money into her underwear. "Fine. Don't say we didn't warn you," she said. She snapped her fingers, and a waitress appeared next to me. "Jolene will show you to the manager's office."

Jolene led me down a hall and up a flight of stairs. I don't need to tell you what her eyes looked like, do I? Yeah, didn't think so. Anyway, she led me up the stairs to a dim little landing. The sign on the door said, "Manager". She knocked and walked away without waiting to see what happened. A voice inside yelled, "Come in," and I opened the door.

Before I say any more about Jose, and about your message, Zachary, let's talk about Winry. Here's what she had to say, once we finally met: The Seekers aren't a religious order, despite the Skull Man's rituals and ceremonial blades and whatnot. They're more like specialists in a branch of the sciences that everyone else thought had withered away and fallen off the tree a long time ago. Like alchemy and phrenology and astrology. Except, in this case, it seems like they actually get results.

Now, of course, you're wondering what I was wondering: what exactly is this science? What results? And here's what Winry had to say: "The Seekers of Dodona are dedicated to the full realization of human potential."

Now, if you're thinking, "That sounds like some motivational speaker bullshit," believe me, I'm right there with you. But Winry explained it a little more, and it started to make sense. Apparently, they've known for a long time that some among us have abilities the rest don't have. Some of these are ones you know about. Some of us are born stronger, faster, smarter. But then there's the other stuff. Like, oh, I don't know, the ability to pull every drop of water from a body without touching it? Or kneading human flesh like clay while keeping it alive? Or transforming oneself into a memory? Yeah. That kind of stuff.

As Winry explained it, the Seekers have been around for a long, long time. And over the generations, they've spent all their time and energy cataloging and mapping and searching for the source of these exceptional skills. Turns out there's way more of that going on than you might think.

"And when they find us, they, what, sacrifice us to the gods or something?" I asked. Winry shook her head. "We're scientists," she said. "We don't do stuff like that. I don't know who that skull guy was or how he found you or what he was trying to do. But obviously he knew something because, well. . ." And she gestured around at this city, this city that has been nibbled at by duststorms and had its youth disappear into the streets and its people reshaped into sculptures. Yeah, he definitely did something, all right.

I asked her if that was what she meant before, when she'd said an apostate might do the things the Skull Man did in that attic. She nodded. "We believe science is the right path. It's slow, and frustrating, but we're taught that it's not just a question of whether or not something works. It's also important to understand why and how things work." The way she described it, it was like rituals and unmapped powers were cheating.

Then I finally got up the courage to ask her about the three words: Grove, Mosaic, Trumpet.

And here's where I started to understand the problem with having Winry as an informant: she doesn't actually know that much. "I don't really know what they mean," she said. "We, the Seekers, we use those words like a secret handshake. But I'm just entry-level. You have to be with them for years and years before you find out what the words actually mean."

That's right. My whistleblower is a goddamned intern. Apparently they operate on a kind of apprenticeship system in which you spend years being vetted and trained and working in basement labs before you finally graduate. Winry says she knows people in their forties who are still apprentices. So I guess it's gonna be a while before she knows anything of real value.

But she did know a little bit more. Specifically, about the "Grove" part. The word among the apprentices is that Grove, Mosaic, and Trumpet refer to steps in some kind of process. Three phases in a plan. Apparently, of those three, only Grove has been completed. And, I remind you, this group has been around for hundreds of years. Winry told me a rumor about the "Grove" phase. The Grove was a place where one of the long-dead Seekers of Dodona acquired information, important information pointing the group toward a way to awaken this human potential they're so keen on maximizing. Essentially, Winry said, Phase Grove allowed them to develop the plan for the Mosaic and Trumpet stages. It gave them the blueprint they've been following ever since.

"That's it?" I asked. "Grove was a planning session? And you're still talking about it, hundreds of years later?"

"Not a planning session. More like an epiphany," she said. "It happened in a grove, obviously, we all know that. And I've heard rumors that it involved someone whose ability let him see the human genome. Like, with his eyes. But how it worked, or how it leads to Phase Mosaic and Phase Trumpet, or what those are, I have no idea."

So there you have it. A guy dropped acid in a grove, or something, and they've been following his plan ever since. Not a lot to go on.

She did tell me something else, though, and that is that the Seekers don't have a lot of money and they aren't all that well-equipped. As in, they have labs in their garages and basements, and they siphon grant money from their real scientist day jobs to fund their work. Based on what Winry told me, they certainly don't have squads of paramilitary goons they can send out to trap people like me. So that brings me to my big question: If those guys pretending to be Bilal weren't the Seekers, then who were they? Who else is after me?

As soon as I opened the door of the manager's office, I saw the old man sitting at his desk. He looked like someone's grandfather, his back a little hunched, his head almost completely bald. But his eyes, though. They were still that beautiful green, and his lashes were still black as coal.

"You're a good tipper," he said as I sat down in the chair across from him. "We appreciate that."

"And you have some good dance moves," I replied. "I appreciated that."

"I make a mean sidecar, too, if you want to stop back at the bar on your way out," he said.

I asked him why he reached out to me.

He sighed. "It was a favor. Something I promised to do for Zachary. He helped me out with a little problem, and in exchange I said I'd try to convince you to move on."

"Move on?" I asked. "Move on from what and to where? How can I move on if I don't know where I started?"

He shrugged. "It's a complicated life we lead, people like us," he said. "Zachary thinks you should just cut your losses and move on. Go to a different city, start a different life, forget about all this."

I said, "Tell Zachary I said tough shit."

Jose sighed. "It's not just for your sake, you know." He gestured around. "Look at everything that's happening to this city. Do you think it's normal that all these strange things are happening, and none of the normals are talking about it? The media hasn't covered it? That's because of you. You and Zachary being in the same place, it's bringing the strange ones out of the woodwork. It's making these things seem normal."

He wouldn't say any more about that. So I asked him something else.

"Tell me about what happened before the attic," I said. "Tell me about people like us."

Jose shook his head. "No. I promised Zachary. And I owe him a big favor," he said. And I could tell from the look on his face that, even if that weren't the case, he probably wouldn't want to tell me anyway. The way he looked at me, it was almost. . . It was almost like he pitied me, or something. I knew I wasn't going to win this argument. So I got up, and I said goodbye, and I left Jose to dance and serve drinks and keep the books and guard the door, all by themselves.

Zachary, I want you to listen carefully. I'm not moving on. Not until I find you. Not until I understand what happened to us in that attic. And you don't have the right to ask me to stop, because this isn't just for you. It's also for me. So either join me, or stay the hell out of my way. Your choice.

Chapter 7
Queen of the Cyborgs

When I started this, I never thought I'd ever have to issue a PSA. Sure, I had to kill Carson and Natalie, but that was all stuff I pretty much managed to deal with on my own, and the threat had passed by the time I made my message. But now I feel morally obligated to warn the people about something, so here it is: "The Sixth Avenue Historic District is now closed to the public. It is now a commune of cyborgs who don't care too much for us old-fashioned flesh and blood types." There, you've been warned.

Ok, I'll admit it. Sage won this round. But, in my defense, she did have a whole lot of people on her side, although I'm using the word "people" pretty loosely, here. Let me explain what happened, and hopefully it'll convince everyone to stay the hell away from Sixth Avenue. But you, Zachary, I know you were there already, although it seems like you were smart enough to stay out of Sage's line of sight.

I had no idea where to find Sage, and from that email she sent me a while back I'd pretty much decided she was mad enough it wasn't worth it to track her down. But then I got an email from the city cops. Apparently they started listening to these messages after they encountered some of the weirdness our friends have been leaving around town. Anyway, they couldn't track down my address or phone number so they finally got in touch by email. I assumed it was a prank and didn't respond. I mean, everyone knows cops don't email people they want to interview, right?

What's next, tweeting my Miranda rights at me?

But, no, as it turns out, they do actually use email when they need to. At least, this one detective does. I'm going to call him Detective Kiyoma since I was watching *Steins Gate* just before I got his email. Yeah, fine, I watch a lot of anime. Sue me. Anyway, Detective Kiyoma tried to get me to meet with him, but I'm pretty sure I got in trouble with the law before the attic and most of what I do now is illegal, so I said I'd pass. Eventually he gave up on getting me to meet with him, but asked if I could send him anything I knew about weird new body modification in town, stuff involving metal. The thing about metal made it pretty clear that this wasn't about Natalie's kids, so I went out to see what I could find.

I didn't see anything weirder than usual on the streets, so I started asking around tattoo parlors. It took a while for anyone to talk, but when I pressed them they'd mention Sixth Avenue, and then follow up with, "Oh, but you don't want to go there." But since when do I listen to reason?

As I got close to Sixth Avenue, I started to notice people looking. . . different. Lots of metal rings and studs in places you don't usually see, like the elbows and between their fingers. Still, spend enough time downtown and you'll see stuff like that eventually. But then I got to Sixth, an old shopping street with hipster bars and sushi restaurants and boutiques. Except the hipsters and the yuppies were nowhere to be seen, now. Now, the only people on the street were covered in rings and studs, and they all seemed to be dressed up for a steampunk convention or something.

I noticed one guy in particular. He wore a top hat and a tweed waistcoat, and he had his mustache waxed into a big twirly shape. But he also had what looked like gold wires coming out of his ear and disappearing back into his scalp just above the hairline. When he turned, I saw he also had a big clockwork piece where his right eye should have been. "Can I help you?" he asked. His teeth were metal, too.

"I was just wondering where you got that stuff done," I said.

"If you're wondering, my dear, then you don't want to know," he said. "Also, I'm with the neighborhood watch association, so I'm asking you to move along."

On a hunch, I said, "Is it Sage? Is she the one who does this?"

He instantly looked suspicious. "How do you know that name?"

I told him we were old friends. He said he doubted that very much, but he'd take me to see her. So I followed him down to the street. There were more like him posted at intersections, I'm guessing to keep out the insufficiently metallic. He took me to a building I recognized but had never been inside, as far as I knew. It was an old movie theater, the kind of historic theater that only plays classics and foreign films. The man with the gear eye walked right past the usher like he owned the place. I followed close behind him, and that's when I saw the cyborgs.

A memory from before the attic: I'm in bed, lying next to a sleeping woman. She's naked and curled on her side. It's dim, but there's enough light coming through the window for me to make out her features. In this memory, her nose is crooked and it really bothers me. That's strange, because I don't think it would bother me now. In any case, I apparently used to be a lot shallower than I am now, because in this memory her nose is driving me crazy. I reach out, and I push the little bump on the side of her nose with my index finger, nudge the bridge until it's a shape I like, make it so it isn't quite as long. Her flesh doesn't spring back the way it should. Instead, it does what I tell it, reshaping under my fingers like putty. The woman stays asleep through all of this. After a while, though, she opens her eyes and walks naked into the bathroom. I hear the moment when she looks into the mirror and screams.

I don't actually know if they call themselves cyborgs. But that's the only word I can think of to describe it. They were all stretched out in the old seats of this theater, talking and laughing like they were waiting for a movie to start. But all of them were more metal than flesh. One woman's arms ended at the shoulder, replaced by bundles of gold and silver cords that twitched and moved around. Another guy basically looked like a human face set into the side of a metal keg. Another person had a vaguely human shape, but two-foot-long metal feathers covered every inch of her skin. Some of them spoke in regular voices, but a couple clicked and hissed through mechanical speakers. All of them wore Victorian-style clothes, lots of corsets and lace, even though some of those clothes had been modified to fit non-human forms. They all greeted my tour guide, in one way or another, some by waving, others by flashing some lights or making an R2D2 sound. He pointed to me. "She says she knows Sage," he said, "wants to talk to her."

"She'll have to wait," the feathered woman said. "The show's about to start."

The tour guide nodded and gestured for me to sit down. I did, but I picked a seat as far away from the others as I could get. The show started a minute or two later. Oh, Zachary, I wish you could have seen it. Or maybe you did. I don't know what you did while you were there.

It started off with Sage just kneeling on the bare boards of the stage. She was wearing a thin leotard, and at first I didn't think she had any modifications at all. Then she lifted her arms, and copper flowed like ribbons from her fingertips and up into the air. She got up and started dancing; the whole time, the copper streamers swayed and flowed around her, like kelp floating in water. Sometimes she froze, but the streamers stayed up in the air. Then she moved again, and the copper ribbons would be like cloth again.

I was so focused on that beautiful dance that I didn't notice someone sitting down in the seat behind mine. Then someone leaned forward and whispered in my ear. Your new message, Zachary, delivered right on schedule: "Zachary says, 'I'll ask you one more time. Please leave the city. I'll find you.'"

I turned around. The girl was small, dark-haired, with metal plates covering her arms and neck. "Do you know where Zachary is?" I asked.

"No." The girl said. "He came here once, and I don't think he'll be back." She looked at Sage when she said that, and I got the sense she was a little scared.

I don't really need to tell you my answer to that request, do I, Zachary?

Sage finished her dance, and all the cyborgs went wild. She took a bow, and the copper ribbons withdrew back into her fingertips, and she stepped down off the stage. As she walked, a thin sheet of silver poured out from beneath her collarbones and formed a corset and long skirt. The cyborgs gathered around her like a bunch of groupies, and she spent some time talking to them and letting them fawn over her. And then she spotted me.

"Oh, it's you," she said, and I think she hated me even more than

Natalie did.

I asked her if we could talk. She said she had nothing to say to me, but she did want to show me something. I followed her out of the auditorium and down a hallway, to an area that might have been the concession stand once. I noticed things about her as we walked. I was wrong about the lack of modifications. They were harder to see from a distance, but up close you couldn't miss them. I'd thought she had a head of long blonde hair, but really she just had countless gold filaments that passed for hair at first glance, but didn't move the way they should. Her eyes seemed like regular blue eyes from far away, until you got close enough to see that her irises were faceted like gems. And her skin. . . I don't know what material it was, but the texture was just a little too smooth and shiny to be real human skin.

A bunch of people waited in line outside the converted concession stand. Inside, there was a chair, the kind you see in dentists' offices. Sage called out, "Next!" and the first person in line got into the chair. She asked what he wanted. He said he wanted wings he could retract into his shoulders, wings with razor-sharp edges. Sage nodded like that was the most normal request in the world. Then she opened a big trunk next to the dentist chair and pulled out a chunk of rusted scrap metal.

"Sage, I just want to know how we got in the attic," I said. "I want to know about the Skull Man, that's all."

"You and Zachary and the Skull Man are on one side. I'm on the other," she said. As she spoke, massaged the metal. It bent and melted and folded under her hands, soft as putty.

I told her I wasn't on the Skull Man's side. I didn't remember much, but I knew that. She finished shaping the metal into a long wing shape, pinching one side into a fine edge. "You're on his side," she said. "Him, and the rest of the Splinter. You have to be." She motioned for the guy in the chair to turn over, and then she held the metal wing against his back. Little metal threads snaked out from the wing and into the guy's skin. Soon, they pulled the wing into his back, and Sage set about making another. The whole time, the guy just dozed like he was getting a massage.

I asked what the Splinter was, but she shook her head. "The more you know, the more dangerous you are to me. I'd kill you, except I don't know what happens if you die. I don't want to risk it." She glared at me. "Natalie was impulsive. She should have known it was too risky, trying to kill you."

I asked her what she thought I could do to her, why she thought I was a threat. She looked at me like I was stupid. "You can take the rest, that's what you can do." And then her expression softened, and for a moment it was like she pitied me. The same way Jose did. "It's not your fault," she said. "You can't help it. But it doesn't matter whether you mean to be dangerous or not. You're like a rabid animal."

That stung. I'll admit it. Finally, I managed to ask, "So why are you talking to me?"

Sage finished working on the second wing and attached it to the guy's back. Her mouth worked for a moment, like she had something stuck in her teeth. She coughed and spat up a yellow gem. She worked it into the guy's back, right between his two wings, watching me the whole time. Then she gestured around at the chair, herself, the line of people waiting outside, the entourage leaning against the walls. She said, "I want you to see what you'll be up against, if you come after us. And I want you to put this in one of your messages, so the Splinter knows it too." She turned to the entourage. "Show her."

And, in the blink of an eye, one of the cyborgs had a hand around my throat and was lifting me off the ground. I kicked and punched, but it was like he didn't feel it. Then I reached out and did the thing I'd done when trying to get away from Natalie's fighters. I slowed time to a crawl, and wriggled out of the guy's grip. And then immediately got punched by one of the women standing next to him.

See, these were people whose movements came from CPUs implanted in them, metal cables woven into their muscle fibers, unbreakable tendons. Even slowed down to a fraction of normal time, they were faster than me. One of them slapped me, and I was surprised it didn't take my head clean off. My ears are still ringing.

They kept hitting me. It was probably only for a minute or so, but it felt like longer.

"That's enough," Sage said at last. Then, to me, she said, "Tell the Splinter. Tell them it's not worth it to come after us." And then, even through her whole tough Queen of the Cyborgs routine, I saw how scared she was.

Her entourage stepped aside, and I left without another word.

So that was my day. I got my ass kicked by a bunch of steampunk cosplayers. Since I don't remember being in high school, I guess this is going to count as my most embarrassing moment for a while. If anyone from this Splinter is listening, I'd recommend taking Sage's warning seriously. Don't mess with her.

I don't remember much, but I know Sage is wrong about me and the Skull Man. I know we weren't ever on the same side. We couldn't be. And you, Zachary, I don't believe you were ever on his side, either. At least, I really don't want to believe that. But I don't know about this Splinter, if it's a person or a group, if it's allied with the Skull Man or if it's different. I just don't know. So, how about it, world? Anyone out there know the Splinter? If so, let's talk.

Chapter 8
The Skull Man

Did you know about all this, Zachary? Did you already know? Or am I about to tell you for the first time? Why would you keep this from me? What. . . Why? What is wrong with you? Did you even know? If you did, then goddamn you, Zachary. Goddamn you.

Oh, God. I've gone back and forth on whether or not to post this last message. Because, Zachary, if you don't know this yet, I'm sorry. I'm so sorry you had to find out this way. And if you did know this already, then. . . Then, I don't know.

It started with Aisha's girlfriend. She asked me not to use her name, so I'll call her Valentine because I was watching old *Cowboy Bebop* episodes when I got her email. Even though I'm guessing she's dead now, so it doesn't matter. Still. I got this email from someone claiming to be Valentine. She begged me to meet, and told me I could pick the time and place, so I decided to check it out.

I went to the place we were meeting long before she was supposed to get there. I circled around, trying to spot any more big men with big guns. But it was just a regular place. Finally, Valentine showed up. I recognized her, but she seemed older than I remembered. Tired. And I didn't know how we'd known each other before. But, even though I knew her right away, she didn't recognize me. I walked past her twice, and she stared right through me into the crowd until I approached her.

"Oh, God," she said when I walked up to her. "You have her eyes."

And she started crying, big ugly sobs, and I felt too guilty to ask her what she meant. Finally, I got her calmed down, and she told me what happened.

Aisha had first disappeared one week before that night in the attic. That's a horrible thought. I didn't know how long we'd been there, but I never thought it was that long. I wonder what happened to her there over that long seven days, but at the same time I don't really want to know. Valentine called the police, organized volunteers, searched high and low. Nothing. Then, the night of the attic, Aisha staggered back home, naked and shaking and smeared in soot and blood. I remember that feeling.

Valentine said, "She refused to go to the police. She refused to see a doctor. She even refused to talk for almost three days afterwards. She just slept and wandered around the house like she'd never seen it before, then slept some more. It was like something had broken in her," she said.

"Was there anything else different?" I asked.

Valentine looked guilty. "Well. . . Yes," she said at last. "Understand, Wren, she made me promise never to come to you. She listened to your messages. I caught her, once, and of course I listened to them, and I figured out pretty fast that it was about her. But she made me swear I'd never reach out to you, no matter what happened. But I don't know what else to do."

Here's what Valentine told me about the weeks and months after Aisha escaped from the attic. She didn't sleep, not after the first three days. She just stayed wake 24/7. During the day she seemed fine, but at night she just sat in dark rooms and stared out the windows. She wouldn't say what she was watching for. But then, one night, Valentine got up and went out to the kitchen for a glass of water. Aisha stood there, smiling down at a kitten playing on the floor. Valentine asked where the kitten came from. Aisha said, "The little girl who lives across the street wants a kitten for her birthday. She's been dreaming of it every night."

As Valentine watched, the kitten rolled over on the floor, and then there were somehow two kittens where there had only been one. And then one of them rolled over again, and there were three. Then Valentine screamed and Aisha did something with her hands, and the kittens all vanished.

It happened every night after that. Not the kitten thing, but every night Aisha would make something appear in their house or in the street outside. A black hot air balloon bouncing along the sidewalk, an old woman who just wandered around touching things in the living room, a desk stacked so high with papers you wouldn't be able to tell if anyone was sitting at it. At first, Valentine tried to understand how she was doing it. But all Aisha would say was that someone nearby was dreaming it. She didn't know how she did the rest.

People saw the things she made, once or twice. Hard to miss, when a giant squid is just swimming around in the air above someone's front lawn. But Aisha always made her creations disappear pretty quickly, and no one seemed to have any idea where they came from.

Until three days ago. Three days ago, as Aisha and Valentine walked home from the park, a man in a black van pulled up next to them and shot them both with what Valentine later figured out were tranquilizer darts. Valentine woke up in an ambulance, and Aisha was gone. When she got home, she found a note in her mailbox. It said, "Tell Wren to come see me if you want your girlfriend back. Only Wren." And there was an address.

After I read the note, I asked Valentine: "Did Aisha tell you anything about me? Do you know how we knew each other?" Valentine said no, but I could tell she was lying. So I went to the address.

It was just a house. Nothing special. Just a small house in a boring neighborhood. I watched it all afternoon and until it got dark, but no one went in or out. I didn't see anyone else watching the place. Finally, I decided I couldn't make this any safer. Going in was a bad idea no matter what, so might as well get it over with. So I went inside. The front door was unlocked, and I knew then something was waiting for me in there.

The house was completely empty inside. No furniture. No personal possessions. Just bare walls and plain carpet, and no lights on anywhere. I wandered through the house as quietly as I could, but in that empty place every single sound echoed and seemed louder than it really was.

I found them in what was probably supposed to be one of the bedrooms. She was unconscious on the floor. He sat in a chair, waiting, holding a gun. He didn't seem surprised when I stepped into the room. He just smiled and said, "Welcome, Wren. It's good to see you again."

You already know who he was. Of course you do. I didn't recognize him at first because he wasn't wearing his mask. But then he lifted up his shirt and showed me the scar from the stab wound. That definitely jogged my memory. "I don't know if you remember," he said, "but my name is Elliot. I've been waiting my whole life to meet you."

"Why?" I asked. "Who am I?"

And then he told me what I was. What we are, Zachary. Did you guess this part? Or did you remember it from the start? Well, if you didn't figure it out yet, here it is. We're the Mosaic.

A memory from before the attic: I'm walking home at night. I'm a little bit drunk, and I take big, swinging steps. In this memory, I feel taller than I normally do, taller and stronger with broad shoulders. I space out a bit as I walk, and some weird stray thought intrudes on my mind. It's a big control panel full of important buttons. But all of the buttons are labeled in a language I can't read, and I know something bad will happen if I push the wrong one, but I have to push something. And, in this memory of walking down the street, I run right into this control panel. It's exactly the way it was in my idle thoughts, the impressive buttons and the unknown language. I stop and look down at it, and in that moment I know I made it happen. I know I pulled it from somewhere else and put it here on the sidewalk. And the idea of that scares me so much that I run away from it, my ankle turning as I wobble drunkenly toward home.

And now, Zachary, it makes so much sense, doesn't it? How I can have all of these memories of being a man and a woman, of being tall and short, of being in all these places and doing all these different things, like I was different people? It's because I was different people. Eight different people.

Zachary, in case you haven't put this together yet, you and I were born four months ago in a pool full of the blood of eight exceptional people. The eight tiles making up the bigger picture that is us. The Skull Man hunted them and watched them and found the best of the best, the ones with the powers no one else has, and he kidnapped them and dragged them into an attic and made them bleed. And whatever he did in that ritual, he made some of them crazy and some of them hateful, and he made some of them leave this world. He did that to them. To us.

All this time I've been walking around thinking there was this life of memories I'd lost, and the ones I had were the only ones I'd managed to hang onto. It's the opposite. Those memories I have are just residue, theft. A bug, not the feature. I haven't been alive long enough to have real memories.

Oh, now there's a big philosophical question. Do we count as "alive", you and I? Or are we just things that exist? Fuck if I know.

And the worst part of it, the worst part of all of this, is that we only love each other because we were designed to. Like Adam and Eve. I feel like that should make me stop loving you, but it doesn't. That's the worst part, knowing what I feel is just some chemical signal and not being able to turn it off. I wonder if that's why you've tried to push me away. If you knew all this.

Or maybe not. Maybe you still have questions, the same questions I still have. Like, what is the point of Phase Mosaic? Why were we made? What possible purpose could this serve? Well, those are good questions, ones I don't have the answer to. At least not yet. Because, just after the Skull Man told me what "mosaic" means, Aisha woke up.

I think Elliot was surprised. I don't know what he did to knock her out, but he definitely didn't expect her to sit up. She looked at both of us and hated us the same. "You did this to me," she said. "You took sleep from me."

I told her that her girlfriend had sent me, that I was there to save her.

But she was way past hearing me. She went on her hands and knees, teeth bared at Elliot. The air in the room throbbed and hummed in a way that made my head hurt. I felt pressure building, like gravity had just gotten stronger. I think both Elliot and I realized then what she was doing, but we couldn't move fast enough to stop it.

"Wake up," she said. And she brought out everyone's dreams at the same time. Even then, in that dark room, I knew it wasn't just right around us. It was the whole city, the dreams of a million sleeping people bursting onto the streets at the same time.

The first thing that happened was a giant stone pillar exploding out of the floor and ripping the roof open. And then there was something outside. I didn't get a good look at it, but it was tall and scaly, and it roared with rage. It batted at the roof and walls of the house. Plaster and wood and dust rained down on us. Elliot screamed and tried to run away, but whatever that nightmare outside was, it reached in and grabbed him and squeezed. It crushed him into nothing, into pulp, and I saw the life go out of his eyes before the thing took his body away.

I reached for Aisha. I tried to pull her to her feet but she fought back. And then, one of the big ceiling beams collapsed, and just like that, she was gone.

If you're out there, Valentine, if you managed to get away, I'm sorry. I tried.

Once Aisha was dead, I waited for the sound of the dreams outside to stop. I assumed she was the only thing keeping them alive. But it just kept going, which you know, because it's still happening now even as I make this message a day later. The monster that killed Elliot still stomped and raged outside, and the pillar still kept growing into the sky, and I still heard the sounds of people screaming and trying to run away from the things coming out of the dark.

The door was blocked by all the debris, and I couldn't make my trick with the shortcuts work. I never can, when it counts. So I just huddled in the corner and waited for the rest of the house to collapse.

But just as I was ready to die, I smelled honeysuckle and clover. And there, in the middle of the wrecked, dark room, was Bilal. I got myself to my feet and I ran for that willow tree, that beautiful stream. Just as I collapsed in the grass, I heard the rest of the roof cave in. But Bilal took me away from there, somehow, because when I looked behind me the house was gone. Instead, it was the place where I've been staying, the street outside my little apartment. I said goodbye to Bilal one more time, and thanked him, and walked away from the willow tree by the stream.

After that, all I could think about was getting out of town. I went inside, packed up my stuff, and found something to carry Akira in. Then I went out to the used car I'd ordered some asshole to buy me, planning on driving away and never looking back. Not even for you, Zachary.

All along my street, people were running and screaming as dreams sprouted around them. Mushrooms three stories tall. A section of street in which a man jogged from one intersection to the next before appearing at the beginning again, in an infinite loop. Dark things you can't quite see, swooping and darting against the sky. Even then, it was obvious that this city was lost.

And I didn't want to be there to see it die. So I got my things and put Akira in a tank in the front seat, and I was just about to leave when a group of people got out of an SUV parked across the street. They were led by a woman. Middle-aged, stocky, blonde, big glasses. Picture a kindergarten teacher, and that's her. Except for the whole being flanked by people with guns thing. Winry was with her. She hung back and avoided looking at me. I assume she was ashamed for spilling my secrets.

The woman must have seen me gearing up to pull the water out of all of them, because she held up a hand. The others all dropped back while she walked toward me with her hands spread out. "It's ok, Wren," she said. "We're not here to hurt you."

I asked her what she wanted.

She said, "I'm the head of an organization you seem to call the Seekers of Dodona." I almost ripped the life out of her right then, but then she told me, "You should know we tried to stop Elliot. He went rogue. He did things none of us would ever do. Your informant told you the truth about that."

Interesting. Still, I didn't want to talk to these people. Even if they didn't condone what Elliot did in the attic, they made him what he was, and that means I hate them. So I told her to stay away from me and started to climb into the car.

"Wait," the woman said. "Please, Wren, we can help each other. We'll explain why you were made. What Phase Mosaic is supposed to do. We'll tell you about the Trumpet. We'll tell you anything you want to know." And then, like she knew it was her trump card, "We can help you find Zachary."

Ah, Zachary. She knew you were the perfect bait to dangle on a hook in front of me. I got out of the car. "My name's Miranda," she said. No, she didn't give me permission to use her name, but I don't owe these people anything.

I asked Miranda what she wanted in exchange, if she helped me find you.

"That's the thing," she said. "We need to find him, too. Elliot wasn't the only one to break away from us. There were others. We call them the Splinter. And we think Zachary might be helping them. We need to find him. We need to make him understand how bad things are going to get if Elliot's people finish what he started."

"And how bad is that?" I asked. I gestured around at the streets, at this city dissolving into dreams and madness. "This bad?"

"This?" Miranda said, smiling but not really. "This is nothing. It can get so much worse than this, you can't even imagine. Come with us, Wren, and we'll tell you everything."

I looked around, and I realized I didn't know where I'd planned on going. I hadn't thought past getting out of the city. I asked Miranda if I could bring Akira with me. She said I could. So I climbed into the SUV, surrounded by the men with the guns, and we drove away. Miranda says I'll get to learn everything tomorrow. What happens after that, I don't know.

Chapter 9
Bonus: After the Fall

I wasn't planning on making another message. At least not for a while. But I keep thinking about something that happened right after I left the dying city, something that happened before I recorded my last message. I didn't want to talk about it, before, because I wasn't sure what it meant. I still don't know what it means.

It was just a few minutes after I'd climbed into Miranda's van. We drove slowly, carefully, as dreams wreaked havoc around us. A painfully thin man, fifteen feet tall, stepped right over the van as we stopped at a light. Another car nearly crashed into us as it swerved around a lumpy pile of red moss that sprouted in the middle of the street. Everywhere, people ran and screamed.

We were aiming for the highway. I guess Miranda thought we could get out early, stay ahead of the crowds who would flood out of the city in the next days and weeks. We were crawling along, bumper to bumper, as the city gave way to desert, when I saw something by the side of the road.

It looked like a kite, at first. A kite, tethered to some jagged shape. Whatever it was moved slowly away from the road, toward an empty stretch of dusty desert land, away from the highway. Another figure moved next to the shape, this one a little closer to human. Close, but not quite. Even from a distance, something told me they weren't just more dreams come to life.

I stepped out of the van. Miranda and Winry asked where I was going, told me to come back. I ignored them, trusted them to either follow or wait for me. But I couldn't just leave, not recognizing the things making their way out into the desert.

The kite and the jagged shape, those were the sculptures Carson had made. One had hung like a curtain in an alley, and another had loomed like a tree over a busy street. I didn't think to go back for them, before. I assumed they died when Carson did. But no. Because here they were, lurching away from the city. I suppose they thought they'd be taken for just another set of bad dreams, madness hidden in more madness.

And the figure walking next to them? Almost a human shape, but long-limbed, with oddly bent legs, as though they could either walk upright or run on all fours. They turned as I approached, and I saw the horns and thick ridge of brow bone. One of Natalie's kids, one of the ones who had managed to consume her flesh after I killed her. The kid bared his teeth at me and let out a low growl. The sculptures made whispery sounds, whimpers almost too soft to hear.

"That's close enough," someone said. And I realized there was another there, one I hadn't noticed before. That was because this one rolled along on wheels, low and close to the ground and hidden in the kid's shadow. One of Sage's, it had to be, a metal and gem creation that looked nothing like a human anymore.

I stopped and watched them from about ten feet away. "I don't want to hurt you," I said. "I just wanted to help."

The machine beeped, and then its voice came out metallic and artificial through the speakers. "You never intend to hurt anyone, Wren. We know that about you. And yet, people always end up hurt, don't they?"

Guilt isn't a strong enough word for what I feel about myself. He was right. Of course he was. Finally I just asked, "What happened to Sage? Is she ok?"

The little metal man didn't answer. Instead, I heard a voice from behind me. "She's gone. I don't think anyone knows if she got out of the city or not. I hope she's safe."

I turned. Jose stood there, eight different bodies with one mind. I recognized some from the strip club. Jojo the dancer, wearing a metallic minidress and heels despite the wind and the desert ground we all walked on. Joey the bartender. Jose the old man. There were others, too. A little boy wearing a Dora the Explorer shirt. A teenage girl with a punky blue haircut. They all watched me with pity. "So. You know what you are," said Jolene the waitress.

I nodded, didn't say anything. There's no apologies for this sort of thing. Behind Jose's bodies, Miranda and Winry and the other Seekers hovered near the SUV. Cars were starting to crowd the road, horns blaring. There was movement beyond the highway, things I'm pretty sure came out of dreams, scattering crowds of frightened people as they moved.

"Where are you going?" I asked them at last. The sculptures shied away from me, the tree one tugged along as the kite caught the wind and billowed like a fleshy sail.

"We're catching a ride," the little robot said. "It should be here soon. Can't stay in this city anymore. And any normal city, we'll have too hard a time hiding. So it has to be this."

I didn't understand what that meant. Before I could ask more questions, Joey walked up to me and touched my arm. "Look, uh, Wren. Listen, you got a raw deal. I can imagine how you might be feeling pretty bad about yourself right about now." He smiled, something pained and awkward. "But, here's the thing. I wasn't sure whether to tell you this or not, but seeing as we ran into you out here. That's, what, kismet, right? That's the word?" I shook my head, not understanding. He went on, "Anyway, listen. We stopped by the sinkhole on the way out of town. You know, just to see if Claire wanted to come out and join us. But she and that sinkhole, they're moving on their own way. But while we were there, she did her thing. You know, she prophesied. There were three. Two about me. You know, us. But the third was about you. Heck, she probably foresaw that we'd run into you out here."

I asked him what she said. He cleared his throat and looked like he was concentrating, like he wanted to be sure to get it just right. "Here's what she said: Wren will fight the Splinter with another Mosaic at her side. Another Mosaic, but not Zachary." Joey smiled again. "So you see, kid? You're gonna meet someone else like you. Someone who's gonna stand shoulder to shoulder with you."

I didn't know what to say to that. I hadn't had time to think about the possibility that there might be other Mosaics. Others like me, like Zachary. What would that be like, to meet someone like myself for the first time? I nodded and thanked Joey for passing along the message. Claire, if you're out there, if you hear these messages I put out into the world, thank you for that.

Miranda called my name. She'd been so calm back at my place, but now she seemed tense, a little frightened. I followed her gaze and saw why. Out in the desert, on the edge of the horizon, a dust storm gathered.

It came in faster than a dust storm should. Faster than any normal dust storm ever has. But of course this wasn't any other dust storm. I knew that. Miranda shouted at me to get back to the car. Instead I waited with the other freaks.

I expected Miranda to retreat into the SUV and wait it out. Maybe drive off and give up on me entirely. Part of me wanted that. But that's not what happened. And this is where I should mention some things I've learned about Miranda in the short time I've known her. She doesn't have gifts, not like me. Her weapons are ones she created, ones she's honed over time. And her first weapon is her appearance. You know that nice kindergarten teacher look I told you about in my last message? The frumpy haircut, the big glasses, the shapeless cardigans? She's chosen that appearance very carefully. Knowing her now, I imagine her sitting down with a focus group and meticulously analyzing their responses to every article of clothing, pearl earrings, schoolmarmish brooches and hairpins.

And all of this she's done so that when she wants to sneak up behind someone and shoot them with a tranquilizer dart, they'll be pretty god-damned surprised by it. I sure was.

I think it took longer to work on me than it would on most people. At least, Miranda seemed a little confused by the fact that I still had my eyes open, that I was conscious enough to call her a fucking bitch. But my legs turned to jelly and I hit the dirt. Miranda and Winry and the two guys with the guns started pulling me toward the SUV, but not before the dust storm hit.

How to describe it. Imagine a storm that, instead of just arriving, the way storms do, rushes toward you. Runs headlong right for you. Like it has a destination. That's what this storm did, this storm that carried Lexi.

Just as it arrived, a column of clean air opened, just wide enough to hold the ones who had waited for it. A space where the dust and the winds didn't whip at them, but curved around. And at the end of that pathway, that column of air, was Lexi's cottage. It was just as I left it, the lights burning in the windows. I wondered how long it had been for her, since that day when I'd gone to see her. Maybe a minute. Maybe a hundred years. Maybe both.

The others made their way toward the cottage. An exodus of freaks. Jose, Natalie's kid, Carson's sculptures, Sage's robot. They all walked away from me without a backward glance. My vision started to go blurry from the drugs, but I saw the door of Lexi's cottage open to let them in. I saw some of her babies swarming around the roof. I reached out, my arm heavy and clumsy and seeming to float at the same time. "Wait," I said, and I don't know if I really got the words out. "Wait. Take me with you." Even though, if you'd asked me before that moment if I'd ever want to go off and escape to Lexi's cottage, I'd have said you were crazy.

Jose, the old one, turned back to me. "Stay strong, Wren," he said. "You still have a job to do." And then he went into the cottage and was gone.

I passed out after that. By the time I woke up, we were far away from the city. Bad things must have happened on the way out, because Winry looked sick and frightened and even Miranda seemed shaken. And one of the other guys, one of the guys with the guns, he wasn't with us anymore. I still haven't heard what happened to him.

So now I'm waiting. Waiting to understand what Miranda wants with me, and waiting to find this new Mosaic Claire promised. I hope, whoever it is, they don't take too long to find me.

SPINES

Chapter 10
Then and Now

These days I spend a lot of time thinking about the difference between now and then, between the person I am today and the person I was just a few months ago. Then, I thought I was a girl who lost her memory. Now, I know I'm too young to have memories, a chimera built from scraps of eight gifted people. Then, I wandered the city where I was born, looking for clues. Now, that city is dead. You know the one I mean. Then, I recorded messages for the person I thought was my lover. Now, I know that person, Zachary, is someone I was programmed to love, someone I've never spoken to directly. And now I don't know who these messages are for.

Then, I stumbled into danger without ever meaning to. Now? Now, when I step into danger, it's because I was sent there. Like today. Today I walked into a living jungle, and I battled monsters, and I came back out with someone a little bit like me. All in a day's work.

I lied, earlier, when I said I didn't know who these messages are for anymore. They're for my kind of people: the freaks, the gifted, the ones who can light fires by snapping their fingers and the ones who accidentally turn parts of themselves into glass. The ones who can eat unfulfilled wishes and snatch thoughts out of the air like paper planes. If that's you, you should know something: you're being hunted. The reasons for this are complicated, and I can't share all of them. You want to hear the full story, go back and listen to all my messages from the beginning. But the short version is that if you have these abilities, then someone might want to use you to make something like me and Zachary. A mosaic. It's best if I don't tell you what mosaics are supposed to be for. Not yet, anyway. The important thing for you, dear listener, is that the pieces don't usually survive the process of making a mosaic. And, sometimes, it's not just the people going into the mosaic who suffer. Sometimes, it's a whole lot worse than that.

Here's what happened today. Today, a woman named Miranda drove me to a bridge at the end of a country road. I'll tell you more about Miranda later, in another message. For now, all that's important is that she's the closest thing I have to a boss. She takes me where I need to go. Today, it took about an hour to get there. For most of that drive, we were surrounded by soft, rolling farmland. The kind of land where people can graze cows and grow corn. The kind of land dotted with red barns and big rambling farmhouses.

Then we came to the bridge. It was an old stone bridge, barely wide enough for a single car. Beyond it, the land changed. On the other side of the bridge lay the jungle. Maybe it wasn't a jungle in the technical sense. It's not a tropical climate, after all. But it was a place of dense, lush plants, trees growing so close together you could barely move through them. Deep, thick shadows. Leaves bigger than most people. It looked like the kind of place no human had ever set foot in, the kind of place people told scary stories about to keep their children away from it. But that's not what it was.

"The compound used to be right there in the middle of all that," Miranda said. "168 men, women and children. More than 25 houses. Livestock. Buildings." She gestured. "I'd be very surprised if any of them were still alive. But there might be something."

I nodded and stepped out of the car. Miranda didn't cross the bridge with me. It's best if I do these things alone. The moment I stepped onto the bridge, I felt another Mosaic nearby. That's what I am, a Mosaic. And one of the things I can do is sense others like me, like magnetism. I got across the bridge and into the trees, and they sighed and pulled back from me. That's not some kind of clunky metaphor or symbolism. They literally exhaled and twitched away. I could feel them looking down at me.

A little path opened up, just wide enough for me to walk on, but the trees loomed close on either side. It's like they wanted me to know they were watching. Still, they let me pass.

I reached a little clearing, a spot where the path widened and there was enough clear space for some light to reach through the canopy. And that's when I saw Shan.

Things you should know about the Seekers: Once upon a time, there was a man who saw the human genome. This man lived long ago, long before electron microscopes or fancy lab equipment or any of the things we can use to see DNA now. He just saw it with his eyes. That was his gift. A strand of hair, a fleck of skin, a beating human heart. This man saw deep down into these things, saw what gave them their shape. Over time, he came to understand what he saw. He recognized the things that make eyes brown, or hair curly, or bones brittle. And, more importantly, he saw the things that gave some people gifts like his. He gathered followers around him, others who had powers or who knew of them. And he took these followers to a sacred grove, and there he looked deeper into the genes than ever before. How he did this, or what made this time different, that's been lost to the ages. The important thing is that he had a revelation. He saw a long, long road. And at the end of the road lay a world in which everyone had abilities. Everyone, not just the lucky or cursed few. There were milestones on this road, milestones generations in the future, that would take lifetimes of careful study and planning and work. One of those milestones is the creation of Mosaics, people with many different abilities instead of just one or two. I can't tell you why the Mosaics are important. It's too risky. For now, I'll just say that they lead to the final milestone: the Trumpet.

For generations, the Seekers toiled away in their laboratories and libraries, snatching up any new technology that came along. They discovered some great things, as they worked, some things they use now. But progress was slow, and some grew impatient. They wanted faster ways to reach Phase Mosaic, the secret paths of blood magic and stolen powers. Finally, those Seekers split off and became something else: the Splinter. And those two groups have been at war ever since, the followers of science versus the forces of the spiritual and the arcane, the slow path versus the short-cut. One side is led by Miranda, and the other used to be led by Elliot, the one who made me. We don't know who leads them now. I fight on the side of the Seekers. You know, on account of the fact that they don't kidnap people and use their blood for their own ends.

And my other half, Zachary? He fights for the Splinter. I wish I understood why.

How to describe Shan? They're about six feet tall, slender, with hair so black it's almost blue. Almond-shaped green eyes. Light brown skin, with a greenish cast to it. Not what people usually mean when they say olive-skinned, something brighter than that. Male jawline, full feminine lips, a body halfway between, with some muscles and some curves. And, well. . . There's no other way to say it. They're beautiful. They wore a tattered, loose shirt with the sleeves torn off, baggy cargo pants. And their arms were wrapped in delicate green vines. Once I got closer, I saw that those vines disappeared right into their flesh, and they moved independently of Shan's limbs.

Shan watched me as I approached. They didn't say anything, just frowned like they weren't sure what to make of me. "You're like me," they said at last. Their voice was low and husky, halfway between male and female.

"That's right," I said. "My name is Wren. I'm what's called a Mosaic, like you. Do you know what that means, to be a Mosaic?"

Shan frowned. "I don't know. But I know I was made, not born." They gestured around at the trees, the plants, this jungle in the middle of farmland. "This happened, when I was made. I don't remember it, but I can. . . See. In a way."

"What about the people who created you? Are any of them still alive?" I asked.

Shan shook their head. "No. They didn't know what they were doing." And then they pointed up at some of the tall, gnarled trees surrounding the clearing. It took me a minute to understand, but then I saw the shape of a torso in the bend of a branch, hands pressing out to get through a trunk, flecks of red on the leaves.

"What about your other half?" I asked. Shan cocked their head and frowned. "Mosaics are always made in twos," I said. "One man, one woman." Although, even as I said that, I knew Shan was neither.

Then Shan smiled. "Ah. Maybe that's what was supposed to happen, two separate ones. But there's only me." And they gestured up the length of their body, and I understood.

"My name's Shan," they said. "I don't know where that name came from. I just know that's what it was supposed to be."

I asked Shan what else they knew. They hesitated, and then gestured for me to follow them along a path, deeper in the forest. "Here. I'll show you." They walked barefoot; whenever they took a step, I could see that the soles of their feet were dusted with grey-green lichen. They took me to another clearing and pointed up. "There," they said.

It took me a minute to figure out what they meant. Then I saw a withered husk, like a giant seed pod as big as a person. It hung from the tallest tree I'd seen yet, and it was split open and dried out. "That's where you were born?" I asked. Shan nodded. Lucky you, I thought. I was born in a kiddie pool. Then I asked, "How do you know this, if there's no one left? Who told you about where you came from?"

Shan held up their fingertips; tiny tendrils of moss or lichen, like on their feet, almost too small to see. But they flexed and moved. "It's. . . one of the things I can do. Anything I touch, I see its history. I touch that pod, and I see how I was made." They shivered a little, then shrugged. "I see how the ones who made me died. The ones I'm made from. The ones who killed them."

I told Shan I understood. They looked a little angry for a moment. "I doubt that," they said. So I held up my hand and told Shan they could touch. "Go ahead," I said. "Take a look." So they did. I didn't see anything, just felt the light, cool brush of their fingertips against the back of my hand. But whatever Shan saw made them shudder and gasp, made their eyes widen and change color from green to violet. "I suppose you do understand," they said after a long moment.

I asked Shan if they wanted to come with me. If they wanted to understand more about where they came from, and why they were created. Their eyes widened. "Oh, yes," they breathed. "That's all I want."

"Let's go, then," I said, turning toward the path. Shan didn't follow.

"You don't understand," they said. I started to feel a low rumble in the earth, to hear a weird buzzing on the air. "I want to leave. But I can't. The forest won't let me." And then one of the trees uprooted itself, and lunged at me.

Being a Mosaic means I can do a lot of things. Some are things my tiles could do, like how I can repair my injuries as easily as you reshape a piece of Play-do. Other gifts are new, powers greater than the sum of my parts, different abilities merged together to make something new. One of those is teleporting. It took me a while to get the knack of it, doing it on command. But now if, just for example, a giant tree monster tries to knock the shit out of me, I can jump away. I did that automatically, by instinct, and now I was on the opposite side the clearing. The tree paused before it got to Shan, stopping short before crushing them. But now all the trees and bushes and plants around me were shaking, twisting, getting ready to move.

They didn't move the way you might imagine trees moving. Not big and lumbering, like the Ents, and not graceful like a willow tree in the breeze. No. More insectile than that. Twitching, jerky-limbed, spindly. And fast. Very, very fast.

"You should go!" Shan yelled across the clearing. "I can't, but you. . . you should." I could see how hard it was for them to say it, how lonely they were. I decided right then I wasn't going anywhere. But I also knew the teleporting wasn't going to work if I was completely surrounded for God knows how far in any direction. So I whipped out another one of my little tricks; I slowed time to a crawl, so slow the branch that had been reaching down to take my head off just kind of drifted over me. I got to Shan, managed to get them in my little pocket of time that lets me move faster than anyone else. I took their hands in my own. They blinked, probably surprised to see me in front of them.

"Can you jump us out of here?" they asked.

I shook my head. "No. I can't carry anything with me. And I can't keep things slowed long enough to get us out of here." I hesitated. "I have another way. But all of this, this whole place, it'll be gone. Can you live with that?"

Shan only hesitated for a moment before nodding. "Yes."

"Ok," I said. "Hold your breath."

This is another thing I can do: As my hold on time began to waver, as the trees lurching toward us sped up, I reached out around us. I felt the water in all the trees, the shrubs, the little crawling bits of moss. I reached out, and I felt it, and I pulled it out. Plants are mostly water, like us. There's really not much of a difference between a tree and a human body, when you get down to the molecular level. When you can pull apart different molecules and elements like I can.

I pulled all that water from the forest, and at the same time I pulled a bubble of oxygen out of the air and wrapped it around us. It took me a few weeks to master that trick, separating out different kinds of molecules at the same time. But it's a good thing I did, because pulling the water out of an entire forest at the same time meant Shan and I were suddenly at the bottom of a lake. It hurt, the sudden pressure of millions of gallons of water pushing down on us. Shan screamed and clutched at their ears. But I managed to hang on, to them and to the air bubble, and we slowly floated to the surface. All around us, along the bottom of the lake, were the skeletons of dead trees, pale and withered and frozen forever. Then there was a forest. Now there is a lake. Does that mean my deeds are balanced out? These are the kinds of calculations I do now.

Shan stared out at their birthplace, their home, and I could tell they were trying not to cry.

We reached the surface and broke through. Now a calm, quiet lake stretched out in all directions, like it had always been there. I saw the bridge in the distance, Miranda's car still parked on it. Water lapped along the edge, but she hadn't been submerged. I'd been pretty sure before I pulled the water that it wouldn't rise high enough to swallow her or the town down the road, but I was still relieved to see her. She got out of the car and watched with wide eyes as we swam over. "I didn't realize you had that kind of range," she called out. I could tell she was already making a mental note for my file. That's how Miranda works. No time for wonder.

"This is Shan," I told her as we climbed onto the new shore. "Shan, Miranda."

Miranda held out her hand to shake, but Shan kept their distance. "I remember. From when I touched your hand," they said, staring coldly at Miranda. "She's a Seeker. She's responsible for all this."

"That's true," I said. "It's true. But she's trying to make it right. All the Seekers are. That's the only reason I'd work with them."

"You can work with us, too, Shan, if you want. We can help each other," Miranda said. She'd said the same thing to me, months before. I wonder if Shan had seen it. Shan didn't look at her. They looked at me instead.

"You can go wherever you want, Shan," I said. "You can leave. Or you can trust me, and come with us." I held out my hand. Shan stared at it for a long time. I could see thoughts moving behind their eyes, slowly changing back to green from the violet. They seemed angry, almost. Then something changed, and they took my hand.

Miranda drove us away, then. Away from a lake that was never supposed to be. Away from the graveyard of a murdered forest.

Chapter 11
Holy of Holies

So I guess I'm some kind of mentor, now. That feels weird, considering I've only been with the Seekers a couple of months myself. And I definitely don't feel like I have my shit together well enough to have my own apprentice. But I'm the first Mosaic the Seekers managed to get on their side, and Shan's the second, so that's the situation. So me and them have been spending a lot of time together lately. It's been. . . Interesting. Kinda nice, having another non-human to talk to.

Today was my first mission showing Shan the ropes, except for the one where I met them. It feels weird, but I stopped to think about it, and I guess I have done a lot of these lately. Here's how it usually works: Miranda gets a call from Seekers in some other part of the country. Most of them have gifted people they keep an eye on. They say either some of their specimens have gone missing, or that people they know have gone missing. And these changes happen to coincide with some weird shit going on nearby. That's when we know someone from the Splinter has tried to create a Mosaic. And that's when Miranda sends me in.

About Miranda: She looks harmless. Middle-aged, average appearance, big glasses and cardigans. That's all very deliberate, I've learned. She does her best not to look like a cold-blooded head of a secret organization, but that's exactly what she is. She'll do whatever it takes to stop the Splinter. If she has to kill half the planet to get there, she'll do it. Or, more accurately, she'll have me do it. Hopefully it won't come to that.

Back to this most recent incident. In this case, Miranda's people zeroed in on the spot pretty fast. It was kind of the obvious choice. A compound of weirdos following some warped new religion made up by some bearded dude with four wives. I'm sure you can guess which state this was in, but if you need a hint, it starts with a T. Anyway, this ranching compound outside a bigger town used to be pretty friendly with their neighbors, but they went off the grid overnight, and some of the gifted folks in the area got twitchy vibes from the place. That's where I come in.

Miranda and some of her people drove us to the dirt road leading up to the compound. I told Shan to stay there. They didn't argue with me. One of their gifts is remote viewing, so they could follow along with everything I did without going anywhere. They touched my arm just as I stepped out of the van. Their skin feels kind of like leaves, dry and cool and. . . Why the fuck am I telling you this? Jesus. Anyway, Shan touched my arm and dusted me with a little bit of pollen from the flowers they have growing out of their arm. "So I can see through your eyes," they explained. Then, "Are you going to be ok out there?"

That stopped me, because I'm not sure anyone's ever asked me that. The folks in the Seekers assume because I'm a Mosaic that I'm a fucking Terminator or something. I wasn't really sure how to respond. "Sure, no big," I said at last, and then I went to check out the compound.

Things you should know about the Seekers: The Seeker plan for creating Mosaics involves a lot of selective breeding and matchmaking between people with certain powers, to make extra-super-duper powered babies. For most of history all they'd have to do is pay the right father an ox or something to marry his gifted daughter off to the right gifted guy. But sometimes people needed a little extra push. Enter the pheromone division. Before most of the world knew pheromones existed, the Seekers had developed advanced technology to distill and control them. They could figure out what pheromones were keyed to each person's biology, and they could use that to their advantage. Let's say there's a woman with pyrokinesis and a man who can hijack the minds of insects. Naturally, the Seekers want those two to make a baby, stat. But they don't notice each other.

Aren't attracted to each other. Aren't the right social class to make the arrangement. So, obviously, you whip up some pheromones the woman will like and smear them on the guy, vice versa on the woman, get someone to ensure they'll bump into each other on the street, and problem solved.

In theory, sure. But the Seekers have always been better at the science than the espionage part of their work. Which led to an incident in Stratford-on-Avon, England, in 1580. The Seekers wanted to get two gifted folks together. Just two servants, not a union that would garner much attention. But the girl had her eye on a handsome young butcher's son, and the guy had an unfortunate pair of ears and horsey teeth, so the local Seeker chapter decided to go with some chemical assistance. The problem? The pickpocket they hired to get the hair samples and then spill the finished product on the targets overstated his ability to read the instructions. He got the guy right. But the girl? He mistook her name for that of a local widow, a beautiful and wealthy woman everyone stared at whenever she took her carriage through the streets. So the pickpocket pulled off phase 1, the Seekers distilled some perfectly matched pheromone concoctions, and then they sent him back out to make the match.

Onlookers remembered it this way. Dull, horsey Jack Button made his way down the street, running an errand for his master. Lady Teresa of Chalon came from the other direction, sitting proud in her carriage. Neither had noticed a grubby man bump into them as they went about their business earlier in the day. But now, as the carriage approached and the breeze carried Jack Button's smell to her, Lady Teresa ordered her driver to stop. Then she leapt from the carriage and kissed Jack Button, and declared him her one true love, right in front of God and the baffled townspeople.

There's no proof that a sixteen-year-old William Shakespeare was one of those townspeople, of course. But years later, when people from his hometown went to see *A Midsummer Night's Dream* in London's Globe Theater, they thought the whole thing seemed awfully familiar.

I met the first one on the road leading toward a row of ranch houses. She was a teenage girl, wearing a shapeless floral dress and a long braid hanging down her back. She looked like something that just wandered in off the prairie. But that doesn't mean anything. I've met killers who looked cute and cuddly right until they tried to rip my throat out. So I hung back a little and asked her if she lived at the compound.

She glanced up, almost dazed. She took a minute to answer. Then she held up one of her hands. "I live on the road," she said, "because I would give only my finger." Her right index finger was severed at the base, the wound still raw. I tried to get more out of her, more about what that meant, but she just stared out at the horizon. I kept going.

I met the next one a little ways down the road. A young guy, maybe in his early twenties. He seemed maybe a little bit happier than the girl, but not by much. When I tried to talk to him, he lifted his leg. "I live on the road," he said, "because I would give only one of my feet." His foot was missing below the ankle, his pantleg rolled over it. As soon as he said that, he started hopping away down the road.

There were more, as I passed the first ranch houses and got closer to the big church in the middle. More missing fingers, toes, another foot. One woman had her entire hand missing at the wrist, but she held her severed fingers in the other hand, like someone had been interested in the palm and nothing else. All of them had the same spacy look to them, the same weird vacant absence in their eyes.

The other thing I noticed was that the missing pieces got bigger, or more important, as I got closer to the church. It had started with the girl with the missing finger, others with missing toes, but now I was seeing an entire leg missing below the knee, an arm gone at the elbow. Finally, I saw a woman sitting on the porch of one of the ranch houses. She was the first one who seemed to live in an actual dwelling, instead of out in the road. She turned to me as I approached, and the lines of her face held dry, crusted blood like tears running from where her eyes had been. "I cannot see," she said, "for I gave my eyes." She sounded proud.

On the next porch sat a middle aged man. He still had his eyes, but the front of his shirt was spattered with gore. He had used it to scrawl letters on the front wall of the house, words a foot high: I cannot speak, because I gave my tongue.

Then I got to the center, the grassy square surrounding the church. A few people lay scattered on the ground, but not like the ones on the road. No, these people were on little carts and makeshift beds, and other people, more intact people, ran around fetching and carrying for them. I stopped to get a closer look at one of them. She had a gash in her chest, one running almost all the way from her collarbone down to the ribcage. She wheezed every time she took a breath, but she smiled all the same. "I can. . . scarcely. . . breathe," she said, "for I gave one of my lungs." She said it the same as the others, the same rhythm, that made me think they'd been saying these words to themselves and to each other, over and over, for days.

I didn't want to go inside the church. No one had threatened me, yet, but things were getting worse as I made my way in, and I was all too aware that Shan was seeing all this through my eyes. I turned a slow circle, then called out, "Where's your Mosaic? And what's your leader's name? Who runs the Splinter now?" Because that's what Miranda's really been looking for, you see. She doesn't really care so much about cleaning up the broken bodies the Splinter leaves behind, putting fatally flawed Mosaics out of their misery. That's why I do it. But not her. She has one purpose and one purpose only: find out who took Elliot's place as the head of the Splinter, and hunt that person down.

None of them answered me. Some glanced over, like I was a minor distraction. Others kept muttering their little chants about what they had given and what it cost. But one, a teenage boy taking water to the ones who had given organs, whispered something else. "Holy of holies," he said. "I could have been in the holy of holies. Could have been holy of holy." I snagged his sleeve as he went by. "What's the holy of holies?" I asked.

He didn't look at me. His eyes darted between the torn open people on the ground and the doors of the church. "Could have been in the holy of holies," he said again. "But. Bad valve in my heart. They didn't want it," and his eyes filled with tears like it was the saddest thing in the world.

Finally, I let him go and went to the place I'd been avoiding: the church. Not just because I'm an unnatural creature of darkness or whatever, although I guess that's true too. No, I'd been avoiding it because it lay dead center in the compound, with all the damaged people arranged in concentric circles around it. Whatever was in there, it was as bad as this place got.

There were seven of them, inside the church. The bodies were propped up in little makeshift shrines, three on the left, three on the right, one in the center in a carved wooden chair like a throne. No attempt had been made to hide the gashes in their flesh. The cuts that had been made to take the liver of one, the stomach of another, the heart of another. One on the right had given his skin, all of it, peeled away from his muscle and bone. The one in the center had a cracked open skull, and nothing left within it.

There were flowers and candles in front of each shrine. People with missing fingers and toes and teeth fluttering around, dusting and tidying and replacing the dry flowers with the new. The place didn't smell like you'd expect. Not like a charnel house. More like a flower shop. Not in a good way, not in the way flowers smell in nature, but in the too-sweet, condensed way they smell when pushed together in an artificial space.

The holy of holies. The ones who gave the organs you can't live without, not even for a little while. They had little woven crowns, just little circlets of grass and daisies that people had placed on their heads.

"They're not Gifted." The voice came as a little whisper in my ear, like something just behind me. It took me a minute to realize it was Shan talking, sending messages along whatever connection their pollen had created between us. "No," I said. "They weren't. I think. . . I think maybe these people, this part of the Splinter, they were going for quantity over quality. Enough recessive gifts in the soup, and maybe. . ." I shrugged. I could tell it hadn't worked, whatever they thought would happen. If there'd been a Mosaic here, I'd have felt them.

But there was something. Not a Mosaic, but something else. There was a little curtained area behind the altar, a little cordoned off space where something moved and breathed. Breathed in big, slow, heaving gulps. I made my way down the aisles, where cut and broken people sat and sprawled in the pews. One of the attendants tried to stop me as I passed by the altar. "Don't go in there!" she said, "you're unclean. You can't lay eyes on the prophet."

I used my compulsion trick on her, the thing that lets me tell people what to do. "Get lost," I told her, and she wandered off in a daze toward the doors of the church. I hoped she didn't take me too literally and go tramping off into the woods, never to be seen again. Although, let's be honest, these people are basically off in Wonderland already.

None of the others tried to stop me as I went behind the altar and pushed past the curtains.

It looked. . . I don't really know how to describe it. Like a giant baby, I guess. I mean. . . It was the size of a man. A really large man. But the proportions were all wrong, the shape of it not the way any adult is supposed to be. It was fleshy and round and bloated, with skin in patchwork colors that changed abruptly at joints and at the end of limbs. It had one brown eye and one blue. Sparse hair of different colors and textures sticking up in tufts from its too-big head. It lay on a makeshift bed, staring and twitching feebly every now and then. I watched it for a moment, reaching out with that part of myself that can sense others like me. But there was nothing. Any magic that had been here had been used up to make this thing and keep it alive. This thing wasn't a Mosaic. It wasn't even gifted. It wasn't even a human. Not even that.

Maybe you're imagining that it was in pain, that it looked at me and begged for death. But life is never that poetic. This thing wasn't conscious enough even for pain. Its eyes were glazed over, its mouth hanging slack. It would never have a thought, much less the ability to move and speak and tell me who created it.

"Tell Miranda there's nothing here," I said, trusting Shan to pass the message along. Then I lifted a hand and ripped the water from that breathing pile of meat. Just in case it ever gained enough of a glimmer of intelligence to get a sense of what it was. The entire compound screamed as the thing died, as though they could each feel one of their parts breathing its last. None of them paid any attention to me as I left. I passed by all of them again, all of the same people I'd seen on my way in, and they were too dazed with grief to notice.

Shan stared at me with wide eyes as I approached the van. "This is what we do?" they asked. "These are the things we see?"

I thought about lying to them. Making up something about how it wasn't always this bad, most of it was fine. But instead I just said, "Yeah. You'll see worse." And Shan went quiet, and said nothing for the entire drive home.

Chapter 12
The Countdown

Today was Shan's debut as pet fixer for the Seekers. I gotta say, they killed it. I wish I could take credit for being a kickass mentor. But the truth is that Shan saved me today. I don't know what would have happened if they hadn't been there. I don't think it'll be the last time, either.

Think about a small town you know of. If you're from a small town, think of another one thirty miles away. If you're from a big city, think of one of the little places you pass by on the highway, a place between where you come from and where you're going. Now ask yourself: how long would that small town have to be gone before you knew about it? Assuming its destruction wasn't reported on the news. Maybe you have a friend there, and at some point you'd realize that friend hadn't been in touch for a while. Maybe you make that drive from your big city to another, and you realize there isn't a place to stop for gas like there used to be. However you found out, the point remains the same: it would probably take you a long time to realize that little town had gone. For those of you who listen to these messages and think the things in them can't be true because how could towns vanish and forests appear and become lakes and how could compounds of people all be dedicated to this secret world you never knew existed, I ask you just one question: when did you last check on that little town down the highway? Yeah. That's what I thought.

But the Seekers are different. They don't wait to find out that a town has gone dark. Especially not now, with it happening all over the country. Now they search for the towns that vanish. And, given the day and age we live in, the best way to spot a town that's vanished isn't by driving past it or looking down with satellites. No. The best way is to keep an eye out for places that aren't posting things to the internet anymore. It's a project headed up by Winry, the first Seeker I ever met. She was low-level then, still an apprentice, but bagging me got her a big promotion. So now she runs the Seekers' digital surveillance operations. Are you picturing a big gleaming control room, like something at the NSA? Haha. They wish. No, for all their struggles to save the world from the Splinter's plans, the Seekers are a pretty ragtag bunch. They only just got their command center, just as I joined up. And it's not a big lab or even an office building. It's a creaky old house one of the older members donated in their will when they died. Just a year ago, all the Seekers were spread out across the country, the world, connected by email and phone calls and all working on different equipment. Now all the ones who can afford it work in the Burrow. That's what we call the command center, the Burrow, because it's full of dark, winding hallways. Those hallways and old ballrooms and forgotten bedrooms are full of equipment, mostly old, mostly begged, borrowed, or stolen.

Winry's digital surveillance room has a big bank of screens and computers, so I guess you probably pictured that right, but they're all mismatched and scratched and propped up on old books. It takes up one corner of the basement, with two separate lab setups in the other corners. Yesterday, like so many other days recently, I made my way down there after I got a call from Winry. The other Seekers still stare at me when I walk through the Burrow, but now they don't stop what they were doing. They stare, but they keep working. That's progress.

I found Shan in the kitchen on my way to see Winry. They've been staying in one of the few rooms in the Burrow not set aside for projects, but they're rarely up there. They're mostly in the kitchen, I think because of something to do with the natural light. Miranda tried to get me to stay in that room when I first joined, but I always have my own place. Winry probably knows where, but not because I told her.

"Another Mosaic?" Shan asked. They held a cup of tea between their hands, and their arm vines pushed and swayed toward the steam.

I shrugged. "Maybe. You coming?"

Shan raised an eyebrow. "Think I'm ready?"

I hesitated. So far none of Shan's gifts seemed very useful for fighting or defending themself. Then again, most of mine weren't so hot for investigating, so maybe we'd make a good team. At the time, all I knew was that I was tired of going into these situations alone. Finally I just told Shan to come with me.

Down the basement, Winry showed us the town that had suddenly stopped posting anything to Facebook, Twitter, or those forums where losers whine about women. It had happened overnight, with not a single shred of internet activity for over two weeks. She'd tried calling businesses and private homes, too, and none of the calls had been able to get through. Yup. I recognize the signs by now. Someone tried to make a Mosaic.

"Why do they keep botching it?" Shan asked. "They pulled it off when they made you and Zachary. So why all these other failures?"

I told them what Miranda told me. Eliot was the only one who knew the secret recipe, the right way to pull off the ritual. He was paranoid and cautious about sharing what he knew until he was sure it worked, and then right after he succeeded he got killed by one of my tiles. All these other members of the Splinter are trying to piece it together from the parts Eliot did share, and from trial and error. "So," I said, "Let's go see what the error was this time around." And off we went.

Things you should know about the Seekers: They came close, once, to making Mosaics in their own way. The slow, methodical way of selective breeding and genetic manipulation, not the way of the Splinter. They managed to produce four people with wonderful combinations of gifts, four people the right age and the right combination of sexes to make two Mosaics. The Seekers saw the end of their quest on the horizon, saw themselves inching toward the culmination of all they'd worked for through the centuries. But then a new year came along, and that year was 1939. You see where this is going, don't you? One of their prized subjects was in China. One in Denmark. One in India. One in Greece, where the Seekers had been based since their beginnings. This is what happened to them: The one in China, a young woman named Yanmei, had the greatest mind control abilities this earth has ever seen. She persuaded entire battalions of occupying Japanese forces to slaughter each other, until the strain of manipulating so many minds at the same time gave her a fatal aneurysm.

The Danish one, Christian, fought with the Danish Resistance for most of the war. His powers were all of the flesh, subtle gifts of biological manipulation. He could make homunculi out of his hair and spit and fingernail clippings and send them into Gestapo headquarters and prisons and private homes to report back on the things they heard. But the Nazis got wind of his abilities, somehow, and they closed in. Just before Christian shot himself in the head, he ordered his lieutenants to burn his body so the Nazis would never be able to use his secrets for themselves.

Then there was Pratitha, the shapeshifter, who made herself a man long enough to join the colonial military and fight her way across North Africa. She's responsible for the British victory in the Battle of El-Alamein, a turning point in the war, although she never got credit for it. A stray mortar ended her life in 1943.

The Greek man, Vasilis, was the only one left at the end. He'd wanted to go and help his beloved Pratitha, but his gifts weren't suited for combat. They both knew he'd only slow her down as she slipped behind enemy lines. So he stayed behind, and the Seekers hooked him up to tubes and beakers, and he helped in the only way he could. He made medicine. He sweated antibiotics, and bled painkillers, and pissed the world's only perfect treatment for chemical burns. His tears cured typhus, and his saliva granted soldiers a temporary surge of superhuman strength. He gave all he could stand, and then gave more. And then, as civil war broke out in Greece and the Second World War came to a close and Vasilis became little more than a withered husk grieving for Pratitha, the Seekers unhooked the tubes and pulled out the needles and told him to stop his tears. Then they smuggled him out of the country, and they settled in the United States, the only place the war hadn't reduced to smoke and rubble. There, they began their mission from scratch, from the remnants of their old libraries and the memories of their surviving researchers. It's taken all this time, all these decades, for the American Seekers to approach what their forbears did. And now we're here.

The town looked fine from the outside. Not like the place where Shan was born, or the compound strewn with maimed remains of people. No, this one seemed like a boring little town. People on the sidewalks. Cars driving down the streets. Nothing exciting. Shan and I watched from the highway for a while, but nothing happened. Finally, we headed for the main road leading down the center of the town.

Things started to get weird pretty quick. People stopped when they saw us, stopped and stared and whispered. But not like the usual small town "who's that" stuff. And not really hostile. More. . . wary, I guess. Fearful. Shan got other looks, too, of course. Even under fear, people can't help but notice beauty like that. They wore a long-sleeved shirt and loose pants that hid the vines twining out around their limbs, but they couldn't hide the skin texture, the other little bits of strangeness people probably wouldn't be able to pin down but together added up to an odd, arresting picture.

I started noticing other things, besides the stares. We passed a house, and towels and pillows had been tied around all the sharp corners. The porch rail, the surface of the door. On the busiest section of Main Street, fire extinguishers sat in a neat row along both sides of the sidewalk. Buckets and sandbags sat a little further back, along the edge of each house and business.

Finally, we stopped in front of a building that was probably the town hall or the community center or something. A big clock had been hung above the main doors. It had the name of a high school along the top, looked like it had been torn off a scoreboard. The big digital numbers ticked down. Right then, it said 2 hours, 14 minutes, and 47 seconds.

"Is it you, this time?" It was a woman's voice, ragged and hysterical. She stormed out of one of the businesses, eyes wide and hair tangled. "Why wait? Just fucking get it over with."

A man ran out and pulled her away from us. "Sorry," he muttered, but not like he was embarrassed. More like he was scared about what we might do.

"We're not here to hurt you," Shan said. They stepped over and let their fingers trail along the inside of the woman's wrist. It looked like just a gentle touch, but I knew Shan was making some kind of soothing potion through their fingertips. Sure enough, the woman settled down. But as soon as the woman calmed, Shan's eyes widened, and they stepped away, blinking and shaking their head.

"What's wrong?" I asked. They hesitated, as though unsure of what to say. So I asked the woman, "Why are you scared of us? What did you think we were going to do?"

The woman's eyes filled with tears. She pointed at the ticking score-board clock. "Is it you, this time? It must be you. No one else gets in. The only things that get in are the things that. . ." She couldn't finish whatever she'd been about to say. I asked what that meant, people not getting in.

The man answered for her: "If you just wandered in here. . . Don't know how you did it. No one's been able to get in or out of town for weeks. And if you got in here by accident then. . . Well. Sorry." And he pointed at the clock, just as the woman had.

Shan's fingers plucked at my sleeve. "Something's wrong," they said, pulling me off to the side. "What I saw, it can't be right. That woman, she died. She died in a fire." I didn't argue. I didn't point out the obvious, that a woman who died in a fire couldn't be standing in front of us now. Those things stop being obvious when you've been in my world for a while. Then Shan reached out and trailed their fingers along the front wall of one of the buildings. "This. . ." they frowned. "This building burned down. But it also got buried in a mudslide. And it also, I don't know, there were people being killed out front." They stepped back and shook their head. "I don't understand how this building can still be here, how it could have been destroyed in all those ways. . ."

I looked around, and I started to understand. I turned back to the man. "How long has that clock been ticking down?" I asked.

"Four days," he replied, automatically. "It happens every four days." I asked him what, what happened every four days, although I was pretty sure I already knew. His voice went weak and dry and fragile as old paper. "We die," he whispered.

There was no way to prepare, because there was no way to know what kind of death was coming. They told us some of them they'd gone through, every four days for the last several weeks. Firestorm, mudslide, drowning, a tornado, a mob of masked people who beat and cut everyone in town to death. A few people survived, most times. Not always. But always, every time, those who had died and those who had survived woke up again, the same as they always had. And then the clock started ticking down, and they tried to plan for a new disaster.

None of them could tell us why it had happened. None of them had heard the words Grove, Mosaic, or Trumpet. I could smell that someone had tried to make a Mosaic in this town, but it wasn't like the compound with the Holy of Holies. This was someone working in isolation, someone hidden from their neighbors.

Finally, as the clock ticked down to the 35 minute mark, Shan and I found where it had happened. It was the house of someone named Dana Johansen, the only person in town unaccounted for, the only one who had vanished and not reawakened when everyone else did. People had checked her house, but they hadn't found the locked room in the cellar. Shan and I did. And inside were bloodstained remnants I recognized all too well. It was a lot like the attic where I was born. I tried not to breathe in the smell of dried blood as Shan ran their fingers over the floors and wall. "There, there, I see you," they muttered. They sighed and rose to their feet. "I saw what happened. The eight, the tiles, they found a way to combine their gifts just before the ritual was complete. They knew it would kill them, but they. . . I suppose you could say they cursed her. The woman who lived here." They looked up at the ceiling like they could see the town above. "They lost control, though. They only meant it for her, but it covered the whole town. One of them had a gift, something with time, that set everything else on a loop."

Well, shit, I thought. I checked my watch. "We should go."

Shan raised an eyebrow. "Aren't we going to save these people?"

"Of course," I said, although I wasn't at all confident that we could do anything. "But I'd rather do it from the outside, where we'll be safe."

But that, as it turns out, wasn't going to happen. We'd gotten in just fine. But as soon as we tried to step onto the highway lining the edge of the town, we turned around. It was like the world twisted and pushed us back in the other direction. We tried again and again. I could feel a buzz in that spot, a hum I hear when I slow time. Someone had played with time here, brought it out of sync with the outside world. Suddenly, that clock seemed to be ticking down a lot faster. Shan and I tried different points around the edge of town. As we moved, people started gearing up for their next death, setting up firehoses, sending their kids down into the basement of the church. But they did it with resigned, heavy movements; they had to try, they knew that, but they also didn't think this time would be any different.

Five minutes left. Four. Three. Shan looked at me. "I don't think we're getting out before this happens," they said, calm, like we were just going to miss a movie.

"Yeah," I said. "Think we should take shelter?"

Shan lifted one shoulder in one of those graceful little shrugs. "I'd rather be out in the open. In the sun." They turned their face up as though listening for what the sun had to say about the whole thing. I just paced, lining up my gifts, ready to pull water from an attacker, slow an assault, compel anyone who came near. Most of all, getting ready to put my flesh back in order if none of the above worked.

"You could try teleporting out, you know," Shan said, quietly.

I shook my head. "I can't take you with me."

"Even so," they said. I just shook my head again. I hoped I stuck with it, when the time came. I hoped I didn't panic at whatever came for us and leave Shan behind.

The clock ticked to zero. There was a moment of calm, everyone watching and listening for what came next. It started as a cloud, a dark shape in the sky. I thought it was a hurricane. But then I heard the cloud chittering and buzzing, and little pieces of it started to break away and swoop down toward the streets of the down. Locusts, I thought. Well. That's not so bad. Then the first of the insects reached the people on the street, and their sharp little jaws opened and bit down on skin, and people started bleeding and screaming and fighting to get away.

A few of them got close enough for me to see, weaving and darting through the air. They were like grasshoppers, but bigger, and with huge beaklike mouths. Mouths big enough to tear out a chunk of flesh the size of a quarter. And there were millions of them. I tried pulling the water from the cloud, and I got a handful, but they were too many and too fast. I braced myself.

Then I felt Shan's hand in mine, cool skin like oak leaves. Their face was calm, focused. Just as the cloud gathered to descend on us, Shan pulled me close.

Then they kissed me.

I understand why, now. But at the time I thought it was just Shan accepting the end, and choosing to go out that way. And I was all too happy to go with it. There are much worse ways to die. I was so lost in that kiss it took me a while to realize we weren't being attacked. I opened my eyes and looked around; the townspeople were shrieking and bleeding, some already dead on the sidewalk, but the wave of insects just parted around us like we were rocks, trees. I pulled back and looked at Shan. They blushed a little. "Repellent," they explained. "I saw how to make it, and that was the fastest way to spread it to you." But their hands stayed on my waist, and I knew that wasn't the only reason.

Sorry, Zachary. I shouldn't be. We've never really spoken, and I owe you nothing. But I still feel like apologizing, just a little.

The next ten minutes were carnage. There was nothing to do but watch and wait for it to be over. It was over soon, but it felt like forever. Once the last one stopped screaming, the cloud of insects shot back up into the sky. And then that hum, that low buzz of manipulated time, started to change. I closed my eyes, feeling it in my fingertips. Shan started to ask me what was happening, but I shushed them. I saw a vulnerable point in the loop. A malleable spot, if I timed it perfectly. I felt time swing back around in its circle, and even without opening my eyes I knew the chewed corpses of the townspeople were healing, damage reversing, hearts returning to a time when they pumped blood. There it was, the split second that took the whole cycle back to its beginning, the moment before everyone woke up in their beds and that clock started ticking down to their next death.

And I. . . It's hard to explain, but it's like I knocked it off its track. I accelerated it when it was supposed to slow down, and the loop broke. I opened my eyes, and the town was clean and boring and normal again. Shan turned a circle as though trying to find something. "Did. . . did something just change?" they asked.

"Yeah," I said. "It's ok. We fixed it." It felt good, getting to save some-one for once. I took Shan's hand and led them out of town. Nothing tried to stop us this time. I saw the clock on the way out. It was broken, burnt and cracked down the middle. I hoped the town left it like that.

Chapter 13
Rewritten

Today I woke up to find that some of Shan's vines had wrapped around me as we slept. Little tendrils wound around my index finger, thicker vines looped around my back, feathery little leaves tickled my neck. That probably sounds horrifying, but it's not. They're just another part of Shan's body, like their eyes or hands or legs. But it did mean it took me longer than usual to get out of bed, which, hey, ain't all bad. By the time I got untangled and dressed and over to where I'd left my phone, I had 17 texts and voicemails from Miranda. I didn't need to check any of the messages to know what that meant. They had another lead, another clue about the new Splinter leader. And that probably meant another attempted Mosaic, more damaged or dead gifted tiles. Shit. And my day started off so good.

Winry started chattering as soon as Shan and I got down to her little computer lair. "That was a lucky break, finding Dana Johansen's house," she said. It took me a minute to remember that was the name of the woman who owned the house where we'd found the ritual remains on the last mission. Winry pointed to a bunch of drivers' license photos pulled up on her screens. "We found emails and calls between her and all these people. All people with the resources to be the one who replaced Elliot." There were five faces, three male, two female, a range of ages and ethnicities.

Shan folded their arms and stared at the screen. "So I suppose the next move is to monitor these people and see which of them coincides with another disturbance."

"Already done!" Winry said, smiling widely. She gets nervous and giggly whenever Shan is around. Granted, the same is true for most of the people we see in the Burrow, but she's especially bad at hiding it. Shan never seems to notice.

Winry sat in her swivel chair and clicked on some icons. "Ok, it's. . . Hm. I must have saved it to the wrong place. Hang on." She clicked and typed some more. Finally, she stopped and frowned at me. "I don't understand. I had it, a disturbance near where one of these people lives." She pointed vaguely first at one of the faces, then another.

"It's ok," I said, "It's just a file. We'll find it again."

"No," Winry said. She started to look panicky. "No, you don't understand. I just found it, just now. And now I don't remember. I know there was something, and I found it, and it was near one of these, but now I don't know. I have a photographic memory, Wren, I don't forget things!" Shan took her hands in their own just as she started to get hysterical. That distracted her a little. Shan closed their eyes and lightly ran their fingers over Winry's palm. Poor girl looked like she didn't know whether to cry or cum. Finally, Shan stepped back, frowning. "It's odd," they said. "It's as if there are two layers in one memory. One's fading, but I know it involved this one." They gestured at one of the drivers' license photos, a guy named Neil Duvalier.

"Yeah!" Winry almost shouted. "Him, and. . . Cincinnati, I think? But. . . I don't know, that's all I can remember." It took us a while to get her calmed down. She's used to great recall, getting her brain to do whatever she wants it to do. She doesn't know what it feels like to have holes in your life. She wasn't the only one, though. I talked to three of the other Seekers who help Winry out on her projects, and all of them were sure they'd found something, sure they had a lead, but they couldn't remember it now. And it got worse as time went on, with even the sketchy outlines of the guy in Cincinnati fading away. Still, it gave Shan and I enough to go on. So we went looking.

Things you should know about the Seekers: This is Winry's story. I don't know if it's representative of the Seekers, since I haven't heard the stories of many of the others I see in the Burrow. I don't know anything beyond the names of most of them, enough to identify them as Zafir or Karen or Magdalena but nothing more than that. I think that's by design. They avoid telling me personal shit. But I managed to get Winry drunk one time, and here's what I found out. It began as a love story, like so many others. Winry and Tasha, two geek girls meeting over a Bunsen burner in advanced chemistry. They were together for nearly a year when Tasha told Winry her deepest secret: she could do things. Things others couldn't do. Winry didn't believe her at first, especially when Tasha had a hard time explaining exactly what it was she could do. But then she showed Winry and that changed everything.

Tasha's gift was language. I don't mean she was well-spoken or she could speak fifteen of them or anything like that. I mean that she could make language do things to the people who heard it, things it's not supposed to do. She explained it to Winry as like being able to unstuff the filling of words and replace it with whatever she wanted. It was tricky, and the effect she wanted to create had to be a good match for the word it hid within, but she had mastered it and developed her own system over the years. Take *bellicose*. That's an obscure word, one you don't see much, and hear even less. But once Tasha was done with it, bellicose wasn't a fancier way of saying aggressive or hostile. No, *bellicose* carried a secret weapon, an inner-ear disturbance so severe it would knock anyone who heard it right on their ass. There were others like that. *Vermillion* could repair astigmatism. *Conclave* reduced body temperature. *Frivolity* produced instantaneous orgasm.

Winry blushed when she told me this. I didn't ask her which words Tasha had used to convince her, but I could guess.

Tasha swore Winry to secrecy, of course. And Winry promised and kissed her and said she'd never, ever betray her. And, at the time, I think she probably meant it. But that scientific mind of hers couldn't let it go. It started small and simple, with Google searches and browsing through medical journals. Reading up on neurolinguistics. She got Tasha to provide some demonstrations. And of course she made it seem like she was just interested. She wanted Tasha to turn her on with *recondite*, get her high with *Pangolin*, fix her headaches with *detritus*. And that was part of it. But then there was the other part. The notes she kept in a hidden folder, the ones she took when Tasha wasn't looking. The little tests she started threading into conversations, hoping to make her girlfriend utter specific word combinations.

The ideas started making their way into her research. Just little footnotes at first. Then bigger ideas. Things she started saying out loud, at conferences, although of course she made sure to avoid that part when she spoke to Tasha about her work.

It all came to an end a year after Tasha had told her the secret. They were living together. They'd started talking, shyly, about getting married. And Winry's lies had gotten so deep and gone on for so long that she knew she could never even begin to undo them. She thought she could keep it going, and she might have been able to, if she hadn't been approached by the Seekers. They kept an eye out for work just like Winry's, research that showed signs of being influenced by someone with gifts. They figured out her and Tasha after just a few short weeks of observation. But they missed one important detail. They missed the fact that Tasha didn't know she was a lab rat. They assumed Winry couldn't or wouldn't have kept that from her. And that's why, when a midlevel Seeker showed up at their home to recruit them both, Tasha grew quieter and quieter.

Winry tried to reach out to her, to hug her, to do something. To explain. But Tasha just looked at her and said one word. Winry wouldn't tell me what it was. But it made her black out. When she woke up, Tasha's things were gone. And Winry couldn't see her. She couldn't see Tasha's name written on paper. She couldn't focus on pictures of her. She couldn't even look directly at things Tasha had left behind. There were just blank spots where those things should have been. So Winry went to the Seekers, because she had nothing left. And because she thought maybe, just maybe, it would be a way to find Tasha again. She wondered aloud as she told me this if she'd been in Tasha's presence since it had happened, standing right in front of her old beloved and unable to see her.

It's easy to find the place where someone tried to make a Mosaic, once you've felt it once. It's unmistakable, like a scent. Shan and I drove around

Cincinnati until we both started to feel the site pull at us like a magnet. This time it was in an abandoned hospital, the kind of place teenagers dare each other to go explore. We found the remnants of the ritual, the pool of blood and the symbols drawn on the walls. And we found something else, too. We found sets of footprints, bloody bare feet, limping away from the scene. My heart started pounding. The tiles don't usually survive, whether or not the Mosaic does. The only other time I knew about was when Zachary and I were made, and that time the tiles were so damaged they destroyed a city. But that's not what it felt like here. I should have been able to feel it, gifted people spinning out of control. I didn't, though. It just felt normal, like any city.

There were other things that didn't make sense. Shan tried reading the history of the room from its surfaces and the objects left behind, but couldn't see anything clearly. "It's like trying to see two completely distinct things happening at the same time," they said, frustrated. "I see a middle-aged woman, with tangled red hair, struggling naked from this room. But I also see a past in which that never happened, in which she was never here. And seven others, just like that. Here, but not."

Finally, Shan managed to get enough of a fix to follow the path of just one of them, just the path of the woman with the red hair. We traced her route down alleys, into an apartment laundry room where she must have gotten clothes, across back yards, winding from one side of the street to the other. We mainly followed Shan's glimpses, the history embedded in walls and trees and telephone poles, but I felt it, too. Little flashes of knowledge that a tile was here, that someone had tried and failed to make a Mosaic nearby. But it was as if it was something in the corner of my eye, something I couldn't quite see.

We ended up at a nice little house with a cute yard and potted flowers on the front porch. "She lived here," Shan said. "She limped inside, tripping on the front step. She'd stopped crying by then. She looks as though she was just. . . numb, by that point."

"Well," I said, "let's hope she's still numb, not pissed off." And I rang the bell.

A guy in his 30s answered. He had olive skin, glasses, a nice haircut. He smiled at us. "Yes?"

I told him we were looking for a middle-aged woman with red hair, someone who might have been involved with an accident several weeks ago. The man frowned. "Oh, I'm sorry, but there's nobody like that who lives here. It's just me and my husband." He held out his hand. "I'm Tarik."

Shan and I both shook his hand. I searched for some sign the guy was lying, but he seemed genuinely concerned about this mystery woman who'd been in an accident. I tried compelling him, asking him to tell us the truth about the woman. But Tarik just smiled and repeated what he'd already said. No woman like that lived here. No one like that had lived here recently. Tarik and his husband Andrew had been here for nearly four years, and didn't share the house with anyone.

I glanced at Shan out of the corner of my eye. They watched Tarik, frowning, head tilted to one side, as though trying to hear something. They didn't say anything, didn't ask any questions, the entire time. Finally, I gave up and we left Tarik alone, in this place where our missing tile's trail had gone cold.

"There are two incompatible histories," Shan said at last, once we were away from the house. "I can see them both at the same time. In one there's this woman, the woman who walked away from that site. In the other, there is this man Tarik and his husband, and they're the only ones who have been there." They rubbed their forehead as though trying to get rid of a headache.

"Let's try something else," I said. I held out my hands. "You can peek into the future, right? So take a look at mine, and see what we decide to do next."

Shan smiled a little. "You realize that makes absolutely no sense," they said. I shrugged. What part of our lives does make sense? But Shan humored me. They took my hands in their own. I still shiver when they do that, even though we've done so much more. Shan was quiet for a minute, then opened their eyes and frowned. "You're searching, a little while from now. But you're carrying Akira. Akira's helping you, somehow."

Of course. I understood right away. Akira is the creation of, or I guess part of, one of my tiles. Bilal. Someone who turned themselves into a place, someone who left the world. If anybody or anything would have a way of seeing through things that both exist and don't exist, it would be him. Half an hour later, we stood close to Tarik and Andrew's house again. We'd gone back to the place we were staying to pick up Akira. Akira always travels when I do. I don't trust anyone else to take care of him. I held Akira in my hands, bundled in a little towel against the cold. He didn't seem to mind.

"Ok, Akira," I said. "Show us what happened to these tiles." He didn't do anything at first. Which was to be expected, because he's a freaking frog. But I waited, and then turned in a circle, and at some point his tongue flicked out at the air. I swung back around, and his tongue shot out in the exact same direction. At every corner, I'd stop and turn in all directions. Sometimes he'd have us continue going straight. Sometimes he'd indicate a turn to the right or left. And so we made our way through the neighborhoods of Cincinnati, walking for hours. Shan never questioned what we were doing. They might not have understood exactly what was happening, but they trusted me and I trusted Akira, so we kept going.

Finally, we hit a spot where Akira pointed directly at a house. We tried going around the block, thinking he was indicating something beyond it. But, no, it was definitely a particular house that he'd led us to. I handed Akira over to Shan. "Hang on to him," I said. "I'll be back in a few."

"You're not going in there by yourself," Shan said.

"Oh, yes I am, protégé," I replied. "Remember? Officially, I'm training you." Even though that wasn't really fair because Shan was really as good at this stuff as I was by this point. I sighed. "Look, I don't want Akira to get hurt, ok? I don't want him in the line of fire if something happens. Keep an eye on him, will you?"

Shan looked like they wanted to argue with me, but finally they just nodded and leaned down to give me a kiss. "Be careful, ok?" they said, and then they settled down on some steps with Akira. I headed over to the house.

It was a squat, in a bad part of town. Most of the houses on the street looked empty, abandoned, coated with age and graffiti. Trash clumped along the sidewalks. This house was different, though. It was clean, even though it hadn't been painted in a while. The sidewalk out front had been swept. When I knocked on the front door, someone called for me to come inside.

The inside was as clean and tidy as the outside, although I could tell all the furniture was mismatched and secondhand. A portable massage table sat in the middle of the room. A tall, curvy woman sat on the couch. She held out her hand as I approached, like I was supposed to kiss it or something. "Welcome, dear," she said. "My name is Thorn."

I noticed her fingernails. They were thick and long and white, but I don't think they were painted that way. They were more like sheets of bone grown out through her fingertips. As soon as our hands touched, she let out a little gasp. "Oh, my dear. I see why you came to me."

I wasn't sure what she meant. I stepped back. "I came because I've been looking for people, and I usually have an easier time finding them. I think you have something to do with the trouble I'm having."

She said nothing for a moment. Then, "If they've come to me for help, then you should just give up looking now. The people you're looking for can't be found."

I told her I didn't want to hurt them. I told her she could trust me, that I was looking because I wanted to help them, to protect them. She shook her head. "You misunderstand me, dear. This doesn't have anything to do with me trusting or not trusting you. I didn't say I wouldn't tell you. I said I can't." Someone knocked on the front door, and she gestured to the couch. "Sit down, and watch, and you'll understand why there's no sense in looking for these people."

Someone came in. I don't know who they were or what they looked like, whether they were a man or a woman, even though I spoke to them and watched Thorn work on them for nearly an hour. You'll understand why in a moment. From what I gather about Thorn and the work she does, this person was most likely desperate, dying, or ready to die. They'd have to be.

Thorn had this person take their shirt off and lie facedown on the massage table. She tied their wrists and legs. "For your own protection, honey," she said. Then she held out her hands, and a tiny corona of blue flame flared out around the tips of each of her white fingernails. And then she started burning designs into the person's back. They screamed and cried in agony, I know that, although I don't remember what those cries sounded like. Thorn murmured to herself as she carved those careful designs. "Born in Chicago on November 4th, 1980. You saw a meteor shower on Independence Day in 1986. Playing in your back yard, you caught dragonflies during the day and fireflies at night." It went on and on like that, pivotal events and mundane details. And, as Thorn worked, the person beneath her hands began to change.

At the end, when Thorn stepped back to survey her handiwork, the person lying on the table was a slim, redheaded woman in her thirties. She wore an expensive-looking diamond bracelet. I don't know what kind of shirt she'd taken off before Thorn started, but I know it wasn't the cream silk blouse that now hung on the hook on the wall. The lines in the woman's back remained, but they were faded, old scars. She sat up. "Oh, goodness. I must have fallen asleep. I. . ." She frowned and looked around. "Wait, this isn't where I usually go for my massage."

Thorn handed over her blouse. "No, dear, remember? The spa is closed today, so we arranged to meet here."

The woman nodded and frowned. "Oh. Right. Of course, I forgot." She laughed. "It must be this new case. I'm just so busy with it."

Thorn smiled. "Of course. You just go home and get some rest, now." And she showed the woman to the door. Now, a silver BMW was parked out on the blighted street. Thorn waited until the woman drove away before she closed the door and turned back to me. "So you see?" she said. "That's why I can't help you. The person who came to me doesn't exist anymore. I don't remember them any better than you do. Their place in the world has been rewritten, and that can't be undone. Now, whoever that person was when they came in, they've always been Audrey Collins, an attorney who has lunch with her sister every Saturday and plays field hockey in her spare time. She's never not been that, now."

I stood. "Well, if that's true, it means the ones I've been looking for are safe. I'm guessing they came to you because they were damaged. If they're like the other ones I've met, they were ruined when someone tried to make them into a Mosaic. I'm glad they found a way to be fixed."

"It's a high price," Thorn said. "It's only for people whose existing life isn't worth living. They have to die, you see, to become someone new." She stepped forward and took my hands in her own. "It's something I can do for you. You have so much pain. I can make you someone else. If that's what you want."

I thought about it. I really did, for just a second. But then I thought about Shan, sitting outside holding Akira. And I thought about the Splinter, and all the lives I hadn't managed to save so far and all the ones they might ruin in the future. I even thought about you, Zachary, God help me. I sighed and shook my head. "No. Not for me," I said. I hesitated. "At least, not yet."

Thorn nodded. I don't think she was surprised. She reached into her pocket and pulled out a card. "If it ever gets to be too much." It had a phone number and nothing else. I nodded and put it in my pocket. I didn't think I'd ever use it, but I also didn't think I'd ever throw it away. I left that house and got Shan and Akira, and we drove away. Whatever happened in Cincinnati, there's no one left to save. We were too late for that.

Chapter 14
Profiles

I suppose someone was bound to try it at some point. No one ever said the Mosaics had to be flesh and blood, after all. Still. We're supposed to be human, sort of. Not sure today's experiment met that requirement. Even so, I'm glad they got away. Good for them.

Shan and I were out following up a lead on some Mosaics when we got a call from Miranda. "Get back to the Burrow," she said. "Winry found something." I asked her what it was. I could hear her irritation through the phone. "Hell if I know," she said. "I'm a cell biologist, not a programmer." Then she hung up.

Winry was practically levitating when we got there, she was so worked up. "So, so, take a look," she said, waving at her monitors. Then she started spouting something about social media algorithms and coding and some other nonsense. I lost her after a sentence or two. Finally, Shan laid a hand on her arm, and that gentle touch cut her off midsentence. "Winry," Shan said, "I'm half vegetation. Computers make me uneasy under the best of circumstances. Could you please explain it in simpler terms?"

Winry blushed and stammered and said she'd try. It took a few attempts and some analogies that probably dumbed it down a lot for us, but here's what she finally managed to get across: the Seekers keep track of the social media profiles of Gifted people, potential tiles. Not only that, they pull some shady strings to read their emails, keep track of their web browsing, stuff like that. NSA shit. "That's fucked up," I said to Miranda, who had been hanging back in the corner with her arms folded.

"You're right," she said, mildly. "We'll stop as soon as the fate of the world is no longer at stake." I didn't really know what to say to that. Anyway. Here's the rest of what Winry had to say. They kept track of thousands of social media profiles, so of course nobody could read them all in depth every day or every week. But Winry had programs and spyware and things that would alert her if certain things happened, weird things that were out of character for those people. Which is what happened a few weeks ago. A few weeks ago, eight people's online existence disappeared. Their Facebook pages, Twitter, Instagram, email accounts, the stupid comments they left on forums. They were just gone. At least, that's what Winry thought at first.

She slid from one monitor to another on her desk chair, typing and talking at the same time. "But then I looked closer, and I found, well, fragments of all eight profiles. Comments that matched old tweets, unique word combinations in a Facebook profile, things that definitely belonged to these eight people." I exchanged a glance with Shan, and then with Miranda. We all know the significance of the number eight.

"Ok," I said, "So someone managed to create a Mosaic. These eight are tiles. So the Mosaic deleted the old accounts and made its own? And we're seeing the composite personalities?"

Winry was shaking her head before I was done speaking. "No, I checked for that. These accounts weren't deleted. There'd be traces, places where I'd be able to see where they used to be. But they're completely and totally gone, like they never existed. And the email accounts? That data should still be backed up to the company's servers, but it isn't there."

"So what are you saying?" Shan asked.

What Winry was saying was this: those online identities comprised of social media pages and electronic information and ethereal communication, those had all merged together to form two new personalities. Lin Lahira, of London, and Phaedra Gutierrez of San Diego. At least, that's what their online information said, but it wasn't true. Lin wasn't really in London, and Phaedra wasn't really in San Diego. And they didn't look the way they did in their profile pictures. They had never existed, not in the real world. And they didn't really exist now. And yet here they were, on Facebook and Twitter and Instagram, and no one could tell they didn't really walk the Earth.

Things you should know about the Seekers: In general, attempts to copy gifts and give them to people who don't have them hasn't worked out too well. There are usually side effects. Like organ transplants. They work, sometimes, but you don't want to have them unless you need to. But there are some exceptions. A few things the Seekers have managed to rip off from folks like me. Or, like my tiles, I guess.

Take their memory storage. The Seekers in the Burrow, if you ask them to recall something that happened or something they read, and they'll do it. Perfectly. That's because all the full members like Miranda and Winry have the gift of perfect instantaneous recall. They apparently managed to isolate that one in the 1960s, and since then it's a standard feature. That one comes without any noticeable side effects. Others, not so much.

Take Antoine. He used to be some hotshot scientist, on the fast track to take Miranda's place when she stepped down. Then he got fixated on isolating one particular gift. He'd discovered a little girl with the ability to reverse entropy. She could make rotten fruit go ripe again. She could make broken objects reassemble themselves. In her presence, computers would become faster and more efficient with time rather than slower and more run down. It wasn't the most visible gift. Mostly people just assumed that she was an unusually tidy child. But Antoine became obsessed with her potential. Rumor around the Burrow was that he saw her ability as a way to eventually conquer death itself. No entropy means no decay. No decay means no death.

But there was a problem. This little girl, with the power to alter the natural progression of the universe itself, this child with unimaginable power, would never be able to teach others about her ability. She would never be able to learn a greater level of control. She would never truly understand what it was she did beyond a basic, instinctive level. And that is because this little girl, for all her gifts, had a brain injury that ensured she would never develop mentally past the age of two. And so, convinced the most important gift in the history of Seekers was going to waste, Antoine set about copying and mastering her ability for himself. I have no idea how they attempt these things. It involves genetic manipulation, engineered retroviruses, things I have no desire to understand. But Antoine tried it.

It was a partial success. Antoine can make a dusty floor tidy, he can make spilled water flow back into a cup, he can reverse the gradual genetic damage that is human aging. But he also can't wear shoes anymore, since his toenail clippings have a tendency to reassemble into five-inch prongs. He has to cover himself when he leaves the Burrow, because the brand new skin of a baby simply doesn't look right on a grown man. He's had surgery several times because the food he ate reassembled in his stomach.

He's not much use as a scientist, not anymore. But the Seekers take care of their own. He has his own room in the Burrow, and Miranda takes him on walks, and all the others take turns checking in and bringing him broken things so he can use his power to put them back together. It makes him feel useful. No one knows if he'll ever be able to die.

Winry spent some time doing her computer stuff, hacking or whatever. Whatever she did, she managed to find some IP addresses of social media accounts and computers that had been interacting with our two Mosaic accounts a lot. From there, she managed to get people's names and physical addresses. And, big surprise, these names were of people who hadn't been to work in weeks, people who had been reported missing. "Once more into the breach," Miranda said, and Shan and I went off to figure out what was going on.

Our first stop was at the apartment of a guy named Dean. Winry sent me a list of tweets and Facebook posts he'd exchanged with Lin's social media accounts. I'll spare you the details, but let's just say the guy had a Confederate flag as his profile photo and the words "feminazi slut" came up more than once. By the time we reached his place, I was half-hoping one of the Mosaics had found a way to climb through his computer monitor like that girl from the Ring and eat his face off.

But no such luck. We got into the apartment and found it empty but tidy. No signs of violent death or struggle. There was one weird thing, though: his computer was missing. We found the desk and the bundle of cables where it originally would have been, but no monitor, no tower.

We checked out Dean's work, too, but he hadn't been seen in a few days. He worked at a software company. That was part of a pattern, I noticed. Everyone on the list, everyone Lin and Phaedra had been in conversation with, they were all computer engineers, software designers, people who worked in programming. And, each house we checked, they were all gone. No people, and no computers or phones left behind.

The missing phones gave me an idea. I called Winry. "Hey," I asked, "can you track cell phones on any of these people? See where they are right now?"

She got back to me a few minutes later. Turns out one of them did have their phone on, and they could be tracked. And, at that moment, they were in the basement of the computer science department of a local college.

Shan and I spent a couple hours watching the place. We saw a few of the missing folks walking back and forth between a van and the building. The way they did it was weird, though. They always had their phones in one hand. Always. And they never watched where they were going. They always had their eyes locked right on those screens. I know that sounds like every asshole with a texting habit out there, but this went way beyond that. It was as though they physically couldn't put the phones away, even as they struggled to haul boxes and armfuls of computer equipment into the building.

Shan tried to do some of the remote viewing stuff they can do, but they cringed and whimpered after a few minutes. "Sorry," they said. "Too much electronics in there. Too much metal. It's painful." And then I noticed the rash breaking out on their arms and neck, like an allergic reaction.

"Ok, stop," I said. "Stop trying. Tech's not your thing, clearly." Then I told Shan to stay outside, and before they could argue with me I teleported my way in. It wasn't too precise, since I couldn't see the inside of the building and my control still sucks, but I happened to land in a deserted hallway outside a door with a sign that said "Computer Commons". I heard movement behind the door, people shuffling around and the whir of a drill and something heavy dropping to the ground.

I went in, ready to slow time or pull water out of folks or whatever else I could do if they rushed me. But none of the people looked up from their work. Their eyes stayed on their phones, most of which were resting on surfaces in front of them. But their hands worked on some kind of machine, some kind of metal tower in the middle of the room. I circled around to one side of it that was open. It was full of circuit boards, metal squares that looked like hard drives, wires and cables. It was like a really big computer tower. But there were other things, things that didn't seem like they belonged on any computer. Like a slim, jointed robotic arm sticking out one side. Or a series of what looked like cameras mounted to the top.

I didn't have the slightest idea what I was looking at, so I called Winry. "I think they might be building a Terminator," I said. She asked me to show her the machine, so I held up my phone and got as close as I could without touching any of the people working on it. Winry took one look at the machine and started making squeaking sounds. I took those for fear at first but it turns out she was just excited. It took a while to get her to explain it in terms I understood, but finally I got that it wasn't a Terminator. So that was good news. Instead, it was a server. But not just any server, Winry assured me; an incredibly advanced server, with new kinds of engineering she'd never seen in a computer before. Engineering that should have been way, way above the level of these missing software designers and programmers.

I asked her about the other parts, the cameras and the limbs. She said, "Well, this is just a guess, but it looks like when this thing is finished it's going to be mobile, self-repairing, it'll be able to see. Basically, it should be able to do everything by itself."

Honestly, that sounded pretty Terminator to me, but I didn't see any weapons mounted onto it and Winry didn't seem to think it was threatening so I held off on smashing it. Instead, I peeked over the shoulder of one of the missing folks, a balding guy named Darren. What I saw on his phone screen didn't make a lot of sense to me. Fast, flashing images and colors. It all looked totally random. A deep green screen, then a picture of an apple, then the words "Elaine's gumbo recipe." And then, almost too fast for me to see, a brief set of instructions. Something like, "Attach circuit 4 to Unit B12." followed by a string of code. I showed the screen to Winry, and she spent some time watching it and muttering to herself. At last she said, "Ok. Here's what I think is going on. I think these images and words and things between the instructions are keyed to this particular guy. I think they're, I don't know, mesmerizing him with the right combination of things. Like, this one, Darren. His wife's name is Elaine. It keeps mentioning her. In theory if you know enough about anyone's psychology and memories and experiences, you should be able to control them."

I thought that was pretty creepy, but I shouldn't judge. I use mind control on people all the time. Still, mine's all-natural. Organic, dammit.

Even with all this info, though, Winry couldn't tell me what Lin and Phaedra wanted. They're a collection of social media profiles, for fuck's sake, they shouldn't have been able to want anything. Winry spent some more time studying the machine through my screen, but she couldn't make sense of it. Finally, I got impatient. "Ok," I said, opening up Facebook. "That's it. I'm asking them."

"I'm not sure that's wise," Winry said. Then Miranda jumped in. Apparently she'd been listening the whole time. "Wren, do not reach out to those Mosaics, hear me?"

Have I mentioned that I don't like being told what to do? Miranda knows that, so she really shouldn't have been surprised when I ignored her and messaged Phaedra. I asked: What's the machine for?

She responded instantly, without hesitation. The message on my screen said, We want a home. A body of our own.

I didn't get it, but Winry instantly gasped. "Oh, of course!" And then she told me what she'd figured out. Social media profiles, accounts, programs, they don't just float around on the internet. They exist on servers owned by companies. Google. Facebook. Twitter. Those servers could get shut down or destroyed or changed at any time. And Lin and Phaedra, they only existed on those servers. Those profiles were them. The closest thing they had to bodies, and it was hard drive space that belonged to someone else. I suddenly understood why this server was so sturdy, why it had cameras to see and speakers to speak and arms to repair itself. They were about to migrate into their own home.

Miranda must have figured it out at the same time, because the next thing she said was, "Wren, destroy that thing. Separate out the carbon, some other mineral, whatever you have to do."

"We don't even know if they're planning anything," I said. My phone beeped. It was a text, with Phaedra's picture. "We're not making a Trumpet," the text said. "We can't. We just want our own home."

I told Miranda what it said. She didn't even hesitate. "They might be lying," she said. "If we can't take them in, we can't risk letting them go. You know what's at stake here, Wren." She was right. I did know what was at stake. I know what it means if someone manages to make the Trumpet. But I just stood there, looking first at Phaedra's Facebook page, then Lin's. They looked like normal women. They were smiling. They listed their favorite movies, their favorite TV shows, just like anyone else. They seemed like people living their lives, or wanting to.

Miranda kept talking, but I tuned out. I stepped back and let the programmers finish the tower. The last of them screwed the big metal case closed, and the second it was done they all blinked and seemed to wake up. Darren shook his head. "What's going on?" he asked. "How'd we get here?"

I never got a chance to answer him, because the entire tower started beeping and whirring. At the same time, I heard a low roar from outside, something in the sky. "They're profiles aren't on the old servers anymore," Winry said through my phone. "They migrated." Miranda cursed and yelled at me, but I kept ignoring her. As I watched, the entire tower started rolling its way to the door of the computer lab. It had little wheels set into the bottom. It used its robotic arm to open the door and make its way down the hall. I followed slowly behind it, because the whole thing looked way too ridiculous not to watch. And, at least in my case, because I was wondering if the two Mosaics now living in that merged body were about to bring the world to an end. I wondered if that was the mechanical roar outside.

But it wasn't. I saw what it was as soon as the tower rolled out those doors. Because that was the moment a drone landed on the street outside. And I don't mean one of those little hobbyist drones. I mean a military drone, as wide as the street outside, the kind that drops bombs on countries we don't like to think about too much. And that's when I understood that these few engineers in this computer lab weren't the only people Lin and Phaedra had bewitched. Somewhere on a military base there was a drone pilot who was about to get in a lot of trouble and who wouldn't be able to remember why they'd done what they'd done. But not yet. For now, the drone just waited for the server to latch onto its belly. And then it took off into the air again, carrying Lin and Phaedra away. A crowd of people gathered, pointing and yelling and not sure whether to be impressed or terrified.

I watched until it was out of sight. I realized Shan had reached me by then, was asking me something. "Did they get away?" they asked.

I held up my phone and asked Winry what was happening. She said nothing for a long moment, then: "I don't see any signs of anything weird happening. No sign of a Trumpet. I think they were telling the truth. They just wanted to have their own body."

Then Miranda's voice came over the speaker. "Do you have any idea what a risk you just took?" she asked. "For all we know, they could have made the Trumpet. You could have ended everything."

"But I didn't," I said.

Then Miranda said, "If you ever become a threat, Wren, I'll put you down. I won't hesitate."

"And if that happens, Miranda, you'll be the next to die," Shan said, in a voice only a complete idiot would ignore.

Miranda didn't say anything for a minute. Then, "Come back to the Burrow. We have another situation," she said, and hung up.

Shan and I stared at the phone for a minute. "Should we run?" they asked.

"No," I said, "Miranda might try to end me one day, if I disobey her too many times, but not now." And, at that moment, I couldn't get too worked up about the possibility. I stared up at the sky and thought about Lin and Phaedra, living in their strange way on their own terms. I don't know where they'll end up. Some remote spot, I imagine, where they can roll their server into hiding and rely on solar power and repair themselves when they need. From there I don't know what they'll do. Live, online, in their strange way, I imagine. Facebook friends with thousands of people who don't know what they are, who think they walk this earth as flesh and blood, Instagramming people who don't know they're just electricity and code.

My phone buzzed just as Shan and I walked away from the crowd that had gathered to watch the drone. It was an alert from Twitter. Two new followers, Lin and Phaedra. Guess us Mosaics have to stick together.

Chapter 15
The Harvester

Someone's killing the Seekers. Up until now, I've been focused on protecting the Gifted. Potential tiles. But now there's something else. And I think it might be more dangerous than anything I've dealt with so far. To any Gifted people out there, I need your help. The Splinter has a Harvester. To all of you listening: I need your help finding it, before it kills us all.

The first one was a researcher who supervised a group of apprentices. He'd worked with Miranda in the past, so she got the call when his body was found. He died at his day job at an infectious disease research center. One of the apprentices got a look at the body before the cops shut the crime scene down and she knew it wasn't a natural death. So she called Miranda, and Miranda sent in me and Shan.

It wasn't easy, getting in there. Local cops and feds and reporters were swarming everywhere. I could teleport in, but there were people in the room with the body, and slowing time would only hide us so long. We watched the building for a while, and then I turned to Shan. "Any tricks up your sleeve that can help us out here?" I asked.

They smiled. "Let me see what I can do," they said. Then they held up their hand, and a deep blue flower bloomed up from their palm. Shan waited until a cop passed by close to us, and then they opened the flower. Little flecks of iridescent pollen blew away and landed on the cop's hair. Shan's eyes rolled back in their head. "It's working," they said. "I can see through his eyes. He's going into the lobby. Up the stairs. Down a hall.

Now he's going past the yellow tape. Oh, dear God."

And I watched Shan's beautiful face go still and terrified. They touched my forehead, and I saw what had shaken them so, like it had been with my own eyes. A body lay facedown on the floor of a lab. Gleaming white walls and lab equipment everywhere, everything metal and white except for the pool of blood surrounding the body. The blood came from a wound in the man's head. But this wasn't any ordinary head wound, not the way a body looks when it's been shot or bludgeoned. This. . . This was like, if a seam ran up the middle of the human head from the back of the neck. Imagine if you could just unzip that seam, create a slit running from the base of the skull all the way up and over to the forehead. Imagine you could crack that slit open wide to get at what lay inside. And, imagine that nothing at all lay inside, just a hollow, bloodstained skull cavity.

"Where's the brain?" I asked, and Shan didn't know. They watched through the cop's eyes for a while, but the brain wasn't at the crime scene. It was just gone. We stuck around and watched for a while, but it was pretty clear we weren't getting anywhere near there so we left. But we both knew, somehow, that this wasn't an isolated incident. We knew others were coming.

The moment I told Miranda about the body, she went pale. "You're sure?" she asked. "You're sure the brain was missing?" I told her I was positive. No grey matter left at the scene. Then she told me what we were dealing with.

The Seekers have encountered Harvesters before. It was an unusual way for gifts to manifest. Usually they aren't physically apparent. Usually Gifted folks can be discreet about it. And most gifts manifest in childhood or puberty, like every other shitty quality people have to learn to cope with. Not Harvesters. Harvesters don't show any signs of unusual abilities until they suddenly activate overnight. It can happen at any age, cradle to grave. When it happens, though, it happens fast. The Harvester starts hearing other people's thoughts. And those thoughts make them hungry. Their body starts to change at the same time, jaws lengthening, sight failing, ears flattening against the skull. Their appetite grows, but regular food doesn't satisfy them. They get temperamental. Sooner or later, their control slips. They crack open someone's head, scoop out the brain, and eat everything that made that person who they are.

But they aren't just eating physical tissue when they do that. No. They're eating thoughts, memories, knowledge, a personality. And while the poor Harvester is too much an animal to do anything with their new information, they can still speak. And the right master, the right person controlling them, they can ask all the questions they want. They can use what the Harvester now knows. And all of that meant that we had someone out there who had inside knowledge of the Seekers, straight for the source. And Miranda's guess was that, given the low-level knowledge they had from their first victim, they'd want another source.

So we waited for the next killing. I spent my time walking around the neighborhood near the crime scene, compelling people to tell me if they'd seen anything useful. None had. Shan spent that time staring into dishes of ink, pots of boiling water on the stove, the patterns of steam floating above a tea kettle. They were looking into the future, or trying. We knew it wouldn't do anything. Shan can only peer into the futures of people they know, or people they have a good description of. And only for specific actions, limited causal chains. I don't really understand it, but, bottom line, Shan couldn't stare into the future and find the next person to be murdered before it happened. Didn't stop them from trying. I'd come home to find them sitting at the kitchen table, looking wilted, Akira sitting on one of their feet. Akira likes Shan.

The next one came a week after the first. Winry called me, her voice high and shaky. "It happened again, Wren," she said. "I'm looking at it through a security camera feed now, and, Oh, God, it's awful." It was the same as before, a split open skull, a missing brain. Except this time the killing had been near a basketball court in the dead of night. This time, the cops could only do so much to keep people out after the body had been carted away. We waited for it to die down, then I compelled the one remaining beat cop to take a walk. Shan ran their hands along the edge of the chalk outline, danced their fingertips along the broken glass on the fringes of the basketball court, touched everything in sight of the pooled, tacky blood on the concrete.

Finally, they shuddered and flinched. "That. . . That was deeply unpleasant," they said.

"Show me," I said. They tried to change my mind, tried to just describe it to me, but that's not how I work. I need to know, no matter how bad. Finally, Shan agreed. They rubbed some light blue pollen on my eyelids. It probably looked tacky, like fluorescent eye shadow. But I didn't really care about that at the moment, because I saw the Harvester. It was on a leash. A leash strapped to a complicated leather harness. It had been human, once. It must have been, to be Gifted. Not anymore, though. Its jaws were too big, toothy and protruding from its face. Its eyes had sunken and shrunk into its wormy white flesh, like they'd just gone unused for so long they'd atrophied.

It was a strange way of seeing, the pictures Shan picked up from the surroundings. They were layered, like I was seeing from different angles and perspectives at the same time. Things were blurred, and confusing, and too busy. Still. I saw the Harvester. I saw it lunge out of the bushes as its victim jogged by, a middle-aged guy in a track suit. I saw it crack open the man's skull and devour what lay within with its oversized jaws. I saw the figure holding its leash. I couldn't tell anything about the person, at first. They wore a ski mask and a baggy dark sweatshirt. I'd never be able to pick that person out of a crowd, I thought.

But then the Harvester lunged forward in a particularly excited motion, pulling its master with it. And that movement tugged the person's sleeve up, exposing a delicate, feminine wrist. Pale as milk. Pale, and tattooed with a trailing violet shape. A jellyfish.

Shan and I went back to the Burrow without another word. I think they felt guilty for showing me something so terrible, even though I asked them to. And I tried to not let it get to me, but that big-jawed thing, unzipping that person's head. . . I hope nobody listening ever has to see it themselves. No one deserves to carry that image around with them.

As soon as we got back to the Burrow, we went down into Winry's computer lair. Miranda was there, she and Winry bent over lines of code on a screen. "Hey, Winry," I said, "when you get a chance, could you reach out to as many tattoo parlors as you can? We're looking for someone who's done a jellyfish tattoo on the inside of a young woman's wrist."

Miranda froze. It was like someone had knocked the wind out of her. "What did you say?" she whispered. I told her the person controlling the

Harvester was a woman. A pale woman with a jellyfish tattoo on her wrist.

After I explained it, Miranda whispered just one word. A name. "Iris." Then she began to cry. She cried, and she said she was sorry, and then she told me why the Harvester is all her fault.

Things you should know about the Seekers: Miranda grew up in the Seekers. Her parents, her parents' parents, her ancestors going all the way back to that sacred grove in Greece. If the Seekers had Kennedies, they'd be Miranda's family. So she grew up hearing about the Grove, the Mosaic, and the Trumpet. But, like most adolescents, she went through a rebellious phase. She read the books in the locked cases in the library, heard whispers about shortcuts to the Mosaic. She studied the abilities of those who would be needed for that shortcut, the blood magic some claimed could make the Awakening happen within her lifetime. She left the Seekers for a time, in her twenties, and she traveled the world, and she learned these strange magics.

She came to her senses, eventually. She saw the insanity of what the people who became the Splinter planned on doing, and she rejoined the Seekers. She even brought her husband back into the fold, her young husband who had traveled with her and learned by her side. And Miranda rose through the ranks, as did her husband, and for a time they were happy. They had a daughter, and everyone assumed she would grow up to be Miranda's successor. That is, until Miranda's husband became dissatisfied with the pace of their progress, and tried to persuade her to leave again. And when she refused, he fled, taking Seeker secrets with him, and he founded the Splinter. And so Miranda lost her husband and gained a nemesis, her handsome, clever Elliot. My Skull Man.

But that wasn't all she lost. There was their daughter, their beautiful Iris, caught between mother and father, Seeker and Splinter. She went with Elliot, but kept in touch with Miranda when she could. Staticky calls from burner phones, emails from a new address every time. Miranda mourned their loss, but she found some comfort in the idea that Iris was with her father, that she might come around, that she might bring him back.

Then came the text from Elliot. A photo of Iris, mangled and bloody and clearly dead. Four words. "This is your fault." Who knows how they faked the photo, or if they even faked it, if they didn't just find someone who could undo such damage. I've seen more impossible things than that. Hell, I see them every day. The important thing here is that they were thinking ahead. Making it look like Iris was off the board. Getting her ready to take Elliot's place.

Neither Shan nor I knew what to say to Miranda after she'd finished telling us her story. Part of me felt like I should be mad. She'd recruited me, gotten me on her side, sent me out to investigate, and she'd done it without giving me all the facts. So that sucked on her part. But she was so miserable, so broken by this new knowledge about Iris, that it was hard to hold it against her.

We were still just sitting there, processing the information, when Winry started clicking away at something on her screen. She cleared her throat, looking embarrassed. "I'm sorry to interrupt," she said. "I know this is a bad time, but. . . It looks like we have another one." This time, she was able to get into the surveillance cameras at the scene. It was a pharmaceutical company. Another day job site. Another poor Seeker working late, not knowing a Harvester was coming for them. Another corpse with a cracked open head.

But this time there was one big difference. Whoever had been there must have known the angle of the security cameras, because they'd used the dead person's blood to scrawl a message on one of the walls, right in the middle of the frame. It said, "We'll talk to your pet Mosaic. Send her or we'll take one every day. 48 hours. The dead city."

Shit. Looks like I'm going home.

Chapter 16
This is Shan

Zachary, it's Shan. Listen. . . I'm aware that I'm probably the last person you want to hear from right now. But it's about Wren. I think she's in danger. And I need your help.

I'm going to tell you what happened, and then I think you'll understand what you need to do, and what I'm going to do. Wren tried to get me to stay behind at the Burrow while she went to negotiate with Iris. She told me she needed me to watch over Akira, that she didn't trust Miranda and Winry and the others to protect themselves with a Harvester hunting them. Those reasons were true, but they were also lies. They weren't the real reason. To me, Wren's lies smell coppery, like old pennies. She doesn't lie often, and when she does it's mostly to herself. This time, the real reason was that she didn't want me to get hurt.

I understand why, naturally. Her gifts make her a fighter. Mine don't. Even so, I wouldn't listen. I insisted on going, if only to be there when she met with Iris. It was a long drive to Wren's birthplace, days and nights in the car, driving across country that became flatter and drier with every mile. That city people on the news speak of as the site of a toxic chemical spill or an example of urban blight or the place no one lives in anymore because the jobs left. That city in the desert no one ever goes to anymore. None of the people who talk about it seem to realize that they're all listing incompatible causes of death.

The traffic started to thin nearly a hundred miles out from the city. The normal probably don't wonder why. They probably all just convince themselves that they simply don't want to go in that direction. Not me, though. Not us. I could smell what happened to that city. I could taste bits of history embedded in dust particles and drifting on the wind. It frightened me, I'm not ashamed to admit. I don't know if I managed to hide that fear from Wren, or if she just pretended not to notice.

We arrived at the northern edge of the city. There were cars now, but not moving. Crashed, rusted, crumbled hulks blocking the highway and spilling off onto the side of the road. Animals moved in the shrubs and cactus patches as we passed, but I don't think they were any animals most people would recognize. The air smelled of chalk and burning plastic. Finally, we reached a point where we could no longer wind our way through the wrecked cars. We got out and walked. Neither of us spoke.

Finally, we reached a ramp leading up to another highway, this one the one that would take us to the center of the city. But there was something blocking the on ramp. Listen carefully, Zachary. This is what it looked like. Imagine a swimming pool. Still, clear water, light moving just a bit along the walls of the pool. Now imagine that swimming pool tipped over on its side, the water somehow staying in place. Imagine the water is grey instead of blue, rippling shadows of charcoal and slate instead of turquoise. Imagine that it smells like crushed sage and pomegranate, strange fresh scents for something so wrong. It is stretched to fill the entire entrance to the on ramp, so that you'd have no choice but to walk through it if you wanted to climb up.

We tried to find another way around it, as you can imagine. There should have been an infinite number of ways into this city, cutting across suburban yards and parking lots and climbing over fallen trees. But no. It wasn't anything obvious. No walls or fences. But every single path that should have existed simply didn't. We found obstacles at every turn, and without speaking we both understood what was happening. I touched Wren's wrist and got one of my little glimpses, a flash of her walking into that vertical grey pool. Alone.

I didn't tell her, but she caught something from the look on my face. Other people can't read me at all. Most people, the ones at the Burrow, never have any idea what's going on under the surface. Wren, though, she sees me. "I have to go through, don't I?" she said, and she didn't seem scared at all. More like it was some kind of unpleasant chore she didn't want to spend her time on. I asked her not to. Please believe that, Zachary. I wouldn't want to place her in danger any more than you would. But we both know Wren can't be told what to do.

She led me back to the gate. That's what I'm calling it, that rippling pool, because I don't have a better name for it. She watched it for a while. Then she touched the surface. Her fingertips slipped right through like it was water, even though I could smell that it wasn't anything like water. "Seems ok," she said. Then she stepped through. And, even though I could see the outline of the highway and cars and all sorts of things through the gate, she immediately disappeared.

I tried to go after her. I went straight for the gate. But where it responded to her like it was water, to me it might as well have been concrete. I tried over and over again. I sifted through my gifts, trying to find one that would help. I secreted an enzyme from my palms that would melt through steel, and I tried using that on the gate's surface. It did nothing. It was solid, but it wasn't matter. So I waited.

I waited for an hour, then two. I got up and searched for other ways through. I read the history of the ground and the stones and everything in the area. It didn't tell me anything useful. I saw hooded figures approach the city, and I saw one of them raise their arms, and I saw the gate appear. I saw three of them walk through it. But that was all. Someone with a gift, obviously, but it didn't tell me how to get through it.

I would still be there, waiting for Wren, except that I started to hear a noise in the distance. Engines. The type of sound that sets my teeth on edge, that makes me want to retreat into soil and forest. Mechanical things, things so far removed from the planet they might as well be from space. And then I saw them, close to the ground, a plume of dust kicked up behind them. Six people on motorcycles. Six people coming straight for me, and I knew even before seeing their faces that they came from the Splinter.

Things you should know about the Seekers: Most Gifted subjects studied by the Seekers never know they are being watched. The observations are made from afar, through stolen lab results and planted surveillance equipment. A few, though, those most prized by the Seekers, like Mosaics, go through other forms of surveillance. Like me. Here is what happens when you are recruited and brought back to the Burrow, as I was. You are taken naked into a cold metal room. Rooms like that are difficult for me. You are told to disrobe, and then you are poked and prodded by people in white coats. They speak to each other rather than to you. They pretend you aren't really there, as though they are studying a body with nothing in it. They pull blood from you, and place it in machines, and study the results on a screen.

Finally, Miranda comes into the room. And she tells you certain things. She tells you the results of the tests, the map that has been created by your DNA. Most of it is things you already know. I already knew the things I could do, the way I can see the future and the past and the way I can alter my body chemistry as easily as you breathe. But some people have a few secrets, ones Miranda reveals. Like me, for instance. Miranda showed me two little slits on the inside of my wrists, described the strange little structures within. She told me to be careful, and to keep these little secrets hidden away. And I did. At least until the Splinter arrived.

Six men got off the motorcycles. They grinned and moved with a swagger. "The Wren ain't here to protect you, is she?" one of them said. "She's a tough cookie, but you, not so much. Freaky, but not scary." He pointed with his gun. I smelled the oil and metal from ten feet away. "Hands up," he said.

I obeyed. I held up my hands, facing out, inner wrists toward the men. And then I let out the things Miranda told me to keep hidden. They don't look like much. Thin little needles, smaller than cactus spines. Translucent. So sharp you would barely feel them puncturing the skin. They were in two little bundles hidden in my inner wrist, and they shot out in all directions with enough force they hit every one of the men pointing guns at me.

It was over quickly. Not as quick as when Wren rips the water out of someone. But they fell to the ground, frothing at the mouth, well before they had a chance to pull the triggers on their guns. Those little needles

I grow in my wrists aren't dangerous on their own. It's the concentrated cyanide coating them that's the problem for humans. I don't think this was an ability any of my tiles had. I think it comes from the part of me that is more plant than human, a kind of plant that makes poison to protect itself.

The men were dead in a matter of minutes. Everything was quiet again, just me alone on the fringes of the ruined city. I wasn't afraid for myself any longer. But I was afraid for Wren. Because, if these men knew where to find us, and if they counted on Wren and I being separated when they arrived, it meant all of this was a carefully planned trap. And that meant that Wren was exactly where they wanted her. That was when I thought of you, Zachary. Wren has described you to me so many times, I feel I almost know you myself. And we're both Mosaics, so there is that thread of connection there already.

It took me a while to find the right tools, the things I need to read the future. Usually I prefer tea leaves, bowls of ink, something fluid I can watch for hours. Natural things, things my body recognizes. I don't actually see the future in the liquid. It just helps send me into the right kind of trance. Finally, I found a wrecked car and stole some of the oil out of it, drained it into a pan. Then I sat down to read your future and see you from afar. And once I found your future swirling in the oil, once I followed your path and watched you walk through the world, I went back to where Wren had left her things in our borrowed car. I found the computer and voice recorder she brings with her everywhere she goes, even though she keeps it hidden from me. And I started making this message.

And now that you know all this, Zachary, you're starting to see why I've made this message. Right now you're seeing how my gifts and your gifts can intertwine to help her. I can follow threads of sound and motion into the future and far away. I see things that happen across the country, and things that won't happen until tomorrow. Like right now. Let me tell you what I see. I see you sitting on a park bench with your phone and your earbuds. This is where you always go to listen to Wren's messages. I think it's because of some scrap of memory of the park you carry from one of your tiles, but I'm not sure. But you can't help yourself. You have to listen to her messages, all of them.

You hear my message, instead of hers. You listen as I describe the place she disappeared into, the threshold I can't breach. And you think about your own gifts, ones I've seen in you. The one that lets you pull things out of time and space and put them when and where you want. Things, or people. Like me. You can't send yourself, but you can send me. You have a clear picture of me, and you have a clear picture of the gate I have to pass through, and that's all you need. That's all you need to send a fellow Mosaic to help the one you love. So let's work together, Zachary. For Wren. On the count of three, send me to her. One, two, three—

Chapter 17
The Trumpet

Miranda's dead. So are most of the Seekers. Shan and Zachary and I played right into their hands, and now we're the only thing standing between the world and the Trumpet. Sorry about that, world.

I appreciate what you did, Zachary. Helping Shan get to me and all that. I think I might have made it out on my own, but they definitely made it easier. So thank you. Still. It was what the Splinter wanted, so you shouldn't have done it.

I guess it's not really important, what happened in the dead city. But telling you will let me put off talking about what happened to the Burrow, so I guess I'll start there. You already know how I went through the gate. Shan told you about that, that watery gate I could pass through but they couldn't. I stepped through the water, and it clung like spiderwebs to my skin. I got through, and there was a destroyed version of a city I used to know so well.

Not everything was dead. There was movement. Moving, lifelike things, although calling them alive might be stretching the definition a bit. But this was a city that was killed by dreams coming to life. Those dreams didn't go anywhere. They just made themselves at home, occupying the spaces humans once did. The first thing I saw was a woman whose body faded into mist right around the navel. She moved slowly above the blacktop of the crumbling highway ramp, watching me out of the corner of her eye. Above her, a palm tree floated upside down, its palm fronds hanging limply toward the ground.

Before I had a chance to explore any further, I heard a sound behind me. A kind of popping sound. I turned, and there was Shan. But you already know all about that, Zachary. Shan blinked at me as if they were the one who should be surprised. "You're still here?" they asked. "How long have you been trying to get back through?"

"What are you talking about?" I asked. "I only came through a minute ago."

And then Shan told me that was wrong, that I'd already been here for hours. And then their eyes widened, and we both realized at the same moment that time was flying by out in the world while we talked inside the dead city. We both realized Iris wasn't coming. She wasn't coming, and the Burrow was undefended, and every moment we wasted here was precious minutes and hours and eventually days out there.

We started searching for a way out, right away. But the gate that had been as soft as water was now hard as concrete, even for me. Shan got to work reading the history of the place, trying to find out how the gate was made. I slowed time in stretches for as long as I could, to try to get it to match up to the outside. But we could both feel it slipping away; we watched the sun outside our bubble careen toward the horizon, and darkness fall way faster than in should have. All the while, itinerant dreams rambled and swirled around us. Just up the highway, a little girl played in a puddle of bright blue mud. A creature that looked like some mix between a giraffe and a bird stalked and clawed at the side of a mini mart off the first exit. A feast of cakes and wine lay meticulously arranged on the surface of an old wooden door hovering a few feet off the ground.

A few yards away from the gate, Shan found a piece of cinderblock, ran their hands over it. "I got something," they said. Their eyes went distant, changing color a little. "Iris was here," they said. "Iris and a few others. They brought someone here. Not the Harvester. Another prisoner. Someone in chains. They. . . They made the gate. And then, once they made the gate, Iris's people took them that way." They pointed down the long, looping stretch of cracking blacktop that used to be a highway. So we set off in that direction, because we didn't have any other ideas.

Things followed us the whole time. Dreamed things, I assume, but maybe not. Maybe there are people living here still. Maybe some of the freaks my tiles left in their wake. Maybe parts of Jose are still hunkered down in their strip club. Maybe some of Natalie's children hunt in the rubble. I know some got out of the city, but maybe not all. Whether the things around us started off as human or not, though, I can't imagine they stayed that way very long, breathing and eating dreams.

Shan started shaking after a while, although they tried to hide it. "A lot of people died here," they said at last. "I can smell it." They pretended they were ok, but I finally convinced them to let me use a little persuasion on them. I told them to ignore the smell of death, to not be able to smell it until we left the city. They did better after that.

We reached a place where the highway curved and conjoined with two others. Back in the day, this is the place where you would choose to go North or South, East or West, to other cities bigger than this one. Now it was just empty. Except, not quite empty. Between the burnt out cars and bits of trash and rotting pieces I avoided looking at too closely, there was something else. A shape that emerged in the center of the highway, right at the juncture. It might have been a discarded duffel bag or something at first. Then I started to see the features, the human shape of it.

I don't know what this person would have looked like, before. Male, female, neither. Old, young, somewhere in the middle. Whatever they had been before, they were now a creature of brick and cement, a living piece of city. They sat in a lotus position, watching me with eyes of smashed windshield glass. Their skin had the marbled texture of old pavement. Shredded newspaper and fastfood wrappers jutted from their head where hair might have once been. They wept antifreeze and motor oil. They spoke, and had glinting bits of soda can for teeth. "Please," they said. "I've done all that she asked."

"We're not with Iris," I told them. "She tricked us. She trapped us here."

"Ah," the thing rasped. "The Wren. You're the reason I'm here. She made me trap you." The way they said it wasn't like they blamed me. More like they were sorry.

"Is there a way to get out of here?" I asked. "A way to get you out?"

They said nothing for a moment. "Not as long as I'm alive," they said, "they. . . they made me this city. They made me put up those walls, and now I can't control it." It wept silently for a time. "I never wanted to. It's just. . . Now it's like it's my immune system. I can't control it."

I didn't really understand what this person's gift had looked like before. I don't think Shan did either. But we both knew what it meant, this person growing into the concrete and detritus of the city. We both knew there wasn't going to be any way to dig them out of the ground.

But that didn't mean we didn't have options. Shan waited awhile, as if they didn't really want to say it. Then: "We can't get you out of here, but what if you were. . . something else?"

The thing on the highway blinked. "Like what?"

"A park. A patch of trees and flowers. Something green."

The thing said, "If I changed that much, it would break my hold on the city. You could go. But I wouldn't be me anymore, would I?"

I didn't say anything. Neither did Shan. We just waited. Finally, the thing took a deep breath and said, "I suppose I'm not me anymore, anyway. And I'd rather be anything but this. Do what you have to do."

Shan pressed their palms together and concentrated. While they worked, I touched the creature and pulled out the things that would hurt plants, like the way I can pull water out of bodies. I pulled out the chemicals and oil and petroleum, everything that didn't belong in a living thing. The thing hissed and shivered as I worked, as motor oil and liquid plastic flowed out of their skin and onto the ground next to them.

Shan pulled their palms apart, and there in their hands lay a pile of little black seeds. They tipped the seeds over the thing's head in a cascade. Where those seeds should have just bounced off and skittered across the pavement, they latched onto the asphalt skin. I saw little white roots, small as hairs, fold out from the seeds and burrow into the thing's body. The thing made a little sound like it was trying not to cry. "My name was Elizabeth," it said. "Will you remember?" And I said yes, and now I'm telling the world so you can remember too.

It only took a minute. The seeds took root in Elizabeth's skin as easily as if it were mulch. The body started to disintegrate as the plants grew out it. The thing's features blurred and collapsed, and then the entire body was a grassy mound with saplings growing out of it. At the same time, I felt a pop as time starting working the way it was supposed to. I knew without looking that the gate was gone.

By the time we turned back and started the walk along the highway, out of the city, the green had spread from where the thing had sat and covered a thirty-foot stretch of the highway. I'm sure it's still growing. Maybe it will never stop. Maybe now there is an oasis in the middle of that desert.

We started trying to call the Burrow as soon as we got out of the city, as soon as we started the journey back. No one answered. Not Miranda. Not Winry. We drove as fast as my car would move, not stopping for anything, using our gifts to lose cops when necessary. All the while, we kept trying to get in touch. Shan tried to use their remote viewing, but couldn't from within the metal shell of a car.

We saw what had happened as soon as we got back to the Burrow. The front door was wide open, and a bunch of computer cables and other equipment had been dragged onto the porch. Then I stepped inside, and I saw the first body. It was a guy named Greg, I think. I know I met him, back when I first came here. I know I shook his hand. I know we passed each other in the halls, and he would smile at me. I feel so bad that I can't remember his name. Greg, if that was his name, lay facedown in the doorway leading from the front hall to the kitchen. His head had been cracked open, and there was no brain left inside.

The rest were scattered throughout the Burrow. Some lay behind splintered, buckled-in doors, near makeshift barricades. Others seem to have been caught by surprise, in the middle of the living room, curled by the toilet, stuffed halfway into a linen closet. Some, the ones higher up, closer to Miranda, had their heads opened. The ones who seemed more on the fringes were just dead.

Miranda was in her office. A gun lay on the floor, near her hand, but I don't think she ever got a chance to use it. Her head was split open, her skull emptied. Shan braced themself and touched Miranda's face. "I see her," they said at last. "Iris." They tilted back on their heels. "She didn't even flinch, when the Harvester took Miranda. She watched the entire thing. It was like nothing." They frowned and ran their hands over the hardwood floor. "But then, after, she took something. Four books from the shelf. And then. . ." I followed Shan down the halls as they trailed their fingers over nearby surfaces, reconstructing Iris's journey through the slaughterhouse her Harvester had created. We wound up in the basement, in Winry's lair. There was an empty space along one of the walls, just a tangle of cords and adapters where a squat grey tower had been. The server. The Seekers' main server, where they kept their database of every gifted person they encountered.

Things you should know about the Seekers: There's no point in keeping the meaning of the Trumpet secret. Not anymore. So here it is: The Trumpet is the person who will have a unique collection of gifts. A collection that adds up to one special purpose. The Trumpet will awaken the latent gifts and powers hiding in the DNA of normal people. Any normal people. All those recessive genes, all those dormant abilities. The Trumpet will have the ability to awaken them all. The man in the Grove saw the path to making the Trumpet. He saw that the Trumpet would never happen by chance, never through random reproduction. And the Trumpet couldn't be conjured or engineered out of thin air. It was too complex for that. No. The Trumpet could only be made in one way. The Trumpet could only exist as the offspring of two Mosaics.

Both the Seekers and the Splinter want to make the Trumpet. They agreed on that. But there's one huge, important difference between the Trumpet each of them would make. The one the Seekers would have made would have been carefully limited, able to activate only one person's abilities at a time. They would have been able to control that through their slow engineering, the selective breeding of their Mosaics. The activation of the human race's powers would have been gradual, and controlled, and we'd be able to prepare for the changes to come. That's not the Trumpet the Splinter is making. The Splinter's Trumpet is something wilder, something left more to chance. The Splinter's Trumpet won't have those limitations. The Splinter's Trumpet will awaken everyone's powers at the same time. Every single gift hiding in the human race's genes, all the things me and Zachary and Shan can do, all of those things will be inflicted on the human race at the same moment. The Splinter calls that the Awakening. Miranda called it the Apocalypse.

So now here we are. The Splinter has everything it needs to make its Mosaics. No more stumbling around in the dark, no more failures for us to clean up. The next time they try the ritual, it's going to work. I can feel it in my bones. And Shan sees that it's going to happen, I can tell from the look in their eyes. So now, between all of you listening and the Splinter, there's just me and Shan.

Or, not quite. Not quite just us. We found Winry huddled behind a file cabinet in the corner, curled into a tight little ball so small I almost didn't see her. Her eyes were screwed shut, and she'd bitten her lip so hard it had broken the skin. Her bundle of dreadlocks was soaked with so much blood I thought at first she had a headwound, but it wasn't hers. I'm not sure whose it was, but it doesn't really matter. They're not here anymore. Iris must have been so focused on getting the server she didn't check to make sure she'd killed everyone in the Burrow. She came close, though. Winry was the only one we found alive. She started screaming the second we pulled her out from behind the filing cabinet, but Shan made some kind of dust with their palms and brushed it over her face and she went into a kind of stupor. Then Shan lifted her in their slim strong arms and carried her out of the burrow. She's still out, tucked into one of the beds in the shitty hotel we're camped out in right now. We went back to the place Shan and I have been stayed just long enough to grab Akira and some clothes. It won't be safe to go back there again. I hope she stays asleep for a while. As soon as she wakes up, we're going to need to get her working on finding Iris. She's the only Seeker we got left.

And there's one other, aside from me and Winry and Shan. Because just after we got to our new hotel, I got an email. It's from Zachary. He says he was wrong. He says things have gone too far. He says he wants to meet, to join us.

Shan was quiet for a moment after I showed them that message. "It could be a trap," they said, but they didn't sound convinced. I didn't say anything. I didn't need to. Shan knows as well as I do that, for all his bad choices, for all his faults, Zachary wouldn't harm me. I took Shan's face in my hands and kissed them. "I choose you," I said, and I watched the relief come into Shan's face because they knew I meant it. I'm telling you this so you know it, too, Zachary. Come to us if you want to help us fight the good fight. But not for anything else. Not for me.

Shan left a note with our address where they knew you'd find it. It should be catching your eye as you hear these words. You should be moving toward it. You should be bending down to pick it up right. . . Now.

Chapter 18
Bonus: The Surgeon

I don't sleep a lot these days. Mostly it's because I don't have time. Every time I finish one mission, Winry finds another. We're in a race, you see, me and Zachary and Shan and Winry. Iris has her list of Gifteds for her perfect Mosaic. We have the same list. Every day is a new struggle to get to someone before she does. So I don't have a lot of time to sleep. But even when I do have time, even when I'm in bed, sleep doesn't come easy. I lie awake, Shan's arm around my waist, their breath on my neck, and I stare at the ceiling, and I think about what happens if we fail. I don't think I'll sleep well until this whole thing is over, one way or another.

Here's the one we were looking for this week, the latest thing to keep me up at night.

Biological manipulation is an essential component for Mosaics. Whether it's my ability to meld wounded flesh back together or Shan's ability to alter body chemistry with a touch, Mosaics need the ability to manipulate flesh on one level or another. So, in this race against Iris, the question came down to which of the potential tiles in the database was the most likely candidate. At the end of the day, there was only one good choice.

Corpse turns up on a sidewalk in LA. It's a well-dressed man in his 40s. A marathon runner, nonsmoker, only occasional drinker. No history of chronic illness, cancer, or heart disease. A healthy specimen. Yet here he is, cold and dead and staring up at the sky without seeing it. Must be some tragic fluke, a congenital defect, right? You'd think so, but then the coroner gets in there and looks around. Except, here's the thing, after he cuts open the body, there isn't that much to see. That's because major organs are missing. Heart, lungs, stomach. There are no incisions, no cuts, no way these organs could have been extracted. No way this person could have lived without them. And yet here he is, only hours dead, missing organs, without a bruise on him.

This sounds like some kind of shitty urban legend, but it's happened at least seven times within the last six months. All in LA, all people in peak physical condition, all without a mark on the outside of the body.

The unusual thing about this case wasn't so much the weird deaths or the physical impossibility of it all. I'm used to all that. The weird thing in this case was the fact that the Splinter didn't know who they were looking for. No names, no possibilities. And yet, of all the biomanipulation Gifteds in their database, this one was by far the most promising. So we made our way out to LA, hoping to get to this Gifted before they did.

We started at one of the crime scenes. It was an alley behind a bar. Near as the police could figure, the victim had stopped there for happy hour, left the bar after two drinks, and then had been accosted walking by the alley. We started there so Shan could read the crime scene. All of us, all the Mosaics, can sniff out a Gifted if we search long enough. There's a certain energy, almost a subconscious hum. But with Shan that gets a whole lot easier. They once told me that moving through the world for them is like hearing five different songs coming from different directions at the same time. There's always the now, and the residue of history, and very occasionally whispers of things to come, all at once. It sounds horrible to me, but they enjoy it. They say it gets dull only experiencing the here and now.

It took them a while to pinpoint what we were looking for. So many people had passed this spot, leaving so many fingerprints and shadows, that Shan had to sit in a kind of trance for half an hour before they found it. "There," they said, and then they downloaded the image into my forehead with a touch. They don't have to ask anymore, we've done this so many times. I'm almost used to it.

I saw why they hadn't just tried to describe what they saw. It's hard enough for me to find the words now. The victim left the bar and made his way toward a parking garage. He had his keys in one hand, phone in the other, idly scrolling and reading something. He obviously didn't know anything was about to happen. And then, just as he passed by the alley, something grabbed him. I say something, because I looked right at it and I still barely saw what it looked like. It was transparent; through its body, the view of the alley wavered and warped, but it stayed visible. The thing was more of a ripple than a body, a distortion of the air. I could vaguely make out the boundaries of its shape. It wasn't human.

It pulled the man back into the alley and pinned him to the ground. He tried to fight back, but he flailed away without knowing what he was fighting. And then part of that creature, a limb I can't quite refer to as an arm, plunged into his chest.

There was no blood. No wound. The victim just went stiff, his eyes staring blindly into the sky. And then he was gone.

The creature pulled out his heart slowly, carefully. The red of it was folded completely within its limb, so that not even a drop of blood dripped onto the victim's shirt. It still beat in feeble little bursts. The thing paused, and even though it didn't have eyes, it seemed to look at the organ in its hand. And then something opened where the face should have been, and it swallowed it whole.

I expected that to be the end of the memory, but there was more. A car screeched up to the curb, and a middle-aged woman jumped out. She looked right at the creature still crouched over the man's body. "Nathaniel!" she said, and the tone of her voice got my attention. It wasn't terror or grief or loss. It was disappointment.

The Gifted scurried away down the alley. The woman walked up to the dead body and stared down at him. She wasn't surprised. She wasn't scared. She just looked exhausted. After a moment, she turned around and got back in her car without doing anything to the corpse. I saw her license plate as she drove away.

From there, Winry had everything she needed. A first name, a license plate. It only took her a few minutes to find our guy. Nathaniel Holloway, cardiac surgeon. His picture looked like a normal middle-aged guy, nothing special, nothing recognizable from the creature in the alley. But the picture of his wife, fellow cardiac surgeon Paula Gallego, was something else. I recognized her right away as the woman from the alley.

I stepped back from Winry's screen and turned to Shan and Zachary. "What do we think?" I asked.

Zachary spoke first. "Whatever's going on with Nathaniel, he's out of control. I don't think there's any appealing to him. But his wife. . ."

Shan nodded. "I agree. If we just try to talk to him or catch him, we'll be going in blind. I think she's the key to this."

About Zachary. There's so much to say there. He works with us now. What he was doing before. . . That's a story for another time. And it's a story that shouldn't be told by me. It's not easy having him around. Shan figured out some ways to negate the weird effects we have on each other, but it's still difficult. That's another story for another day. The important thing, for now, is that Zachary is here, and he's one of us.

Shan and I waited for Paula Gallego outside her house. Zachary hid out of sight just in case something went wrong and we needed backup. Nathaniel wasn't there, and when we looked in the window it was pretty clear that the place hadn't been cleaned in weeks. It was 1:00 am before Paula's Mercedes parked in the driveway and she stepped out. She looked like she was about to collapse under the weight of her exhaustion. She wore a windbreaker over her hospital scrubs. Her nails were bitten to the quick. Dark circles stood out under her eyes. She saw us as soon as she stepped onto the porch. She took a close look at Shan, and resignation came over her face.

"I don't know where he is," she said.

I stepped forward. "My name's Wren. This is Shan. We're here to help."

She didn't shake my hand. She just stared at me, and then she said, "If you're here to help, you're way too late." But she let us into the house, and there she told us her story.

They'd met in medical school, she and Nathaniel. They competed, each of them fighting to be the top-ranked member of their cohort, and as they competed they fell in love. Even then, Nathaniel's success didn't make much sense to Paula. He was smart, and he worked hard, but she was smarter and worked harder. And yet, whenever they practiced on cadavers, when they moved up to internships and residencies, every time he lifted a scalpel, every surgery he performed went better than anyone could hope for.

It wasn't until after their residencies that he told her the truth. A patient had flatlined on the operating table, and Nathaniel had reached into the chest cavity and done. . . Something. She didn't know what. He had somehow, impossibly, restarted the patient's heart, and everyone at the surgery talked about it like it was some kind of miracle. It wasn't. It was, Nathaniel explained to her when she confronted him, a simple matter of reaching through flesh without a scalpel. That was his big secret. It wasn't technique, or knowledge, or luck. It was just that he could reach through flesh like it was water, find the part that wasn't working, move it or tweak it or give it a thump and get it started again.

Paula didn't believe him, of course. She thought he was insane. But then he demonstrated for her. He reached into her abdomen, and he very gently touched the outside of her lungs. She said it was the strangest thing she'd ever felt, and she told him that she'd leave him if he ever did anything like that again. But he had convinced her. She knew it was true. Nathaniel could perform the most complex surgeries on the planet with nothing more than his hands.

And for a while, nothing bad happened. Nathaniel only used his Gift during real surgeries, when he needed a little extra room to maneuver. Paula made peace with the fact that he would always have this edge over her. They were happy.

And then came the day they were mugged in a parking garage. Paula and Nathaniel were on their way to their car after dinner out. A man with a knife attacked them, jumping out of the shadows and demanding Paula's purse. She screamed, thinking she was about to be killed. And Nathaniel defended her in the only way he knew how. He reached into the attacker's chest, and he pulled out his heart.

Paula didn't blame Nathaniel for what he did. He'd feared for their lives. It was justified, and she knew that right away. What frightened her wasn't the bloody organ in his hand, or the cooling body of their attacker on the pavement. What frightened her was the expression on Nathaniel's face. It wasn't frightened or devastated or shocked. It was joyful.

He started staying out late after that. He wouldn't tell her where he was going, what he was doing. Most women would have suspected an affair. Paula suspected something far, far worse.

Then, one night, Paul awoke to the sound of Nathaniel moving around their room. She rolled over, turned on the bedside table, and saw. . . Something. Not her husband. Something translucent, formless, something more empty space than matter. She screamed, and the shape collapsed into the form of the man she loved. When she asked him about it, all he would say was that it was the technique he used to fix organs, the way he could make his hands slip through matter. Except now he could do it with his whole body.

He wouldn't say what he was using this newfound ability for.

The first time she followed him was about three months before Shan and I spoke to her. She waited for him to leave work and then followed his car to a bar. He parked outside, but he never went in. He just walked into an alley and stayed there.

The rest of the story we already knew. We'd seen Nathaniel pull the man into the alley, Paula speed over and pull her car up to the curb, jump out to see what he had done. What we didn't know was how many other times it had happened since. Seven times. On four of those occasions, she'd managed to get there and intervene before Nathaniel killed anyone. Three times, she was too late.

"Why eat the organs, though?" I asked. "I'm sorry to be blunt, but why does he do that?"

Paula sighed. "He said once that doing what he does, even when it was just during surgeries, it took a lot of energy. He was always ravenously hungry just afterwards. Back in the day a burger and a shake would take care of it, but I think, once he started pushing himself. . ."

I chose my next words carefully. "Paula, we need to stop him. And we need to keep him from falling into the hands of irresponsible people. We're going to do our best not to hurt him when we capture him, but. . ."

"No," she said, interrupting me.

I exchanged a glance with Shan. "No what?" I asked.

"No. Don't take him alive." She shook her head. Her eyes shone with tears. "Nathaniel's dead. That thing, whatever it is, it isn't the man I fell in love with. It's a monster, and it needs to die."

"We're still going to try to help him," Shan said. Paul looked skeptical, but she didn't say anything.

"Do you know where he is?" I asked.

She shook her head. "No. But he still answers the phone, sometimes, when I call. Should I?"

I nodded. "Yes. Tell him you need help. Thank you, Paula."

From there, it was easy. Paula called him and said she was in trouble, that she needed him. She hung up before he could ask questions. He showed up less than twenty minutes later. I saw him from where I hid beside the house. He didn't even bother driving over. He just oozed and glided along the ground, a shapeless, formless thing. He coalesced into a human figure just outside the front door, just before he would step inside to see his wife. I saw his face, in the seconds before Shan and Zachary and I sprang our trap. He was wild-eyed, half-crazed. But his eyes were also full of love. Through all of it, through all of what he had become, he still loved his wife.

I won't tell you where he is now. Whether he's alive or dead. That would be too much information for the Splinter to have. What I will say is that, if he died, it's because a brave woman sacrificed the love of her life to save the innocent people he would have killed in the future. And if he's alive, it's because we know Gifteds who can help when the Gifts spin out of control. It's because we're more interested in healing someone than harvesting them.

Either way, Iris, you don't have him. And you never will.

Chapter 19
Rite of Spring

Hey there, Iris. Winry says I shouldn't talk to you. She says you'll have a bunch of profilers and analysts picking up clues about my surroundings and my psychology based on things I say. She's right. I shouldn't talk to you. But. . . I don't know. It feels wrong to be this involved with someone I've never spoken to. It feels wrong to hate someone this much when I've never met them. Let me tell you about my day, Iris. Let me tell you about who we killed, you and I.

There's a lot about the last year or so that's been surprising. In the short time since I came into this world, I've found out about the Seekers and their quest to improve the human race. I've learned about the Splinter and their insane plans to speed up the process by awakening every hidden power in the human genome at the same time. I've seen terrifying and amazing things. I've fallen out of love with one person and in love with another. I've seen too many friends die. But nothing, absolutely nothing I've seen in my time, is as shocking to me as the idea of gifted people working with the Splinter. Working with people who kill and experiment on their kind, all for the benefit of the normals. And yet, even with all that, there's gifted people who work with the Splinter. Who work for you. That I don't understand.

Or, at least, I didn't understand until I heard Zachary's story. But, that's not my story to tell. I think he will tell it, at some point, but not until he's ready.

Anyway, the fact that you've got gifted people working for you, Iris, that's a neat trick. And it's definitely made this fight a lot more difficult. And, by the way: Iris, I know you know what this fight is about, but for those listening at home and wondering what we've been doing the last few months: Basically, Iris has her secret recipe to make Mosaics, which is what she needs to make the Trumpet. That's the person who's going to wake up everyone's powers. A few months ago I spent most of my time cleaning up the messes the Splinter made in their failed attempts to make Mosaics. Now they have the information to make one the right way. The problem, though, is that this Mosaic recipe calls for some pretty specific tiles. They can't just snatch any gifted person off the streets. We have the same list they do, which means we have a pretty good sense of who they're going after. And so the last few months has been all about trying to save tiles before they get snatched. We've saved some, and we've lost some, and even when we save someone you fuckers in the Splinter just move onto the next best option. It never ends.

A quick word about who I mean when I say we: there's the ones you know about. Me and Shan and Zachary and Winry. But there's more, now. I'm not going to describe who they are, because that would give you too much information. But we've got a whole lot of gifted people on our side now, ones we've saved and ones who've come out of the woodwork since this whole mess started. Just in case you were getting cocky and thinking it was just the four of us against the whole Splinter, Iris. It's not. Way, way more people than me want you dead.

But today, as it happens, really was just the A Team, so I guess that's another reason I feel like telling you about it. You know the setup, but for the rest of my dear listeners: Winry put together a list of the most likely candidates you and the rest of the Splinter might go after to make your Mosaics. And right at the top of that list was a singer named Erin Cho. The Seeker files on her were a little vague, but it was clear that her gifts had something to do with mind control and emotional manipulation. That's an essential component for any Mosaic; I have it in the form of an ability to compel people, Shan can produce consciousness-altering chemicals, and Zachary can make people bond with him like a baby bird imprinting on its mother. So we knew the Splinter would be going after somebody like Erin Cho, and we had some other leads telling us she was the top choice.

And so Shan and Zachary and I found the nightclub where Erin was singing, and we went to check it out. We split up as soon as we got there, Shan and me to one end of the club, Zachary to the other, Winry keeping in touch with all of us remotely through earpieces and watching our progress through button cameras we all carry with us into these things. That's how we always do things. Shan and me as a team, Zachary on his own. It's always like that.

The club seemed pretty normal at first. Mostly college students, dancing and drinking and hanging out near the bar. It was a little grungy, the smell of BO wafting on the air, but it wasn't a complete dive. Erin's band wasn't playing yet, and the speakers blasted a bland series of EDM songs. As we moved, Shan ran their fingertips over the bar, the walls, even a few of the people there. They winced as they did it, as their delicate ecosystem encountered hairgel and hand sanitizer and artificial perfume. But they kept it up, because if you set up a trap for us Shan could get a glimpse of Splinter agents who were here in the past few days and hours and minutes. At least, that's what we thought at the time.

"Nothing," Shan said at last. "Iris hasn't been here."

At that moment, Erin's band appeared on the stage. She's the lead singer of a band called Ritual of the Rival Tribes. I didn't think much of that, but Winry piped up in my ear. "That's one of the parts from Rite of Spring," she said. And then, when I didn't know what that meant, she said, "You know, the Stravinksy ballet? The one that caused a riot in 1913?" Because of course Winry would carry around a little tidbit like that. I didn't think anything of that connection at the time, although in retrospect maybe it should have made me realize what was about to happen.

Erin Cho and her band started up. Their music was some kind of postpunk stuff, not really my thing. I planned on waiting until the performance was over, making sure she wasn't being watched by the Splinter, and then letting her know she was in danger. Most people we intercept like that end up going with us. Most, not all.

But that's not what happened here. A few lines into the first song, Erin looked right at me. Recognition came over her face. She glared at me like I was the enemy, like I was someone she knew. Then the pitch of her singing changed, and everything started to go to shit.

Maybe you wonder what it was like, when Zachary and I met face to face for the first time. We're programmed to love each other, after all, to fuck and reproduce and make your Trumpet. So maybe you think the first time we saw each other, in that shady little hotel room with Shan standing at my side, Winry still catatonic after your attack on the Burrow, maybe you think our eyes met and everything went slow motion and soft romantic music started to play in the background.

It wasn't like that at all. It was. . . It was like smelling food you used to love but that you're allergic to now. Part of me was pulled toward him, but part of me was repulsed by him at the same time. I could see from his face he felt the same way, that same queasy push-pull. "Hello, Wren," he said at last. "It's good to finally meet you."

His eyes darted back and forth between me and Shan. There was something in the way he looked at Shan, recognition, devastation, that I didn't understand at the time. I do now. But, again, that part isn't mine to tell.

He looked the way I remembered. Bilal's dark curly hair, Jose's light brown skin, Lexi's eyes. His fingernails were still black. They aren't painted that way, I learned later. They're just naturally that color. When he spoke, his voice wasn't what I expected. An accent he got from Natalie, I think, traces of one of the languages in our makeup. Strange, isn't it, thinking that I didn't know what his voice was like before that moment.

I hit him. I'm not proud of it, especially now that I know his story. But it was like my arm was possessed, like all that weird contradictory energy had to go somewhere. He just stood there without fighting back. Shan put their body between me and Zachary and held me back. "Stop it, Wren!" they said. "This isn't you. Stop it."

"I don't think she's just angry," Zachary said. "I feel it, too. It's. . . Chemical."

He was right. There was heat and aggression and something sexual, too, a blend of feelings that didn't belong together. I scratched at my own arms, bit the skin of my hand, needing that energy to go somewhere. Zachary suddenly turned around and punched a wall.

"Go outside," Shan told Zachary. "Just go outside. I think I have a solution." Zachary went outside, and then Shan sat me down on the sagging hotel bed and told me what they wanted to do. I thought about it for a minute, but I finally nodded and gave them permission. "Do it."

Shan pulled out a few strands of my hair, then went outside and pulled some hair from Zachary. They were outside for a while. I assume they had a conversation with Zachary, but I've never asked either one about it. When Shan came back in, they held our combined strands of hair between their palms for a while. When they opened their hands, the hair was gone, absorbed into their flesh. Slowly, beads of dark liquid welled up on their fingertips. They smeared some of it on my forehead, went outside, and did the same to Zachary.

When Zachary came back in, those feelings were gone. All of them. I remembered what I used to feel for him, but it was just that. A memory. There's a part of me that's sad to lose that, but it's a pretty small part. Zachary, though. It hit him hard. I could see that. But we both knew it had to be done. Mosaics aren't meant to be out on their own in the world, you see. They aren't meant to have separate lives and fall in love with other people, like I had. It warps the connection. Shan explained all this to us. They'd suspected for a long time that the Mosaic connection depended on compatible pheromones, chemicals in me and Zachary keyed just to each other. And whatever they had just given us, it canceled out that warped connection entirely. Zachary and I can be alone in a room, now, and the only feelings we have are the ones that have grown from months of fighting side by side. Like our shared hatred of you, Iris. That's our strongest connection.

But the memories. The memories are still there. It means that no matter what happens, being around each other will always make Zachary and I a little sad. And so we avoid that, working apart. Me and Shan. Zachary and Winry. Tasks as far apart as we can manage.

And that's why, in the crowd at Erin Cho's show, Zachary and I were on opposite ends of the room. That's why we weren't close enough to be much use to each other when everything went wrong.

Here's what I saw. Notice I'm not saying, 'here's what happened', because later I came to understand that not much of what I saw in the next few minutes actually happened. Still. Here's what I saw. Eight of the people in the crowd turned around to face me. And, suddenly, whoever they had been before, those eight people were my tiles. The eight people who were brutalized to create Zachary and me. And that was weird on a couple of levels. For starters, I knew for sure that some of them were dead and some of them had transformed into different forms. Yet here they were, the way they had looked before they encountered the Splinter. They stared at me and I could feel their hatred.

Then they ran at me, snarling like animals, and I screamed. Somewhere close by, I heard Shan scream, too, but when I tried to see where they were my tiles were all around me, scratching and clawing and biting at me. One of them got an arm around my throat and pressed down on my windpipe. I reached back and pulled the water out of them. That's one of the things I can do, separate one kind of matter from another. The person around my neck shriveled to the ground, and when I looked down I couldn't tell which one it had been. Because, somehow, when I looked up and tried to fight my way through my tiles, there were still eight of them.

I caught a smell on the air, a kind of piney odor Shan produces through their skin when they're making a defensive chemical. It doesn't work on me or Zachary or Winry, which was something Shan worked into the potion's design. Anyone else, though, it lays out flat. So Shan was still alive, I thought, still alive and conscious enough to fight, even if I couldn't see them through the crowd. Knowing that gave me enough of a boost to start throwing punches, kicking, trying to fight my way through the wall of people boxing me in. Except I couldn't seem to land, like there was a gap between what I saw and what I could touch.

At some point, I realized someone was shouting in my ear. Winry. "Wren! What's happening?" she asked.

I jumped behind the bar, trying to put some distance between myself and these monsters that looked like my tiles. "Can't you fucking see my tiles? They're trying to kill me. What's happening to Shan?" I shouted.

Winry didn't answer my question. Instead she said, "Wren, I don't see any of that. You're just flailing around at people in the crowd. And they aren't doing anything to you. It's the same with Shan and Zachary."

I asked Winry what the fuck she was talking about, couldn't she see what was happening, and as I spoke I realized that I was much, much more afraid than I should have been. This was scary, sure. Any ghost encounter is. But I've seen so much worse than this. I shouldn't have been so terrified. Winry seemed to realize the same thing. "Hang on," she said through my earpiece. I imagined her at her workstation, sliding around from one keyboard to another, her screens lighting up with information I can barely comprehend. "Just hang on, guys," she said, "I'm trying to figure this out." From across the room, I felt a blast of cold air. I thought I knew what that was; Zachary can do the same thing with energy that I can do with matter, pulling heat out of a body or pushing heat into it. When I leave a body behind it looks like a mummy, but when Zachary kills it usually leaves them frozen solid, coated in frost and cooling the air all around.

That made me realize something else. No one had noticed the mummified body I'd left crumpled on the ground. The whole crowd should have been losing their shit, running for the doors, but they were ignoring it.

"I got it!" Winry shouted. "Infrasound! I think Erin's producing infrasound. It must be directed infrasound, too, if it's only affecting you three like this and it's making everyone else oblivious." When I asked her what that meant, she told me infrasound was a frequency that caused paranoia, hallucinations, even psychosis. Later, when it was all over, she would explain that infrasound was usually produced only in very specific natural environments, caves and old buildings that had the right shape, or else with specialized equipment. That infrasound was one explanation for why people thought certain buildings were haunted, that some part of the house was shaped in such a way that it produced sound that interfered with people's thoughts and emotions.

But something about that wasn't right. It took me a second to sift through the paranoia and figure out what it was. "But somebody grabbed me around the neck," I said. "I felt them." I realized Winry couldn't have seen that through my button cam, that it would only have given her a view of the room in front of me. As she and I had this conversation, my tiles snarled and batted at me over the top of the bar.

Winry figured it out first. "Shit! Everyone, close your eyes. Wren, turn to your 3 o'clock. Shan, to your 11 o'clock. Zachary, to your 6 o'clock. Now hold still. That gives me almost a 360 degree view of the room."

It was a little better having my eyes closed and not having to look at my tiles, but I still felt the pressure of being watched, still fought the panicked pounding of my heart with every word of Erin's song.

"Ok, listen carefully," Winry said. "There are guys moving through the crowd. Four of them, that I can see. They don't look like they're here for the music. I think they're here to take you down in the confusion."

"Winry," I said, "If I just try to defend myself without knowing where they are I'll probably kill a civilian."

She said she knew that. She said I needed to trust her. I knew I could trust her, I knew I should, but that paranoia was starting to creep into my thoughts about Winry. Some small, hysterical corner of my mind start babbling. What if Winry was a traitor? What if she had led us into a trap? I did my best to squelch that part of my mind, because I knew beyond any doubt that Winry was on my side, but it felt as real as anything I'd ever felt.

"All of you be ready to defend yourself when and where I say," Winry said, and I forced myself to listen.

"Wren, coming up at your 2 o'clock, moving behind the bar, reaching for your arm. . . Now!"

I felt the hand on my arm, coming from the direction Winry had said. I turned to him and, eyes still closed, said, "Leave the club and forget everything you know about us." I held my breath; my compulsion abilities are pretty strong, but if they knew enough about me to set this up they might have come prepared with earplugs or something. But no; the guy dropped my arm and moved away.

I heard more orders from Winry, ones directed at Shan and Zachary. I said a silent prayer to a God I don't believe in that Shan would come through it unharmed. Then I waited and listened until Winry said, "Shan's clear. Zachary's clear. Wren, one more incoming from the left."

I got rid of that one just as easily as the first. I was just starting to think that we were going to come through this without a whole lot of bloodshed. We'd just need to get out the door and find a way to intercept Erin another time. But then the first song ended, and Erin moved onto the second. And this second song wasn't so much music as a piercing, nonstop shriek, a sound so loud everything sounded like I was listening from underwater for days afterward. Erin screamed and screamed and screamed into the microphone, and she somehow did it without ever having to pause, without having to draw breath. My own paranoia faded, and when I opened my eyes my dead tiles were gone. My tiles were gone, but the crowd, the real crowd, was still there. They froze for a second, listening to Erin. And then they turned on me.

This time there was no question they were real. I felt their hands, their nails, their teeth. They yanked at my hair and tried to bite my skin. I screamed commands for them to stop, but Erin's howl into the microphone was too loud for my compulsion gifts to work. I slowed time, but they were packed so tightly around me, gripped me so hard, that there wasn't much I could do even then.

"Shan!" Winry shouted. "Anesthesia! Put them all to sleep, now!"

I caught just a glimpse of Shan through a gap in the crowd. Some of the people closest to them staggered and started to fall, but the effect didn't spread the way it should have. The crowd was packed too tight for Shan's pollen to travel on the air currents the way it was supposed to. Shan pushed and fought and struggled, but blood already stained one of their sleeves, dripped from a cut in their neck.

Part of the crowd on the other end of the room suddenly started floating up toward the ceiling; that was Zachary, manipulating the gravity in a six-foot wide circle.

"Wren!" Winry said into my ear. "Incoming on Shan! Guy with a knife!"

I saw what she was talking about right away. A big guy, holding a switchblade, shoving people aside to get to Shan. Shan had their back turned, their arms held by others in the crowd.

I didn't hesitate. I did what I'd been hoping I wouldn't have to do ever since the crowd went berserk. I ripped the water from a dozen people, ended a dozen lives. You see, I can control the size of the area from which I separate matter. I can limit it to the size of one human body, or an entire forest. But one thing I can't do is reach over a seething crowd of bodies and pull water from one specific person. I can't do it from that kind of distance. I could only include the man with the knife in the part of the crowd I decided to kill.

Water sloshed over everyone's shoes, and a column of space opened between me and Shan. At the same time, Zachary got himself free of the people who had been tearing at him. He climbed up onto the stage. And then he killed Erin Cho. She froze instantly, mid-song. Her body fell, and as soon as it hit the stage it shattered into a thousand pieces, as though she'd been dipped into a vat of liquid nitrogen.

Most of the crowd ran for the doors then. The moment Erin died, the moment she stopped singing, the spell broke. They fled, along with whatever Splinter agents were still in the room. And then it was just the three of us, and the bodies.

Shan looked at the row of dead civilians I'd had to kill to take out the Splinter assassin that had been reaching for them. They looked sad, and they shook their head. "I'm sorry you had to do that," they said, and it was just the right thing at that moment because they didn't bother pretending that I could have let them die, even if it meant taking out innocent people along the way. Shan took me in their arms, and I let myself stay like that for just a minute. And then, before the cops could arrive, we left, none of us saying anything. There was nothing to say. Our mission was a failure.

To the people who survived that club, to Erin Cho's band, Zachary and Shan and I are the villains of this story. We're the ones who came in and killed people for no clear reason, and then vanished without a trace. So congratulations, Iris, on turning us into the bad guys here. It'll make recruiting the next Erin all the easier.

But you and I, we know the truth. We know who made that massacre happen. We know how much blood is on your hands.

I'm coming for you, Iris. And every innocent person who gets caught in the middle, every assassin you send after Shan, it just makes me that much more determined to reach into your chest and rip your heart out.

Chapter 20
Iris

This story isn't for you, Iris. You already know this story better than I do. You know what came before, and what happened behind the scenes. So I'm not speaking to you. I'm speaking to any gifted people who are with the Splinter now, or who are thinking about joining them. I'm speaking to anyone who believes Iris's lies about the Splinter and the Seekers and what's going to happen when the Trumpet sounds. I know how easy it is to believe her. I know, because I believed her, too, once, before I saw her for who she really is. My name is Zachary, and I'm here to tell you exactly who Iris is.

I want to be clear about something. I'm not telling this story to make excuses for what I've done. Wren and I came from the same place, had the same experience, and she managed to avoid doing the terrible things I've done. She saw through lies that I fell for. So this isn't to absolve me of my crimes. This is just to tell you what happened, what you need to know about Iris and the things she's capable of.

If you're listening to this, then you already know what happened in the attic. The blood, the Skull Man, the fire. I won't get into any of that. I'll start from the part where my story and Wren's story split into two. You know this part. Wren killed the Skull Man and we escaped from the attic. I grabbed her hand, and all I thought about was getting her to safety. But then we ran down the stairs and onto the street, and her hand slipped from mine, and I got lost in the smoke and the dark. I can't even describe how that felt. Like losing a limb, like losing everything in your entire life. The only person I loved was gone, and I was naked and alone on a dark street.

There's some blankness, after that, some parts of my memory I've never gotten back. But I do remember when I was rescued. I was hiding outdoors, somewhere, maybe a park. I was curled up in a hollow behind some trees. And then I looked up, and a woman stood there, staring at me. She was tall and slender, with strong features and long black hair. She didn't seem scared of me, even though I was a naked, blood-spattered man babbling to himself beneath a tree. She held out a hand. "Come on, Zachary," she said.

"Is that my name?" I asked. And it seemed so, so important for me to have a name.

"Of course it is," she said. Then she frowned and asked me what I remembered. If I remembered her. I tried, but there was almost nothing. Fragments. Flashes of life I now know belonged to one or another of my tiles. The woman shook her head. Her eyes filled with tears. I felt guilty, in that moment. I didn't know who this woman was, but I knew I'd disappointed her.

"Oh, Zachary," she said, "it's going to be ok. My name is Iris. I'm your wife."

Iris took me home, and cleaned me up, and fed me, and told me a story. I know now that's all it was, a story. A lie. For a while, thought, it was the reality I lived. There are times, looking back, when it still feels true. Here's the story she told me: She told me about an evil organization called the Seekers. She told me about how they looked for people with special gifts, like mine. The way I can move things through time, and manipulate energy, and control gravity. They hunted people like me. Iris and I managed to work together to stay ahead of them for a long time. That's how we met, how we fell in love: we'd been brought together by a shared desire to defeat this evil organization and save innocent people from destruction. And that's what we did. But, one day, she came home and I was gone. She wasn't sure what happened, but she knew the Seekers wanted to harness my powers for their own. She went out looking for me, and she eventually found me in that park, but only after the Seekers had done something terrible to me and nine other people.

"What should we do?" I asked, after she finished her story. "Should we leave town?"

And Iris shook her head slowly, with this really convincing look of regret on her face, and said no, she wished we could just run. But we had a responsibility to help people like me. We had to protect them from the Seekers. I looked at her and I thought, oh what a brave woman I married. How wonderful she is. And then I felt so guilty, because even though I admired her and I believed her and I accepted that she was my wife, I didn't feel love when I saw her.

The only time I felt love was when I closed my eyes and I saw that strange blood-spattered mystery girl from the attic. But I knew that was wrong, so wrong, so I kept quiet and I told Iris I didn't remember the people in the attic at all, because I didn't want to have to explain what I felt for that one girl.

After I recovered a little from what had happened, Iris told me what I had to do to help people like me. Gifted people. The first step was finding them. They would be mistrustful, for good reason. They would be used to being hunted. They would trust Gifted people much more than they would trust a normal like her. I had to find them, using my talents, and gain their trust, and then my brave, lovely wife would get them to safety. She made it sound so noble. A kind of rescue network for those the Seekers wanted to exploit. So I went out into the city, and I followed leads, and I used my abilities to track down Gifted people.

They weren't my tiles. Iris wasn't interested in them. She wasn't even interested in Wren, not until she started making trouble for the Splinter. Wren and I are flawed Mosaics, you see. Not what the Splinter was aiming for, although I wouldn't learn any of this until later. We were the closest thing to a successful attempt at that point, but Wren interrupted the last crucial bit of the ritual when she stabbed the Skull Man. We were useless for the Splinter's purposes after that. No, Iris was already thinking about the next version, the next attempt. So I found Gifteds. I found the girl whose consciousness could travel along rivers by hitching a ride on the water molecules. I found the man whose blood acted as a powerful halluci-nogen. The twins who could communicate telepathically across continents. I found them, and then Iris sent me on my next mission while she whisked them away from the Seekers.

I asked her why I couldn't help with that part. I asked her where they went, how she saved them. She told me it wasn't safe for everyone in the network to know more than their part. If anyone was captured, if anyone was interrogated. . . Well, that made perfect sense to me, and so I kept finding them, and Iris kept lying about what she did with them. I always pictured them living simple lives in secluded cabins. I pictured them safe and free and living off the land. I never pictured them in chains.

Then Wren's messages started showing up online, and there were more lies. The second I heard Wren's first message, and the words Grove, Mosa-ic, and Trumpet, and the part where she said she loved me, I went straight to Iris. I asked her what the hell was going on. I asked her about the little fragments I'd been remembering, odd bits that didn't feel like my life.

Iris's eyes welled up with tears and she looked at me like I'd broken her heart, and she said that the Seekers had made Wren to mislead me. That they had conjured my perfect match like a golem, that she was designed to drive a wedge between me and Iris and the people we fought to save. That they were trying to seduce me into their ranks. She cried and said she was sorry and told me this meant she wasn't my dream woman, and again I felt so guilty I thought she must be right. This was my fault.

But I started keeping secrets from Iris. Some part of me must have started to suspect her, even if the rest of me didn't want to believe that she was lying. On some of my trips out of the house, the ones where I was supposed to be searching for people on our list of Gifteds, I went looking for my tiles instead. I listened to Wren's messages and tried to anticipate her movements. Iris told me I should kill her if I ever got close, because she was just a Seeker plant. If anyone had asked during that time, I'd have said that's why I was looking for her. But it wouldn't have been true. I'm still not really sure what I was looking for back then, what I thought would happen.

One day I found the sinkhole Claire had disappeared into. I tossed in my coins, and I heard my future. The first coin bought me this prediction: "Wren will learn your name in this place."

The second said, "Jose will tell you where you came from."

And then came the last one. The one that almost destroyed me the first time I heard it, and the only thing that brings me hope now. That prediction, the last thing Claire said to me, was, "You'll watch Iris die in a field a long way from here."

I tried throwing in more coins, begging, screaming Claire's name, but she wouldn't tell me more. She wouldn't tell me if this future could be avoided. So I went down into the pit. I didn't need a rope, not like when Wren went. Manipulating gravity is one of my Gifts, so I just floated to the bottom. You've already heard about what's down there. It didn't change between when I was there and when Wren visited. I searched for Claire, but she stayed silent. And so, once I gave up on finding her, I left a note for Wren. It said, "Dear Wren: You don't need to keep doing this. You're safe. Please just try to live a life. I love you."

After Wren found out what we were, she thought I had already known. She thought that note was me trying to protect her from the knowledge of what we are. I committed that sin later, but not then. Then, all I could think of was trying to prevent the fight to the death Iris said Wren and I would have if we ever met. I thought about what it would mean if it was Wren who would try to kill Iris in that field, and I would have to fight her to protect my wife. I thought about how that choice would feel. I thought she was just a creation of the Seekers, but that didn't stop me from loving her. It didn't stop me from wanting her to walk away from this whole mess, and live whatever life an artificially constructed dream girl could have. I didn't know at the time that I was every bit as much of a construction as she was.

Even then, I didn't ask the right questions. I didn't think about the right things. I didn't go to see Jose. Why wouldn't I, you might ask. Claire said he would have the answers, the truth. And I could have found him earlier than I did. I think some part of me knew I wasn't going to like what I heard, so I made up excuses for why I should go. Maybe it was a trap. Maybe Claire was lying. Maybe this, maybe that. And all the while, I kept finding Gifteds for Iris.

The last time, the one that ended it all, was a girl named Lily. Lily was fifteen years old. She was bright, and hardworking, and she was a talented musician. She was popular at her school, which was odd, because she didn't fit the usual popular girl image. She didn't wear the nicest clothes or use makeup, and her sense of humor was quirky in a way most teenagers fear because it's too different. She was the kind of girl that my fragmented memories told me would be a little bit on the fringes in high school, but would find her place in college. Not at this school, though. At this school, the other kids flocked to be around her, to sit with her at lunch, to adopt her mannerisms.

I know all this, by the way, because Iris and her people got me into the school as a substitute teacher. I spent a few weeks pretending to know something about writing and composition, while in reality I was there for a very different purpose. I was there to find out why the school had changed so dramatically over the course of just a single year. In that time, test scores saw an unprecedented improvement. Truancy basically vanished. And then there were the little stories. Teachers and parents whispering about how much nicer the kids had gotten. How bullying and the little acts of cruelty one sees every day among teenagers had just stopped. It wasn't like a body snatchers situation; the kids were still themselves, still had personality, still had bad moods or off days. They just seemed like better, nicer, more open versions of themselves.

When I started my mission there, we didn't know why any of this happened. All we knew was that only the influence of a Gifted person's abilities could explain such a dramatic change in such a short period of time. Now, of course, I know that everything changed because Lily started high school that year.

I figured it out the day Lily's grandmother died. I was helping supervise the lunch room. The kids milled around, ate, gossiped, did everything as usual. Lily was just one face among many, although maybe one I noticed a bit more because she was so popular with the other students. In the middle of lunch, she answered her phone. Her smile slowly faded. She nodded and said a few words, then hung up and continued eating her lunch. She didn't tell anyone what had happened. But, as I watched, the spark went out of every kid in the cafeteria. Their smiles disappeared. They stopped talking to each other. Some even started to cry a little. And most of them weren't even looking in Lily's direction. Their faces just matched up with hers.

It all made sense, after I saw that. Lily was an influencer. A real one, not one of those obnoxious wannabe trendsetters online. What Lily did, others wanted to do. When Lily got interested in something, others followed. As luck would have it, she was a sweet kid who studied hard and didn't bully anyone, so that's what became popular at her school. She didn't do any of this on purpose. This wasn't mind control. It was much subtler than that.

Finding Lily, that was the end. I didn't know it at the time, but that was the end of everything.

As soon as I identified her, I. . . Um. No. I'm sorry. Yeah, you know what, I can't finish this story now. The world needs to hear this, but not today. For now, just remember: Iris can't be trusted. The Splinter can't be trusted. When I can finish this message, you'll find out why.

Chapter 21
Iris, Continued

It's Zachary again. I started to tell you my story last time. I told you about waking up in the attic, and being found by Iris, and how she lied and pretended and made me believe she was my wife. I told you about how I was stupid enough to be tricked into hunting Gifteds for the Splinter. That's just the background, though. That isn't the important part of the story. So today I need to do the last thing on Earth I want to do. Today I need to finish telling you about Lily.

Lily was the last one before I found out the truth. A sweet, good-natured girl, a girl whose Gift made the other people around her better. I found out who she was, and for a little while I thought I was saving her.

Once I'd identified Lily, I brought it to Iris, same as always. I told her I'd figured out that one of the students was an influencer. Iris smiled when I told her that. She smiled, and she seemed just ecstatic about the news, and that made me wonder. Why? Why would it make her so happy to know that the Gifted person being threatened by the Seekers was a fourteen year old girl?

She must have realized that she'd reacted too strong, because she looked serious again. "What's her name?" she asked.

I hesitated; I knew in that moment something was wrong. I knew I didn't trust Iris on some deep level I wasn't quite aware of. Instead of giving her the name, I asked what would happen with Lily's family. Would they go into protection, too?

Iris just seemed confused by the question. "Yeah, yeah, of course," she said at last, but I could tell she was lying. "So what's her name, Zach?"

She tried to be casual as she asked the question, but she wasn't. She looked. . . Hungry. That's the only word I can think of to describe it.

An odd, unrelated thought crept into my head: had I seen any pictures of me and Iris before the attic? Shouldn't we have a wedding photo? Shouldn't there be mementos and souvenirs and photos from our time together?

But I didn't ask that. I didn't ask anything. Suddenly, my heart was pounding. I'd been with Iris every day since the attic, months by that point, and now I was afraid in a way I had never been before.

"Come on, Zach, what's her name?" she asked, and I saw her real face for just a second.

I gave her a name. Not Lily's. I should have just refused and confronted her right there, but I was too paralyzed with the jumble of thoughts and doubts and suspicions running through my head. I wish I could tell you that I made up a name, or that I gave her the name of someone who deserved what they got. But that would be a lie. Instead, I panicked and I said the name of one of Lily's classmates, a girl who didn't deserve the attention of the Splinter any more than Lily did.

After Iris left to find the girl, I searched the house. I went through the dresser, the cabinets, under the bed. There weren't any pictures. None at all. None of me, but also none of Iris. There were other things wrong, too, things I hadn't noticed before. All my clothes were new. Not fancy or special, but like they'd only been bought a few months ago at most. The furniture was cheap Ikea-type shit, but it also seemed new. There wasn't a junk drawer, and the only clutter we'd accumulated was stuff I remembered bringing home since the attic. Receipts, rubber bands, candy wrappers, all that stuff that gets into couches and into the back of drawers, there was almost none of that. No evidence whatsoever that Iris and I had been together before the attic. And no evidence that anyone at all had lived here before a couple months ago. It was like I woke up and suddenly realized I was living in a movie set, or a dollhouse.

I went looking for Jose. It didn't take me long to find them. You've heard about it from Wren. The strip club, the one mind divided among half a dozen bodies. None of them wanted to talk to me at first. Joey reached under the bar, and I knew he had a gun stashed there. Jolene looked me right in the eye and told me they'd die before they'd let themselves be taken again. I didn't know what they were afraid of, or I thought it was the Seekers. They seemed confused when I said I wasn't with them.

Finally, I said, "I just want to know about my wife. Iris. Do you know anything about her? What she and I were like, before?"

They all blinked at me. Then Jojo, the dancer, took my hand. "Oh, honey," she said. "You don't know anything, do you?" She sat me down, and she told me everything. How the tiles got into the attic. How Wren and I were made. How I couldn't have had a wife from before, because for me there was no before.

It took a long time for all of it to sink in. A lot of it still hasn't, even now. But, at the time, all I could think of was Wren. I'd thought before that there was nothing worse than the idea of her being a tool of the Seekers, but the thought of her finding out what she was, what I am. . . I couldn't take it. "Don't tell her," I begged Jose. "Please, just don't tell her what we are."

There's a lot of stuff I've done in my short life that I regret. That one's top of the list. She had a right to know, and I tried to keep it from her. That, more than anything else, is something I can't take back or make up for. But I asked, and Jose's bodies looked at each other, holding some silent conversation that didn't include me.

Finally, Jojo turned back to me. "Ok. We'll keep quiet. And we'll try to get Wren to move on. Leave town. But we want something in return." She gave me an address. She told me what I would find at that address. She told me what I needed to do there. So I left, to see if what Jose had told me was the truth.

It looked like a normal house. Most of the Splinter's bases do. It's easier to hide what you're doing when your headquarters doesn't look like a shadowy base of operations. I spotted a few people on lookout, sitting in cars or pretending to be out for a walk. But I'd gotten pretty good at moving through the world unnoticed since I started hunting Gifteds. I used to say "rescuing". Now I know "hunting" is the right word.

I got to the house and slipped through one of the walls at the back. I can't teleport the way Wren can, but I can phase through solid matter. Once I got through the wall, I found myself in an empty office. Filing cabinets, computers, that kind of thing. There was nothing obvious on the desk or in the computer, nothing that blinked "You've been lied to, Zachary!" in giant red letters. I started to wonder if Jose was lying. It would make so much sense, if this was just a fantastical story by the Seekers to throw me off. But if they were right about what was here, there was no other explanation. It would be proof they were telling the truth.

So I slipped through the wall into the next room, and that's where I found my smoking gun.

That smoking gun's name was Josie. A teenage girl with blue hair, sitting on the floor in the middle of a bare, padded cell. She wasn't surprised to see me. She was still linked to her other bodies, to the rest of Jose, even from this padded cell. The others had known for days that she'd been captured, had seen and heard and felt everything she experienced, but they hadn't been able to get close enough to save her. And she'd refused to help the Splinter get to the rest of her. "It's about time," she said. She stood and wiped tears from her face. "Let's go."

I lifted her and phased back through the locked cell door. I asked Josie if Iris was here. She shrugged. "I don't know. They make sure I don't see too much. But she's come to talk to me almost every day I've been here."

I told Josie to stay behind me, and then we moved down the hallway. I could hear movement, people talking, from the place where the living room should be. I stepped around the corner, and there she was. Iris. Sitting at a desk and peering at a folder full of papers, in a house with a kidnapped teenage girl.

There were about five other people in the room, most with guns and commando gear. They reached for their weapons, but I told them not to move.

"Listen to him. His energy transfer abilities are extremely fast," Iris said. She was calm. No, not calm. Cold. She was cold in a way I hadn't seen before, in a way she had managed to hide from me. Now I saw that it had always been just under her performance, this real self. She looked at me for a moment and said, "You gave us the wrong name. That girl you named at the school isn't Gifted."

Josie pointed at Iris. "Just kill her. Kill the bitch. Trust me, she deserves it."

But I needed to know. I needed to know for certain. "It's all true? The Mosaics? All that?" I asked.

Iris didn't bother playing dumb. She saw the look on my face, made the calculation, and decided there was no point in denying anything. "Yeah," she said. "It's true."

"Why?" I asked, and I wasn't even sure which part I was asking about by that point.

Iris shrugged. "There's no one better suited for tracking Gifteds than a Mosaic. It seemed easiest to fabricate a preexisting relationship. It's not the only way to ensure compliance, but it's the least messy option."

I thought of the time we'd spent together, the things we'd done, all the things Iris did to make me believe she was my wife. Thinking about it made me so sick I almost vomited right there. I shouted and screamed and ranted. I cried. I called her every name I could think of. She didn't even flinch. She just waited for me to finish, and then she said, "Just in case you're thinking of killing me now. Icing, boiling, whatever you would do. You should know that a sniper is positioned to kill Wren the second they receive word that something has happened to me, or that you've gone AWOL."

I told her I didn't believe her. She leaned back in her chair and folded her arms. "You've listened to her messages," she said. "You know she was intercepted and shot by one of our teams. You know she can self-heal, but she wouldn't have time to do any of that if she were shot in the head rather than the leg. So, you're going to keep working for me. You'll keep locating Gifted people necessary for our project. And, in exchange, Wren gets to live."

I thought about bluffing. I thought about saying I didn't care, that Wren and I didn't really know each other, that I couldn't be in love with her if we were just created months before. But it wouldn't have worked, and Iris and I both knew it. She nodded and said, "And one other thing, Zachary. I know it doesn't seem like it now, but I promise we really are working to create a better world. A fairer, more peaceful world. What you're going to help us do, it's going to require some hard choices, but you'll be on the right side. Just try to remember that. It'll make things easier."

When I could finally speak, I just said, "I'll do it. But I'm taking Josie home." It was my one, tiny rebellion, the one thing I could put right.

Iris glanced at Josie, and it was clear she'd forgotten about her. "Oh, that's fine. She didn't turn out to be as useful as I thought," she said. "We weren't sure if tiles could be recycled. It was worth a try. But it seems like the process changes them too much for reuse." And then she looked me right in the eye. "We're still not sure if Mosaics can be liquidated for parts. Some of us are looking into that possibility, but I've put that option on the back burner. For now."

Of course, I didn't know it at the time, but that was a lie, too. Breaking down Mosaics for their parts was Elliot's big project, the one that led him to try to capture Wren. And Iris knew what her father was up to, obviously, but she managed to keep that part of things hidden away from me. I didn't even know Elliot was still alive until I heard Wren's last message before the city died. I didn't know he was Iris's father until much later. But at that point I didn't see any other option than to believe Iris, and do what I had to do to stay alive and keep Wren safe.

So I took Josie back to her family. I went back to Iris. And then, for the next year, I did terrible things. Lily. . . I didn't save Lily. Iris took her, and I helped her do it. For a long time, I didn't know what happened to her. All I knew was that she was taken out of state, to be one of the tiles for a Mosaic attempt based in a small town in Ohio. I later heard from one of Iris's minions that the Ohio attempt had failed, had killed everyone at the site and created an environmental disturbance that almost exposed the whole project to the outside world. That was all I knew about what happened to Lily for the longest time.

Then I met Shan. Wren's love. I met Shan, and I saw their crooked smile and the way they tilt their head when they're listening to something, and the soft kindness in their eyes. I met Shan, and Lily's ghost stared back at me, and I suddenly understood what they had meant when they talked about that environmental disturbance in Ohio. That impossible forest that became a lake.

I told Shan this story, eventually. I thought they had a right to know, and I've learned not to keep secrets from people who have a right to know them. Shan listened, and was silent for a long time. Then they said, "I thought I remembered you. I was right." And then they said, "I'm not Lily, Zachary. I'm not her, but I think she'd forgive you." They touched my arm, and smiled, and I thought that at least some tiny shred of good came out of all the things I've done.

But there were so many other things, things I did after I found Lily. Things I won't talk about. But as I did those things, I waited, and I watched, and I gathered information. I waited until I could be sure that Iris was lying about the sniper team following Wren around. And then, when I was sure I could do it without getting Wren killed, I ran. I ran, and I took a computer full of Splinter secrets with me, and I brought them straight to Wren and Shan and Winry.

I won't say I've paid for my sins, because I haven't. I'm alive, and innocent people are dead, and that means there's been no justice. But the Splinter made sure I suffered. I've learned that everything I believed in was a lie. I learned that I was bred like an animal, made to reproduce and be discarded like trash. I've learned that the woman I trusted, the one who cared for me and helped me and protected me, that woman is a monster. And now I live with the knowledge that Wren has moved past me, that she and Shan have grown around each other and have something I can't even understand, much less be a part of. I'm not angry about that, or jealous. Wren and I would poison each other if we were ever together, and we both know that. Still, it doesn't make it any less painful to see.

I'm sharing this because I want everyone listening to know that this is what happens if you let Iris near your life. She ruins and defiles and uses everything she touches. You will lose everything you love and care about, and you will do evil things in her name, and, worst of all, you'll think you're one of the good guys. And then, when you're no longer useful, Iris will leave your empty husk behind.

But I have things that have kept me going. Top of the list? Claire's last prediction. I know I'm going to live long enough to see Iris dead in a field somewhere. I hope it happens soon. I hope I'm the one to do it.

Chapter 22
The Loch

I'll be the first to admit that I've gotten pretty cynical about all you normal folks out there. So far the ungifted folks I've encountered have tortured Gifteds, killed or kidnapped them, and created me to exist as a fucking brood mare, all for their benefit. Interacting with Iris and the Splinter has only made that worse. But today gave me a little bit of hope for the normals. I know, I know, don't tell anyone I'm losing my edge. Still, I want to tell this story not just because I like talking about the Splinter's defeats, but because a lot of you Gifted folk out there must be wondering if we can ever live with the ungifted, if preventing the Awakening is even worth it. And so, for those of you looking for a little bit of faith in humanity, here's the story of how one tiny village in the Scottish Highlands looked the Splinter in the eye and told it to fuck right off.

Shan and I went to Scotland thanks to some of Winry's research, and also some tips we've been getting from Gifted folks and allies all over the world. When this race to put the new Mosaics together started, Iris and her people were focused on the US. They were trying to get their tiles assembled as fast as possible. But with all the interruptions from us and our allies, they started casting their net wider. We've been hearing about Splinter agents showing up in South Africa, Japan, Costa Rica. And now two simultaneous high-priority sightings; one in the highlands of Scotland, and one in Hong Kong. Winry couldn't say for sure what the more likely target was, so we decided to split up. Me and Shan to Scotland, Winry and Zachary to Hong Kong.

One of my tiles visited Scotland before. I think it was Lexi. I remembered the heavy grey sky, the thick accents of the people, the constant smell of rain. The moment we got out of Edinburgh and into a long stretch of road looping through cow pastures and moors, Shan asked me to pull the rental car over. They stepped barefoot onto the grass and let out a long, happy sigh, like a burden they'd been carrying for years had been lifted. Their arm vines unfurled and fluttered in the air. "Yes," they said, and even though we were on a clock to get to our destination before the Splinter, I couldn't make myself hurry them along. I just stood there and watched them walk on the clean earth, and that walk was more like dancing.

But, after a while, it was time to go. We got back in the car, and we made our way to the tiny village whose name I'll never tell.

We were spotted the second we arrived. A young woman in tights and a leather jacket leaned against the wall of a grocery store, smoking a cigarette. The moment she saw us, her eyes narrowed. She crushed the cigarette under her boot and marched inside. From there, as we parked, as we got out and walked the streets, we saw the news spreading. People walking briskly from pub to bakery, from bakery to house, from house to gas station. No one said hello to us, even though the people in other towns along the way had been open and friendly.

"It feels like they know something," Shan said after a while. They were right, I thought. These people did know something. And that meant our usual strategy wasn't going to work. Whenever possible, I like to be subtle. Slip into a town unnoticed, watch and learn what I can, and involve civilians as little as possible. That usually results in a lower body count. But sometimes, like today, blending into the background just isn't an option. So I decided to take a more direct approach.

We walked into the town pub and each ordered a beer. Men leaned on the bar and smoked, even though smoking in pubs has been illegal in Scotland for ages. I guess anyone tasked with enforcing that law took one look at these guys and decided it wasn't worth it. They didn't hide the fact that they were watching us. They just took long drags on their cigarettes, blinked, and stared at us so hard I thought they'd burn holes into my skin.

I took a sip of my beer, set it down, and turned to address the pub. "So, gentlemen. If you don't mind me asking, who do you think we are?"

One of them answered in an accent so thick I could barely understand it. But it was something like, "I think you're with them that keep snatching special people out of their homes."

That's what I thought. "Well, that's not who we are," I said. "The people you're thinking of, they call themselves the Splinter. We're not with them. We work against them."

"That's what one of them would say, if they was trying to gain our trust," the bartender grumbled. I couldn't really argue with that one. I could have used compulsion on all these guys in quick succession, but that felt wrong. It felt like it would prove their suspicions right.

I was still trying to figure out the best way forward when Shan grabbed my arm and pointed out the window. A blue minivan with rental plates moved slowly past the pub. Two people sat in the front seats, both craning their necks to see the town around them. "Some of your friends, then?" the bartender asked.

"Kind of the opposite, I think," I told him. I wondered what we should do. I wanted to follow these guys, see what they were up to, but it also seemed smart to stay hidden. So I moved to a seat by the window, tried to ignore the cigarette smoke, and watched. While I did that, Shan subtly checked out the place. It would have looked like idle taps of their fingers across wooden surfaces, but they were reading the place's history like Braille.

"Splinter hasn't been in here," Shan told me in a low voice. "But there's been meetings late at night. With all the villagers. Couldn't tell what they were discussing, but it seemed very secretive."

The phone behind the bar rang, and the bartender answered. He listened in silence as someone spoke on the other end, too quiet for me to hear. Then the bartender just said, "Aye, will do," hung up the phone, and picked up a shotgun from behind the bar. He pointed it straight at us and said, "Don't either of you move."

I froze. I could fix the damage from a shotgun blast, as long as it missed my brain, but at this distance it would shred Shan's flesh, too. That wasn't something I was willing to risk. But I also really, really didn't want to kill some guy who honestly thought he was protecting someone. And compulsion works pretty well, but if the guy's trigger finger just happened to twitch as I ordered him to put the gun down, we'd be done. Shan put their hands up and asked, in a steady voice, "What's your name?"

The bartender blinked. He seemed unsettled by the sound of Shan's voice. "Ian."

"Ian, whatever's happened, we're probably the people best equipped to help you."

"Save your breath," Ian said. "We know your friends are going after one of our lads. If they take one of ours, we'll sure as hell take two of theirs. Two at least."

"One of your lads," I said. "Who? Who are they after, Ian? What can he do?"

Ian blushed and seemed to realize that he'd given away information that we didn't already have. One of the men at the bar leaned toward him, careful to avoid the barrel of the shotgun. "Maybe they're telling the truth. They could help us."

"Nothing they can do that we can't do ourselves," Ian snapped.

"That's not true, Ian," Shan said. Ian seemed to waver at the touch of Shan's voice, and the skin above his collar grew tomato-red. He swallowed and wiped sweat from his forehead. I suspected that Shan was pumping some subtle pheromones into the atmosphere, in addition to just doing their usual thing. "Ian," Shan went on, obviously seeing that they had him, "if you just lift the shotgun, my comrade can provide a demonstration of the sorts of things we can do to help."

The phone rang again. Ian answered it, cradling the receiver between his chin and shoulder. "Fuck," he whispered at whatever he heard. "Ok," he said, hanging up. "Show me what you think you can do to help."

I turned to Ian's friend and told him to turn a complete circle, whistle Camptown Races, and slap himself across the face, in that order. He did it. "See, Ian?" Shan said. "Wren could have ordered you to put that shotgun in your mouth the second you pointed it at us. But neither of us wants innocent people to get hurt. We won't be taking anyone away from your village when we leave here, we promise you that."

Ian wavered for a moment. Then he let out a curse and put the shotgun down. "Get Agnes on the phone," he told one of his wide-eyed customers. "Tell her we might have some reinforcements here."

He led us down narrow alleys and passages between houses, keeping us out of sight of the main road. "We've got people trying to put them off the scent," Ian whispered. "But if they find where he's hidden, well, we'll need to make a stand there."

The sound of splintering wood stopped us in our tracks. Ian peered around a corner, then told us armed men had started kicking doors in. "What are they looking for?" I asked.

He wouldn't say. All he said was, "You'll see."

We ended up in a house like any of the others, tucked between two similar buildings. Ian knocked quietly on the back door and said, "It's me." It opened, and a middle-aged woman holding a gun waved us inside.

Half the town was there in that house's living room. Most were armed. In the middle of it all sat an old woman, tiny and wrinkled as a doll, a halo of white frizz standing up from her head. She looked me right in the eye and said, "If you've come to take one of our lads, you had better be ready to kill the rest of us on the way there."

"That's right," said a teenage girl standing next to her. She was terrified, trembling almost too hard to hold the shotgun in her hands, but she glared at me and chambered a round.

I told them we weren't here to take anybody. I told them we were Gifted, we were the kind of person the Splinter hunted, even though that was a little bit of a fib. Even so, Ian nodded and said I was telling the truth. That I could do things that might come in useful.

Agnes stared at Shan and I for an uncomfortably long time. Finally, she made a decision. She nodded. "Right, then." She rose from her chair, tottering and reaching for a cane leaning against the table. "Let's show them what these Splinter cunts are after."

She led Shan and I down into the basement. "It's alright, Gareth," she said. "They're here to help."

Sitting on a bed in the basement was a young man, perhaps twenty years old. He stared at us with wide, fearful eyes, and wrapped his arms across his middle. His belly swelled against his shirt. A young woman sat next to him. She stood, hands balled into fists, as though ready to fight for him.

I blinked, not sure what to think. Maybe he was trans, I thought, a pregnant transman, but that wouldn't explain why the Splinter was interested. But I was wrong. "It happens to about one in four of our lads," Agnes said. "They've got no womb, no women's parts. Still, about one in four, when they're about Gareth's age, they birth a child."

"Me wife and I have three kids. I birthed one of them," Ian said, following us downstairs.

"May I?" Shan asked, moving close to Gareth. He nodded, and Shan ran their hands over his belly. "Fascinating," they said. "She's right. There's no uterus, no ovaries, no birth canal. And yet there's a baby in there."

"This is how it's always been here," Ian said. "Hundreds of years. Thousands, maybe. As long as there's been records, there's been birthing fathers in this village. Old legend says it comes from drinking the water in the loch, but I don't know anything about that."

It all fell into place, why the Splinter would take such an interest here. Most Gifted occurrences were isolated, random, a genetic mutation surfacing seemingly out of nowhere. This was different. This was a genetically isolated population, a village full of people carrying a Gifted trait. One that would change everything we thought we knew about human reproduction. The implications sank in. Shan seemed to realize it at the same moment. Their eyes widened.

"What?" Agnes asked.

"They don't need Gareth," I explained. "If this is common among the men in your town, then they just need one of them. It doesn't have to be one who's pregnant right now. Are any of the men out there alone right now?"

Ian cursed and pelted up the stairs. "Get to MacDonnel's!" Agnes shouted after him. Shan and I followed, and we were soon joined by half a dozen very heavily armed people. We rounded a corner onto one of those windy little roads, and there we found two Splinter agents pushing a young man into a van. A shot cracked through the air, and one of the van's tires deflated. I saw Ian holding a rifle to his shoulder, advancing on the agents.

One of them grabbed the young man, wrapped an arm around his neck, and pressed a pistol to his head. "Don't come any closer!" he shouted. The agent's eyes met mine. "Wren, take another step and this kid's dead. You can slow time, but not enough to get to me before I cap him." He cocked his head so that I could see the noise-canceling earbuds he was wearing. "And don't try that compulsion shit, either."

He was right, dammit. I eyed the distance between us, and I knew I couldn't cross it in time, not if this guy was well-trained. "Can you nail him with your spines?" I asked Shan under my breath.

They shook their head. "Not without risking hitting the boy. My aim isn't that good."

Everyone stayed like that, frozen, for what felt like forever. Really it was probably only a minute or so. But then Agnes hobbled down the street. She was tiny, frail, barely able to stay upright even with her cane. But her eyes were fire, steel, pure strength. "You let that lad go," she said, and although her voice was quiet and quavery with age it carried to the agents.

"We're not going to hurt him, ma'am. We're working to ensure the safety of the public, to make sure that—"

"Oh, shut your stupid face," Agnes said. "We've protected our own for hundreds of years. We're not about to stop now. We've survived witch hunters and Jacobites and MI5, you bloody idiot. And we've never willingly given up our own. Now, you'll either hand over that boy, or you'll have to kill each and every one of us to get him away from here." She peered at the collapsed tire at the front of the van. "If you start walking out, now, alone, we'll give you a ten minute head start before we follow."

"This is the best deal you're going to get," I added. "Even if you kill every person in this village, you won't get me and Shan before we get you."

Everything froze again, but this time we all felt who held the power. We all knew which way it was going to go. The moment broke, and the agent shoved the frightened young boy away from him. The two men from the Splinter backed away, slowly, all while the people of the village watched them in contempt. In the end they turn and ran down the road, out of sight.

Ian lowered his rifle. "Well, they're gone now, but they're sure to bring more. Should we scatter?"

Shan and I looked at each other. "How long can you survive in this town? Cut off from the world?" I asked.

"Months," Agnes said. "If not years. We've always stored food and water and prepared for the worst."

I told Agnes we might have a solution. She listened to what we had to offer, and then she turned to her people and asked for a vote. A forest of hands shot into the air.

We said goodbye to everyone in the village. We wished Gareth and his girlfriend good luck. We told Agnes to take care of her people. And then Shan walked in a slow circle, all around the perimeter of the fields and lakes and moors surrounding the village. It took an entire day, hours of walking. I kept them company, made sure they paused to rest and drink water, but it was their task. They walked in a complete circle around the village, and as they walked they dropped a special mix of seeds from their palms. The plants had already started to grow as we walked, were already forming a thick tangle of bramble and thorns in a ring around this place. But it wasn't the thorns that made these plants important. No. It was the pollen they gave off, a perfume stronger than the poppy fields in the Wizard of Oz. The people in the village wouldn't feel a thing, Shan made sure of that. But anyone else, any outsiders approaching, they would collapse into a stupor the second they got too close.

By the time Shan and I drove away from that village by the loch, the entire place was hidden in tangled brush like a hedgemaze. It would take a tank to get through there, a bomb. Maybe the Splinter would go to those lengths. I don't think so. They'll be too scared of the other little traps Shan left behind, the stronger poisons dripping from some of the thorns.

Thing is, though, this place didn't really need us. We gave them an extra layer of security, a last line of defense. But they saved their own today. They stood toe to toe with the Splinter, and they didn't blink.

That's what you're up against, Iris. The little old ladies who protect the lads of their village, the people who fight for their children, the ones who close ranks around the ones they love. Those people, Iris, are the ones who will be your downfall. I just hope I'm still around to see it happen.

Chapter 23
The Citadel

Hey, um, Iris? I can't actually be 100% sure that you're listening right now, but that's a pretty high-quality camera you have in the corner of the cell up there, so it would be a shame not to use it, and I'm guessing you're probably curious about what your prisoner is doing, so, you know what, I'm just going to assume you're there and you're listening. And if Iris isn't listening, then, whoever is, you should go get her, ok? There's some stuff she's going to want to hear, and I wouldn't want you to get in trouble for not letting her know.

Ok, um, so. . . You don't know me, not really, but you probably know of me. If you listen to Wren's messages, and I know you do, you'll know me as Winry. The Last Seeker, they call me. Ok, nobody calls me that, but still. . . Uh, maybe I should just start by telling you what happened just before you captured me and threw me into a Splinter holding cell. Yeah. That's a good place to start. So. Here we go.

I imagine you're probably wondering what I was thinking, breaking into the Citadel. Fair question, definitely a fair question. Awesome name, by the way, for a headquarters. I mean, you have the Citadel and we had the Burrow, so, yeah, maybe in retrospect the outcome of that was a little obvious.

Anyway, Wren and Zachary and Shan and I have known about this place for a while. I mean, it's a fortress, it's not like it would have been easy for you to hide it. We've known about it for months, but of course we couldn't really get in. I mean, the anti-Gifted protections you have on this place, they're something else. Like really, really impressive. You probably know we tested the waters a few times, got close enough to set off the alarms. So we tried, but of course the Mosaics weren't going to get anywhere close to this place. So, yeah, kudos on that part of your system.

But then the other day I thought, hey, they have all this anti-Gifted defense set up, but what do they have for regular garden variety humans like me? Turns out, not so much. I'm not saying your defense system sucks, or anything, but. . . Yeah, actually, fuck it, I'll say it, your security people left stupid big holes in the system. And with the number of people you have coming in and out of here each day, I thought, you know, maybe it's worth a try.

I should have told Wren or Shan or somebody about this. Ok, that was dumb, I admit it, but I knew they'd try to stop me. But, look, I want you to know I wasn't focused on sabotage or assassination or anything like that. I didn't break in here to hurt you or any of your people. I just wanted to help the prisoners. I mean. . . Look, I know you and I have our differences. I know we want different things with the Mosaics and the Trumpet, but. . . I mean, I have to believe you have regrets about the way you treat Gifted people. Even if you see it as a means to an end, I don't think you're a monster. I think some of this has to keep you up at night.

Or, I don't know. Maybe I'm giving you too much credit. But, look, you've been with the Splinter a long time. You've gotten used to how this organization works. Maybe you're just too close to it, too close to see what this has turned into. So I'm going to tell you the way I saw it, what it looks like through my eyes, because I want to believe that you're capable of rethinking this.

Anyway, like I said before, your security has holes big enough to drive a truck through. So I made myself up a fake key card and ID, and I got myself a lab coat.

A side note, about the lab coat thing. I get that it seems all professional and all to have everyone in white lab coats, but come on. It makes it so much easier to blend in. And besides, people in real labs don't even wear lab coats most of the time, I mean I did most of my dissertation research in a Sandman t-shirt, so it really just makes it seem like you're trying too hard. Sorry, you know what, that part doesn't really matter, you do you, I don't care.

Where was I? Um. . . Oh, right, so I got in with my little lab coat and my safety goggles and my key card, and I went looking for the prisoners. I had a pretty good sense they'd be in this wing, based on the architectural plans, but you guys must have done some renovations at some point. The steel doors and vaults definitely weren't part of the original design.

Moving around in this place, it was like. . . I went to Catholic school when I was a kid, a really old-fashioned one, the kind where the nuns still got away with slapping you with a ruler. Kids were so scared of those nuns, they'd whisper and tiptoe past Sister Mary Eustace's office even when they were allowed to be in the halls. That's what it felt like, walking around in this place. Even people going over files and clipboards together, people sitting in the same computer pod, it's like they were afraid to talk above a whisper.

That makes me wonder, who's the Sister Mary Eustace in this situation, Iris? I'm guessing it's you. I would hate finding that out about myself. I wonder if you hate it, or like it, or if you don't care either way.

Even after I found the prisoners' wing, it took me a while to get in. My keycard didn't have high enough security clearance, so I had to find a terminal and reroute. . . Well, I'm sure your security guys figured out how I did it by now. Doesn't really matter. The point is, I eventually did it. I got into the prisoners' wing. This wing.

It feels different, being in a cell instead of being in the hall, walking past them. In a way, as scared shitless as I am right now—and, believe me, I'm really, really freaking scared, no point in pretending I'm not—I think looking into the cells from the outside was almost worse.

This is the part where I hope and pray that you listen, Iris. Really listen. Listen to what this looks like to someone who isn't used to it. Think about what you've done here.

The first was one I recognized. Amina Abdullah. We'd never met, but I've studied her file in our database. I've looked at her picture. I've wondered what she thought about her Gifts, what she was like, whether or not we'd get along if I met her in person.

When I looked through the little slot in the door, she was huddled against the far wall of a padded cell. She was almost too drugged to sit upright. Spit dripped down her chin. Her wrists and forearms were bandaged, and she looked thin. No, not thin. Emaciated.

Amina's a third-grade teacher, Iris. She has a sister, and two parents, and she swims laps twice a week at the gym. Her Gift is one of the most harmless I've ever seen. Hyper-acute sense of smell. In the past few years, she's experimented with using that sense of smell to track missing persons, find lost things. Nothing about her could ever be a threat to normals. I don't even think she'd be useful as a Mosaic tile. And still you took this real person and turned her into a drooling husk in a padded cell.

What could be worth that, Iris? I sure can't think of anything. Does it feel like you're doing the right thing, still, hearing what this looks like through my eyes?

Or how about the second one. Peter Sanderson. The padding had been stripped out of his cell, along with his mattress and all of his clothes. Anything flammable, it had been taken out of the room. Everything was coated in a layer of soot. The walls, the floor, all of Peter's body. I know his file, too. He's pyrokinetic and, sure, they can be dangerous, but his control's been just about perfect since we started monitoring him three years ago.

He's fifteen years old, Iris. Fifteen. That's why I decided to save him, and not the others. I hoped when I first went in that there would be a single wing-wide locking system that I could deactivate. I hoped I could release all of them at once. But that wasn't going to work. I could only open one cell at a time. And then, once I did that, I'd have to sneak him out.

That part turned out to be easier than I thought. Some wet wipes to get the soot off, some scrubs and a white lab coat snagged from a locker, and Peter almost looked presentable. He was too young, obviously, but some of your interns come straight out of college. They're only a couple years older than him. But his age wasn't what worried me. It was the shell shock in his eyes, the thousand-yard stare. Anyone would take one look at that kid and wonder what had happened to him.

I finally just got him a clipboard and a manila folder and got him to walk with his head bent down as though he was reading something fascinating. I walked next to him, pointing and saying nonsense about whatever was on the clipboard. That walk from the prison wing to the exit was the longest walk of my life. Every step, I was sure someone was going to sound the alarm, grab us, drag us off to the cells. But it didn't happen. Not then, anyway.

Somehow, miraculously, I got Peter out of the Citadel. No one challenged us. No one stopped us. I just got him out the door and through the parking lot and I pointed to the road and told him to walk until he reached a pay phone, and then I gave him the number he could call collect for help. Shan's number.

That could have been it. That could have been the end. But I went back in. I wanted to save one more. Just one more. I wasn't going to try for the whole wing. But just saving one, only one, it felt wrong. So I went back in, and I made it to the door of the prison wing, and that's when one of your security people grabbed me.

I just keep reminding myself that I saved Peter. He's alive and out of that cell. No matter what happens, no matter what you do to me from this point on, at least I have that.

And. . . Ok, you know what, I'm just going to stop the story there. And, Iris, I really hope you're listening, because I fudged a lot of the details I just gave you. Or outright fucking lied about some of them, if I'm being honest. But what I tell you right now is completely true, I promise. My earpiece just beeped, which is Wren telling me all systems are go. Yeah, that whole thing about me not telling Wren where I was going, that was a lie. They know exactly where I am. Also, I kinda fibbed about why I came here. I care about the prisoners, I really do, but freeing them wasn't really my goal. Except for Peter. His mother is an ally of ours, an important one, and we agreed to help her get him out.

But that wasn't really the main reason I was here. Getting Peter out of the Citadel was Phase 2. I kinda skipped over what I did right before I went into the prisoners' wing. I skipped over Phase 1. I just needed you to think that so your people would focus on checking prisoners' cells and not on some other stuff. Specifically, the servers and the firewall.

[Alarm sounds]

Now that I have your attention, I need you to listen. There's three things you need to know to understand why you need to evacuate this building immediately if you want your people to survive more than ten minutes into the future.

Point 1: Your anti-Gifted defense systems are outstanding when it comes to detecting someone with Gifted physiology approaching the building, but they aren't so great at picking up trace elements of Gifted biology. Specifically, the pollen concoction Shan made and then dusted onto my skin and hair before I brought it inside. That blurred vision and confusion you've been feeling since this stuff started circulating through the building? That's the reason none of your people noticed some important little details, like my earpiece. And the flash drive I left in one of your servers. We knew it wasn't going to be enough to get your people to let me go completely, not without setting off a whole shit-ton of alarms, but you were definitely suggestible enough to think the flash drive I handed over was the only one I brought in.

So, here's the thing, there's no point in even trying to undo the damage at this point. Your firewall's been breached for over an hour by now, and all your data's compromised, so you've taken a big hit no matter what happens from this point on.

Ok, moving on to point 2: According to a geological survey, the Citadel rests on a shelf of limestone, and far below that is a system of caverns. In case you're wondering why that's important, and I sure would be, that brings me to Point 3:

The Citadel's anti-Gifted defense system has a reliable range of about 100 yards, but Wren and Zachary's matter and energy manipulation skills are reliable up to a minimum of 300 yards.

If you have any halfway smart people back there then they're already explaining to you what that means, but I'll spell it out just in case. In about two minutes, Wren's going to pull out the small amounts of water absorbed by the limestone beneath your headquarters. Once there's no water there, any supercooling event will cause the remaining calcite to contract, causing this entire part of the surface to fall into a sinkhole. So you should really get your people out of here right away.

Zachary wasn't a big fan of warning you about this, by the way, and I don't think Wren was, either. They were in favor of just ending you right here and now. That's what they think is happening. So this is a present from me. I meant what I said earlier, Iris. I want to believe you have humanity I can reach. I want to believe you can change. Wren and Zachary and even Shan might just want you dead, but I'd rather save someone if I can.

And, in case you're wondering whether they're ok with letting me and all your Gifted prisoners go down with the ship, well, if I did the calculations correctly—and I really, really hope I did—then the collapse should shear off the northern half of the building and leave the southern half, where all the cells are, intact. We should be just fine. Pretty much. I'm pretty sure.

Goddammit, Wren, how did you talk me into this? I mean, ok, it might have been my idea but, Jesus, why didn't you tell me how dumb this was?

Oh, God. Ok, that little tremor just now was Wren removing the water, which you should be able to see forming a new stream somewhere if any of you are still stupid enough to be listening to this and you can see out a window. Ok, so now we're sixty seconds out from the supercooling stage. Come on, you got this. There you go, crash position, practiced it a hundred times. They're not going to let you get crushed. You got this, you're good. You're the Last Seeker. Yeah. I'm going to make them call me that if I survive this. I've earned that much.

Shit! [Winry screams. The rumbling gets louder, and the audio cuts out].

Chapter 24
The Trade

I'm speaking now to Iris's second in command. Winry has some thoughts on who you might be, but your name doesn't matter. Not to me, and not for the purposes of this message. Yes, Winry survived, as we knew she would. Her calculations were perfect. The building cracked exactly where she said it would, and she and the Gifted prisoners came out of it without a scratch. We'd hoped we'd be able to capture Iris in the chaos, but she escaped. At least, she escaped that time. Not today, though. And that's how I know I'm talking to her second in command, who has just assumed control of operations.

I know that because I'm looking at Iris as I say these words. She's alive. Alive, but bloodied and bruised and tied to a chair. You know why that is, why I haven't stung her with my venom or stepped aside to let Zachary rip the heat from her flesh. We have Iris, and you have Wren. So. Let's talk about a trade.

Wren's going to be furious at us for making this trade. We've discussed these scenarios before, what to do if one of us is taken. We've all of us, Winry and Zachary and Wren and I, nodded and agreed and said, yes, the world is more important, we won't risk the mission to save one of us. But I've smelled Wren's copper-penny lies as she said that, as she looked at me. And I've always known that I'll never leave her behind. So I'm choosing to make the trade, because at the moment the choice is mine to make.

I don't know where you have her, or I would have taken her back already. But I do have a sense of how you're holding her.

It came at a quiet moment, a moment none of us expected to become dangerous. We were conducting surveillance, about a week after the fall of the Citadel. I suppose you must know where and on who. Zachary and Winry had taken the first shift, and Wren and I were on our way to relieve them. We approached the car where they sat, visible in the front drivers' and passenger's seats. All seemed well, both of them looking bored and tired.

We were in the middle of the street when it happened. I smelled something above us, something like melted glass and burning cloth. Ten feet in the air hung a kind of bubble; it looked like the bubbles children make with those plastic wands and bottles of soap. Except this one smelled all wrong, and stretched three yards across. It felt as though it watched us. And then it descended, and before any of us could move, it snatched Wren off the ground.

She flailed and kicked. I felt the buzz that sizzles through the air when she uses her gifts, the ones that slow time or separate matter or teleport. I felt her try all of them. I tried my own, a hasty mixing of chemicals and pheromones that I thought might puncture the thing, weaken its structure. Zachary was there in moments, lashing out with his own gifts, floating up into the air on reduced gravity, trying to reach through the wall of the bubble. But nothing worked, and that bubble holding Wren sped away over the rooftops and into the sky, taking her away from me. I don't know what gifted person you bought or bribed to help you, but I know it wasn't something you developed yourself. That was scavenged from someone with real talents.

All of which you know, of course. But I think it's important to provide some context here, just to make it clear what you are dealing with and how little I am prepared to negotiate when I issue my demands.

Ten seconds after Wren disappeared into the sky, a bike courier pulled up on the sidewalk next to us. He probably has no idea how close he came to dying in several different supernatural ways, but we held back and the last moment. He gave Zachary an envelope, asked for a signature, and sped away. Zachary opened the envelope and found a voice recorder inside. On that voice recorder was a single recording, just a minute or so long. We all recognized my voice right away. It said, "Send me and Winry to Vienna." And then it gave a date and a time, three weeks in the past. Finally, it closed with: "Shan: you'll need to go to the Blue River Bar on Alterplatz. Knock on the door in the back and ask for Ilsa. She'll explain the rest."

By the way, second in command, I'm telling you these details because any meaningful intelligence you could have derived from them is in the past. These places are now abandoned, the people in them already known to you or have moved on. Don't waste your time looking for them. You'll understand why soon enough. Or, if you're really clever, you've pieced it together already.

Zachary looked like he wanted to kick something, as soon as that message ended. He and I have been down this road before, him able only to send me into battle instead of going himself. He has a need to be a hero and a protector, Zachary does. It's brave, in an egotistical sort of way. And I can't fault him for wanting to save Wren. But we had no time for such things, and I told him as much. "This must have worked, if we sent this message back," I told him, even though we could be sure of no such thing. Even Zachary, who can pluck things out of the future and the past, doesn't truly understand how time travel works.

"Just get her back," he said, and then he made some motion with his hands, and Winry and I stood in the biting cold of the Vienna winter.

"So," Winry asked as we made our way to the front door of the Blue River Bar. "Who do you think this Ilsa person is? Info broker? Security contractor?"

"I don't know," I replied as we moved through the crowd of drinkers and toward the back room. "But the place behind this building is a brothel." I could already hear the groans and grunts through the soundproofing layer separating the two businesses. I could already smell the sex and sweat on the air. No one else in the bar would be able to, though. They had hidden it well, whoever ran this secret place.

I readied my spines and knocked on the door. A little slot slid open at eye level, and someone spoke in German. I answered in the same language, the language of one of my tiles, that I was here to see Ilsa. The door opened, and a slender young woman led us down a hallway. This place was not your typical brothel, to say the least. The bouncer, this slight young woman instead of a beefy man, gave off the scent of a Gifted. From what I heard later, I gather that she can crush granite between her fingertips.

We saw others as we moved down the hallway, through the bar, past the rooms where clients and employees met. The workers were men, women, as well as some like me. Each and every one of them was Gifted. Some looked human at the first glance. Others would never pass in the outside world. One woman floated, cross-legged, in the air. One man had scales studding his face and torso. One person, a tall, genderless figure with a shaved head, moved by crawling, gecko-like, along the wall.

All, without exception, were beautiful, whether in human or inhuman ways. And they were surrounded by men and women who watched them with awe, with lust, with hunger. I saw diamond tennis bracelets and designer gowns and three thousand dollar suits. I saw people who run the world, or think they do, groveling at the feet of a Gifted man with two extra sets of arms. In a room off the main bar, I saw a male client strapped to a chair, his chest hair being singed off by a Gifted woman with fire-wreathed hands.

At the end of a long hallway, past the flurry of the main rooms, the bouncer knocked on a wooden door. "These people are asking for you," she said.

"Thank you, let them in."

Ilsa sat at a desk, a computer and stacks of papers in front of her. She didn't dress like a prostitute, or a brothel madam. She wore a cardigan and reading glasses, and her dark hair was pulled back into a messy ponytail. The only odd thing about her appearance were the long silk gloves she wore up to the elbow. She eyed me across the desk. "Well, if you're here for a job, you're hired," she said. Then she turned to Winry and her eyes narrowed a little. "I'm afraid we employ Gifted courtesans exclusively."

"That's not why we're here," I said. "We're here about the Splinter."

Her eyes widened. "You must be Shan. And you're the one Wren calls "Winry", if I'm not mistaken, you're working with Zachary."

"Whatever," Winry snorted. "He's working with us."

I asked Ilsa how she knew Zachary. She hesitated for a moment before answering, then folded her hands on the desk and said, "He leaked a lot of information to us back when he was with the Splinter. Some of our best leads started with him."

I asked Ilsa what she had that would be useful for making an enormous demand of the Splinter, the kind of demand that would be nearly impossible for them to consider. Ilsa watched me carefully for a moment. Then she stood. "This will only take a moment," she said. "I need to make sure you're telling the truth." She took off one of her gloves, and then she touched my hand.

Her appearance didn't change. She was still a normal-looking woman in a ponytail. But, the moment her skin touched mine, she became the most erotic creature on this Earth. I forgot about Wren entirely. It's a terrible thing to say. But all I wanted was to carry Ilsa to a bed and never leave it. It was all I could do not to rip her clothes off and have her on the desk right then and there. She was asking me a question, but it took me a minute to realize it. "What?" I asked.

"Do you work for the Splinter?" she asked again. "Are you here as a spy?"

"No. No, please I'll do anything, just let me—" I begged her.

She stepped back, and all that lust vanished just as quickly as it had appeared, so fast in made me lightheaded. I can secrete pheromones and develop substances that increase sex drive, but I can't do anything approaching what Ilsa could do with a touch. She touched Winry's arm, and asked the same question, and I watched Winry's eyes glaze over, her knees almost buckling. "Good," Ilsa said when she was done. Winry staggered and stared, wide-eyed. "You're not spies. We can work together." She sat down at her desk, reached into the neck of her blouse, and pulled out a key on a necklace chain. She used that key to open a drawer in the desk, and then she pulled out a leatherbound ledger. And then, with those silk-gloved hands, she flipped open the book to reveal columns of names, addresses, and notations. "Shan, Winry, I'd like to introduce you to some of my best clients."

It makes perfect sense, if you think about it. Of course the same people who are so fixated on superhuman gifts would include Gift fetishists among their number. I say that without judgment; there's nothing wrong with being attracted to my kind. But the people who visited this brothel, many of them treated it as a kind of menagerie. A place to sample curiosities. And visitors to a menagerie always imagine themselves as the spectators. They never imagine that the curiosities might be watching them.

The lesson here, dear listeners? Don't underestimate the people working in a brothel. Especially not Ilsa's brothel.

The ledger was full of information about prominent people from around the world. There were ambassadors and CEOs and heads of state. There were celebrities and warlords, bishops and Nobel laureates. Their habits, their preferences, secrets they had whispered in their sleep or screamed in ecstasy. There were things in that ledger that could have started wars, brought down governments, ended lives. But we weren't here for them. We were here for the Splinter leadership.

You'll have figured out the traitor by now, but just in case: his name was Lars Halvorssen. A wealthy youngest son of a financier, some distant connection to the Swedish royal family. The third cousin twice removed of one of the princesses, or something like that. Enough status and prestige to never have to work or struggle, but not enough to ever have to worry about running the family business or holding a real title. In other words, the perfect sort of person to get involved in obscure hobbies and secret societies, the perfect sort of person to become fixated on the stranger members of the human race.

I suspect that Lars got into the Splinter on the basis of his money and connections alone, and not because of any skills or knowledge he might have possessed. But he must not be entirely useless, because he worked his way into Iris's inner circle, four or five places from her position at the top. He would never lead the Splinter, not with his lack of scientific or medical background, but he had Iris's ear, and that was what interested us.

Lars made a habit of visiting Vienna once a month, ostensibly to attend board meetings for one of his family's charities. In reality, though, he suffered through those dull meetings every four weeks just so he could go from the board room to his favorite place on Earth: the Blue River Bar. The ledger showed that he had made his way through a number of the employees, but he had eventually settled on a favorite: a woman named

Vision. That wasn't her real name, just the one she used with the clients. The clients didn't expect to hear names like David or Maria or Annie. They wanted creatures who called themselves Vision, Nightwalker, Death-shroud. They wanted spandex-clad heroes and villains, archetypes rather than people with history or family or politics. Lars never thought about the possibility that Vision was also a mother and a sister and an anti-glo-balization activist who knew exactly what questions to ask a man like Lars, a man with mediocre talents and superb connections.

Vision joined us in Ilsa's office, and there we hatched a plan to take your leader.

Vision's gift is immersive illusion. She can not only make clients see a fabricated scene, she can make them smell and taste and hear and touch it. The sexual possibilities of this gift should be obvious. She never touches clients. She merely takes them into a room, listens to their fantasies, and spins beautiful dreams of things they would never be able to have in real life, not even from another Gifted.

This is what Lars saw, on his next visit to the Blue River Bar two weeks after Winry and I arrived. He went to the back room, had his drinks, eyed the men and women working the floor. And then Vision sidled up to him, even more beautiful than usual with her thick black hair and beestung lips. She ran a hand along his leg, and he was hers for the taking. They went to one of the rooms, and had a glass of wine, and he told her about the sce-nario that had occupied his fantasies lately. The details don't matter. What matters is that Vision held out her hands and conjured his fantasies into being, and he fell into them without a moment's hesitation.

Afterwards, as he lay on the bed and tried to catch his breath, the illusion seemed to fade, and he found himself back in Vision's room, or something very close to it. Perhaps he would have noticed some details wrong, the colors and textures a bit changed from before. But the wine and the fucking let him slip into a drowsy haze, and he was none the wiser.

His cell phone rang. That was odd, because he was certain he had set it to vibrate before. But it rang, and he groaned and reached to answer it. And out of the phone barked the voice of Callum, Iris's right hand. "Lars! Do you know where Iris is?"

Lars blinked and sat up. Callum was as rough and abrupt as Lars was refined, and he didn't have any respect for money or aristocracy. Lars always felt small in Callum's presence, and couldn't quite summon the confidence he usually had. "No, I don't know where she is. What's wrong?"

"What's wrong is we've got a major Mosaic asset loose in the Austrian wilderness, and I have to supervise Operation Extraction here. We need a senior officer on the ground to coordinate the teams. It's Zachary, Lars. That motherfucker's planning on wrecking the project, I can feel it."

Lars's heart started pounding. This was his chance. This was where he could prove himself at long last. "I'm in Vienna. I can be there in—"

"No, no, you stay put. You can be there for the op, but Iris needs to take charge. And you spend some time calling her, I don't have time to brief her and deal with operations here at the same time. I'm sending you the file on the asset and the teams I'm sending out, you just take charge of getting ahold of Iris and getting her out there to take care of this thing."

"I will. I'll take care of it." Lars hung up the phone, already giddy with the possibilities. Perhaps he noticed a slight shift in the room at that point; maybe he noticed that the texture of the sheets felt a bit more authentic, that the colors dimmed. But if he noticed these things at all, he quickly forgot them as he opened the mission dossier that had just been emailed to his phone, as he called up Iris and told her that he had located a major asset in Austria, that he had called in the extraction teams and was waiting for her arrival. He paused dramatically before telling her that it was Zachary, that they had him cornered. She said only that she was heading to the airport and would be there in 24 hours.

That's always been Iris's weakness. Maybe you were aware of it on some level, maybe not. She formed a far deeper attachment to Zachary than she would ever be willing to admit. Not affection. Not love. More like. . . ownership. Any other asset, maybe she would have held back. But not Zachary. Zachary, she would want to capture personally.

The ambush was easy. Lars did most of the work for us. We'd spent the last two weeks laying the groundwork for the rest. Calls to the supposed strike teams rerouted to Winry, a phone hack on Iris used to track her location, all the things we needed to follow and grab her when the time was right, all the things needed to ensure that she would go in believing she would be supported by armed strike teams, and that she would really be alone. Now we have her, and we've spent the last two weeks making sure none of your usual methods of tracking and locating her will work. Winry has anticipated all of your moves, so there's no point in fighting us. Your only option is to trade.

To be clear: I fully understand that the people I'm speaking to are prepared to let Iris die for the cause. I know you won't save her out of any attachments or personal loyalty. But consider how many secrets she has. Consider the vast array of creative methods at my disposal by which I might extract those secrets. Consider what she knows, and how that knowledge could destroy your plans. I assure you, I have no qualms about doing what I have to do to learn her secrets.

So, if you want to avoid that, you have one option and one option only. Bring Wren, alive and well, to the coordinates Winry is about to text to you. Follow the instructions to the letter. And if Wren has one scratch on her, please understand that I will burn your entire world to the ground.

Be at those coordinates. Twelve hours. There will be no negotiating.

Now get moving.

Chapter 25
The Trumpet Sounds

They weren't planning on having to trade me back. They had other plans for me, things Shan just managed to stop from happening. It meant that I survived. It also meant that I got to see other things, things I wasn't supposed to. Here's what I know now: The Mosaics have been created. They've bred. The Trumpet is on its way.

You've already heard from Shan how I was taken. One minute I was walking across the street, and the next I was suspended in the middle of a clear, shiny bubble, like Glinda the Goddamn Witch. That bubble that didn't respond to anything I tried, not slowing time, not matter manipulation, not teleporting, nothing. I could still do all of those things inside the bubble, but I couldn't make contact with the walls. They just flexed and shied away from me as I rose into the air, as it took me away. I watched Shan's face as they tried to stop me, until they disappeared from sight.

For a long time, I was up in the clouds. I couldn't tell how fast I was traveling, or how far I was going. Turns out it was a few thousand miles, which meant I must have been going faster than a jet. After a while, the bubble started to descend. I could make out a city beneath me, something hot and sunbaked and unfamiliar. Later I found out it was Madrid, but I wouldn't know that until after the trade.

The bubble carried me down toward the roof of a warehouse, something remote and removed from the main part of the city. I thought we were just going to crash into the building, but the bubble just passed through the rooftop like it was water. It carried me down through layers of pink insulation, stucco, pipes, wooden ceiling beams. I emerged into a room lit with bright blue lights. One entire wall was clear Plexiglas, and behind that were banks of computers and people bent over screens. In a kind of booth on the other side of the room was someone strapped into a chair, electrodes attached to their skull. I think they were the Gifted controlling the bubble, although they didn't really seem conscious. In the middle of the floor was a sunken area, like an emptied pool. Set into the floor of that sunken area were two metal trap doors, each about six feet across.

The people behind the Plexiglass saw me, but they weren't surprised. They'd obviously expected me to come floating down through their ceiling in a bubble, which said a lot about who they were and what they were used to. I screamed and struggled and tried lashing out with my Gifts again, but they didn't speak to me or pay that much attention. They were confident in their captured Gifted's ability to keep me imprisoned.

Time passed. I don't know how long. Maybe an hour. They kept working at their computers and work stations, kept speaking and gesturing to each other. Finally, they all gathered near the Plexiglass and watched the sunken room. It started without any warning, without a countdown or a big red warning light or anything. The metal doors in the floor just flipped open, and it started.

Keep in mind that I didn't know what they were, at the time. I was just floating, trying to understand what I saw. So I'll tell it the way I saw it, before I understood. The things that climbed out of the pits were fleshy, with muscles and soft hairless skin. They were obviously mammalian, even if I'd never seen anything like them. But their shapes were all wrong, not like any warmblooded creatures you've ever seen. There were two. One was shaped almost like a giant crab, with a flat, disc-like body and six scuttling legs. On the top of its flat body were two sets of eyes. They were compound eyes, like when you see a closeup of a fly and there are hundreds of tiny dots making up the bigger eye. Except these compound eyes were different. Each one had eight pieces instead of hundreds. Those pieces were different colors: blue, brown, green, grey. They were human.

Human eyes in blinking clusters, standing out from the back of this inhuman thing.

The other one was smaller. It had an entirely different shape. I would have taken the two creatures for completely unrelated species, except that both had that warm-looking skin stretched over an impossible, arachnid frame. This one was long-bodied, skeletal, about seven feet long with ten or twelve tiny legs. It had no eyes that I could see, compound or otherwise. It did, though, have a small orifice at the front of its long torso. When that slit opened, I saw pearl-colored human teeth.

The things crawled out of their pits and circled each other, ignoring me entirely. They came close enough to nearly bump noses, or whatever they had in place of noses. Then they hopped away from each other, and the big one raised two of its legs like it was ready to fight. They kept doing that, coming close and darting away, testing each other. Even though they never looked at me, I was more terrified than I've ever been in my short life. I didn't need to see them do anything to understand how wrong these things were. All the while, the people behind the Plexiglass just watched and took notes and checked their computer screens. Whatever this obscenity was, it was going the way they planned.

At last, the big crab-like one turned its back on the smaller one and hunkered down low on the floor. The other one, the centipede, inched closer and closer. It stopped still just before reaching the big one. Then, in a motion almost too fast for me to see, its tail whipped over its back, past its head, like a scorpion's stinger. That stinger stabbed right into the other one's back, and blood started oozing out and onto the floor. They stayed still like that, the stinger of one embedded in the back of the other. The big one quavered but didn't struggle, didn't fight back. And then, just as quickly as it had struck, the stinger pulled out, and the smaller creature tipped over onto the floor.

The big one stood and shook itself. Blood still oozed from the wound on its back, but it didn't seem like a serious puncture. It turned back around toward the crumpled centipede. The big one opened a mouth I hadn't realized was there before, a mouth that extended across the width of its entire flat body. And then, with a mouth studded with spiny teeth, it ripped and tore and gobbled the flesh of its cellmate. The entire body was gone in less than a minute, and then there was just the breathing, heaving form of the surviving creature. The moment it had eaten the last shred of flesh, it started sniffing and nosing around the pit as though to find something else.

That's when my bubble started moving. It had been on the edge of the pool before, but now it started floating toward the center, between the two open trap doors. I panicked as I moved closer, clawing at the walls of the bubble even though I knew it wouldn't do a damn bit of good. Behind the Plexiglass, someone was watching the Gifted with the electrodes on its head, tapping some handheld device and watching my progress across the pool. No one would meet my eyes.

The bubble stopped directly in front of the thing, and it seemed to notice me for the first time. I wondered if I would be able to pull the water from it between the moment when the bubble vanished and the moment it consumed me. I'd seen how fast it moved when it ate the other one, and I knew I wouldn't be fast enough, and I wouldn't have time to slow the scene. Still, I got ready.

And then, something happened. I didn't know what at the time. But someone in the control room shouted into a phone and waved his arms around, and everyone else stopped what they were doing to stare at him. They all turned to look at me, then back at the man, and then the creature circling my bubble. Whatever was happening, it was interfering with their plans.

As the people in the room argued, the creature's movements started to get more agitated. It started clawing at the floor of the pool, circling the bubble, moving faster and faster. Suddenly, it took a leap at the bubble and bounced off. I didn't feel a thing.

It went on like that for a few more minutes. The more agitated the thing in the pit got, the more frantic the people behind the glass were. One woman started crying. A man pulled at his hair and kicked a trashcan. People darted back and forth to the booth holding the Gifted controlling my life. Most of the argument seemed to be there, around my status, what would happen to me next.

I think that argument would have gone on forever, except that the creature in the pit stopped biting and scrabbling at the walls and started gnawing on its own leg. It quivered and cringed, and blood started to flow, but it kept trying to take a bite out of itself. The people in the control room panicked. One grabbed the controller for the Gifted in the booth, and someone else punched him to take it away. Finally, the guy who seemed to be in charge said something that stopped all the other activity in the room. He pointed at me, pointed at the Gifted, pointed up at the roof. And then he opened the door to the control room and jumped down into the pool. He landed, and knelt there on the tiles, and closed his eyes.

The thing was on him in seconds. It was a quick death, this sacrifice. Quick, but I don't know if it was painless. The people still in the control room screamed and cried and hid their faces. He was respected, whoever he was. As the creature devoured the rest of his body, my bubble started to rise back toward the ceiling. I passed back through the ceiling, the roof, back up above the warehouse. I just hovered there for a while, until some people came outside, got into a car, and drove away. The bubble started to move again, then. I traveled much slower this time. I didn't know it at the time, but it was keeping pace with the members of the Splinter who went to make the trade for Iris.

I should mention at this point that I wasn't really thinking straight for that hours-long journey. You've probably figured out what happened in that sunken room in a converted warehouse. You've probably put together what that was. But at that point I was just trying to get past what I'd seen, what it had felt to be sure I was about to die. Then there was the fact that I didn't know where they were taking me. I didn't know if I was about to be fed to something worse. I thought a lot about Shan as I floated through the sky. I thought about how I might never touch them again. I might never kiss them again. I hadn't told them I loved them in too long. I won't let myself make that mistake again.

I touched down in a field outside a small village. I found out later that it's part of the countryside outside Vienna. There were three figures alone in the middle of the grass. Shan and Iris. Iris was tied up, gagged, looking about as haggard as I felt. Standing across from them was one of the men from the control room. The bubble settled on the ground next to him, then dissolved, letting me fall to the ground. For a second I could barely move. The smell of fresh air and grass, and the sight of Shan, it was too much.

"This is a trade, Wren," Shan said. "Don't do anything. They have a sniper set up, aiming at you, and we've got Zachary out of sight, ready to take down Iris. We're all going to walk away from this." They reached over and undid Iris's gag. She stared right at me, her eyes wide and piercing.

"Was it successful?" she asked the man beside me, as soon as the gag was out of her mouth. She didn't seem scared, just frantic, like she needed to know something.

The man hesitated before he answered, looking over at me. "There were complications. Since we couldn't. . . use her. But it was successful."

Iris smiled then. A wide, joyful smile. I wondered what could make her so happy in a moment like that. So happy that being kidnapped and tied up didn't even matter to her.

I thought back on what I had seen in the warehouse, and I realized what most of you probably have already. I realized the one thing a member of the Splinter would be prepared to sacrifice their life for. "Those were the Mosaics," I said. "That was them mating."

It was perfect, I realized now. All the genetic advantages of Gifted people, without any of that messy intelligence or free will. Just two creatures operating on pure animal instinct. A male to impregnate and die, a female to gestate and consume until the Trumpet was born.

"They'll have already moved it," the man said, quickly, to Iris. "She won't be able to tell them where it is, even if she can find the site again."

"You were going to feed me to it," I said, and I saw Shan's face settle into a mask of cold rage.

Iris nodded, not even a little guilty. "That was the most nourishing choice, another Mosaic." She turned to the man. "I assume you found an alternative?"

He nodded. "Callum sacrificed himself. He was a good man. And we have some of the lower-value Gifteds ready for the next feeding cycle."

"Not as good as a Mosaic, but it should do," Iris said.

"Let's make this trade," Shan said, pushing Iris harder than they had to.

Iris and I passed each other as we crossed the field. Our eyes met for the briefest of moments, and then she joined her comrade and I joined Shan. I wrapped my arms around them, breathing in their fresh leafy scent. "Are you ok?" I asked.

"Yeah," they said. "Are you?"

"Yeah." And then, in a low voice, I whispered in their ear, "Where's the sniper?"

"At your five o'clock," they said, kissing me on the cheek.

I hugged Shan close to me and told them to keep low. "Iris," I said without turning to look at her.

"Yes?" she asked. I could tell from the sound of her voice that she had already started to move away. She'd already turned her back on me, the fool.

"I want the last thing you know to be that this isn't for Zachary, and it's not even for me. It's for the people you used to make those abominations I saw today."

Iris realized what was happening. "Take her-" she started to say, before I pulled the water from her body, and the body of her comrade. The sniper's bullets hit me a second later, one of them puncturing my lung and another blowing out my left kidney. It hurt like hell, but none of them went through, so Shan was safe, just like I'd planned. They pulled me to the ground until the last of the shots was fired, and we heard the tearing sound that meant Zachary had reached the sniper and taken their heat.

Shan helped me sit up. I coughed up some blood, but I managed to massage out the bullet and push the shreds of my lung back together before I passed out. It's harder, repairing internal wounds, but I've had enough practice at this point. Iris's people made the mistake of assuming that bullet I took to the leg was the only time I got shot, or the worst injury I've had to self-repair. It's not. It's not even close. There's been so many times I haven't shared in these messages, so much about my healing Gifts I didn't want the Splinter to know about. This wasn't the first time I've had an injury that would have killed a normal, and it probably won't be the last. I've reattached limbs. I've regrown most of my intestines. I've gotten third-degree burns over half my body and was up and walking the next day.

By the time Zachary reached us, my lung was back to normal and my kidney was on its way to working again. He stopped and stood over Iris's remains. I think he probably didn't know what to feel. He wanted her dead, of course, but he also wanted to be the one to do it. In the end, though, he just looked up at me and said, "Thank you."

Shan helped me up. I took their hands in my own and told them the thing I'd been dreading. I told them that I'd seen the Mosaics, that they had bred, that the female was pregnant with the Trumpet. I told them I had failed to stop it while I was there. Zachary cursed and ranted and kicked at a rock as he heard the story. Shan just listened without saying a word until I was done. Then they said, "Well. I guess we better get to work."

And we did. We got back to the new headquarters and told Winry what happened, and she got to work figuring out where that warehouse had been and where they could have moved the pregnant Mosaic. That's what we've been doing nonstop since I got back. I stopped to record this message for two reasons. First, I want the Splinter to know that their fearless leader is dead. I killed her, and I didn't even bother to look her in the eye while I did it. The second reason I'm making this message is to ask any Gifted listening for help.

I don't know how long that thing needs to gestate. The Mosaics they created were so far from human, I don't think we can assume we have nine months. We need to move fast, now. All of you Gifteds out there, all you who know about us, and about the Splinter, everyone needs to move. Everyone needs to help us find where they're keeping the mother of the Trumpet. We need. . . Wait, what is that? Is that. . . [High pitched whine in background]. Oh, no. Oh, no, no, no [screams in pain, then whining static sound comes to a halt].

[Breathing heavily] Oh, God. That was it. That was the Trumpet. I'm sorry. I'm so sorry. It's over.

Chapter 26
2033

Hey, Wren. It's your old buddy. . . Wren. You're probably pretty surprised to hear this. Actually, scratch that, I know you're surprised to hear this, because I remember being surprised to hear it. I remember where I was when I heard this. Where you are. You're sitting on the ground. You're thinking it's the end. You can't look Shan in the eye. I remember all that. But I also know you're going to make it. You're going to make it, because I did, and I lived long enough to sit down and record this for you. So. Sit back, relax, and let me tell you a little bit about the year 2033.

I'm going to start by telling you about my day so far. I woke up next to Shan, the way I have every morning for fifteen years. I got my breakfast from a fruit tree in our yard, one Shan designed for us. Then I went out and did some work for other folks in our commune. Today was an easy set of tasks. Someone's garden got flooded, so I pulled the water out and channeled it toward the river. Someone else needed to retrieve their dog after it escaped from their yard, so I slowed time long enough to catch up with it. This work is more of a barter system than for pay. Currency stops having meaning when you have people who can assemble a new computer system out of random matter, when there are people who can heal your cancer with a touch, when a beautiful dryad has created a continent of fruit trees that supply all the food we could ever need. Once the 1% couldn't control what we needed anymore, their reign ended pretty fast.

Now, we live in small communes. We owe our community our gifts, and in exchange we get access to everyone else's gifts. There were a lot of casualties of the Awakening, and capitalism is one of the ones that hasn't been missed.

After I did the work people needed, I went to visit Winry. She has a wife and a daughter, now, a beautiful little girl named Kira. The Awakening brought out a few gifts in Winry, but most of what she does these days involves making quantum computers with not much more than a glance. Figures.

There's a playground at the center of our commune. It was built by an antigravity Gifted named Jo. It floats, a giant sphere, a few feet off the ground. Playground equipment is arranged around the inside of the sphere, so kids step inside and bounce from place to place. They float instead of fall, and no one worries about their safety. Kids this age don't know how dangerous the world used to be. Winry and I watched Kira play for a while, and talked about mundane little things, gossip around the commune. For a little while, we speculated about what Kira's gifts are going to be. Most gifts don't show up until puberty, so kids Kira's age are pretty much like kids the way they used to be. This kind of speculation is pointless; gifts don't have much to do with a parents' gifts, and there's no way to tell from their interests or talents or appearance. Still, this is what people wonder about when they wonder about children. It used to be people asked whether little Jonny would be a doctor or a football player or an astronaut. Now, like Winry and I did today, we wonder whether Kira will be a pyrokinetic or an anatomorph or whether she will command the movements of hydrogen molecules. We imagine all the things she might be, whether she'll grow wings or extra limbs or whether she'll never age past the point she's at now. This probably sounds like an anxious, fearful conversation, where you are now. It's not. People have learned that most gifts are nothing to fear, and that most children adjust to their new powers with little difficulty. It's amazing, the things you get used to.

Just as I was about to leave, Winry turned to me. "You're making that message soon, aren't you? I know you make it after coming to the park with me and Kira."

I nodded and told her I thought she was right. Today's the day. And she smiled and gave me the message she remembers receiving. "Will you tell the old me something?" she asked. "Tell her it's going to be ok. Truly ok, even though where she's at then, it doesn't feel like it'll ever be ok again. Also, don't use my wife's name, or say anything about what she's like. I don't want to spoil the surprise."

So make sure you pass that message along, Wren. Tell Winry what her future self has, and that it's going to be ok. And as far as her wife goes, I don't think there's a lot of mystery once they lay eyes on each other. It's a pretty obvious first-sight kind of thing. Still, pretend you don't see right through it, it'll help preserve some of the mystery.

After that, I teleported to a commune in what used to be Buenos Aires to help out on a project for a friend you won't meet for another seven years. There aren't that many airplanes, not anymore. I still can't take anyone with me when I teleport, but there are Gifteds who can move a whole busload of people from one continent to another with a snap of their fingers. They have their days full moving people around. That's another thing that more or less came to an end with the Awakening, the nation-state. Some national borders still exist, in some places, but they're not fooling anybody.

You might be wondering what happens to the rest of the Splinter, once Iris is dead and the Trumpet sounds. I know right now you're angry enough to hope for some terrible vengeance, but the truth is that they stopped being important. Once the Trumpet sounds, there are new things to worry about, and you forget about them pretty fast. I'm guessing most of them died fast, or are already dead by the time you hear this, at least the ones in the main lab. There's rumors that the creature that was the Trumpet, the creature that made its call and awakened all these gifts, that that creature was just as monstrous as its mother. That it ripped apart not only the building but an entire city block, feeding on everything it found. I doubt many members of the Splinter in the vicinity got away from that.

Like I said, though, you'll stop thinking of them pretty soon. Other things are going to occupy your attention. I want to be clear about something, though: the fact that we have this world now doesn't mean Iris was right. It doesn't mean she was justified. Nothing could ever make up for what she did. I never would have chosen the carnage that comes right after the Trumpet sounds. I don't forgive her, and I never will. All this means is that you get past it, and survive, and that things get better eventually.

At the end of my day, I came home. Our house is inside a giant tree, every part of it grown rather than built as part of the tree's trunk. Shan and I made our dinner, and we told stories about our day, and then we listened to music being played in what used to be Portugal, broadcast by the singer's will alone. Then we climbed up to the roof and lay back and watched the sky. Oh, Wren, wait until you see what the night sky looks like now. There's no more industry, no more smog, so the stars are so much brighter. But it's more than that. There are Gifteds who don't need oxygen to survive, Gifteds who can protect their bodies against the chill of space, Gifteds who can feed off solar radiation alone. They've made homes in orbit around Earth, space stations and satellites and new moons. You can see them at night, floating above. There are some who set out for other planets. They solved all the technological problems preventing deep space travel, and built the ships, and gathered colonists. They found Gifteds who could scout out other planets from afar, who could reach out across the stars with their consciousness and find new homes there. They're flying through space like comets right now, and the people who will reach new planets will be so unlike what we were fifteen years ago.

When we'd had enough of the sky, Shan turned to me and said, "To-day's the day, isn't it?" And I said yes, and we went back into our home and I started recording this. They have their arms around me right now, as I'm speaking, and they look a little sad as they remember the time you're in, the things you're going to see.

As you listen to this, Wren, I want you to touch Shan's face. I want you to look into their eyes. If you remember nothing else, remember this: this is the face that will guide you and keep you strong and give you a reason to survive when none of the others matter. This is the face that will save you. You will come to owe them more than you'll ever be able to repay, and they never once make you feel the weight of that debt. Touch their face, and let their vines curl around your wrists, and you'll know that I'm telling the truth.

After I finish recording this message, I'll have to get up and do one more thing before returning to my spot in the bed next to Shan. You've probably got at least a general idea of what this is, since the message is there with you in 2018. You know the last thing I have to do after I record this is to give it to Zachary.

Zachary doesn't live in my community. He survives the wars to come, and in some ways he's much more at peace than when you know him. But things happen to him that make it hard for him to be around a lot of other people. Whenever I want to see him, I have to teleport to a plateau in what used to be the Utah desert. In the middle of this plateau is a circle of huts, kind of like Mongolian yurts. Different people are living in them every time I visit. Zachary is the only permanent resident. The rest are the unlucky kind of Awakened, the ones whose Gifts rage out of control, the ones who possess abilities that are more of a curse than a blessing. For every dozen or hundred people who gained the ability to fly or heal or see into the future, there is one whose consciousness comes untethered from their body, one whose dreams set their bedroom on fire, one whose skin unzips and falls to the floor when they're threatened. Zachary helps these people now, teaching and comforting and accepting them when others can't. He usually can't fix all of their problems, but they leave his monastery a little bit more whole than they were when they arrived.

Actually, I have to amend something I said before. Zachary's one of only two permanent residents. The other is Akira. That little frog is still alive, after all these years. He decided to go with Zachary when he settled down in his retreat. He has a soothing effect on the residents, like a little therapy frog. Holding him has stopped people from summoning hurricanes, opening portals to other universes, shedding their humanity entirely. He's probably saved the world more than once, to be honest. And he keeps Zachary company. Bilal's shown up there a few times, so I think Akira helps him keep an eye on things.

I'm not sure what Zachary will say when I show up tonight. I imagine him coming out of his yurt and joining me in the center of the village. I imagine him looking up at the sky, the same sky Shan and I watched earlier. I imagine him asking if tonight's the night, and I'll tell him yes. Then I imagine him looking at me and asking something like, "Are you telling her everything?" and I'll have to shake my head and admit that I'm not, even though he already knows what's on this recording. And then he and I will look at each other, and not say anything, and we'll both remember some of those things I'm not telling you. Some of the terrible days that I can't bring myself to talk about, and some of the transcendent ones I wouldn't dream of spoiling for you. He and I will remember those days, and then I'll hand over the recording, and he'll make one of those rips in time and space and drop it through. After that, we'll say goodnight, and I'll come home and crawl into bed next to Shan.

I'm telling you this, Wren, so that you have a beacon. I know how important this beacon is going to be to you. I know that you have times of agony and loss ahead, times when you think you're going to die, times when you want to. But you won't. Because you have this perfect day to look forward to, this world that you'll live to see. This will carry you, because it carried me.

Thing is, though, this world I live in now doesn't just happen. It has to be fought for. You have so many battles ahead of you, and some of them you're going to lose. You'll try to save the place that used to be Australia, and you'll fail. That land and all its people are trapped under a single continuous sheet of diamond, placed there by an enraged and power-mad new Gifted. Warlords are going to emerge and tear apart much of the East Coast of the US before you and Shan lead an army against them. Half of India is simply going to disappear, leaving a new swathe of ocean behind. Most of the population of the Scandinavian countries fell into a kind of trance just after the Trumpet sounded, and they never came out of it. Millions are going to die. But the world survives.

You're realizing something, now. You're realizing that this isn't the story you thought it was. When all this began, you thought this was a story of starcrossed lovers finding each other again. Then you found Shan, and you realized that wasn't right. Then you thought this was the story of the girl who saved the world, but it wasn't. And, for a few hours, you've been thinking that this is the story of how the world ends. It's not that, either. Right now what you're figuring out is that this is the story of a girl who helps make a new world.

But this world doesn't happen on its own, Wren. So now it's time to begin. It's time for you to get up, and dust yourself off, and dry your tears. It's time for you to take Shan by the hand, and stand shoulder to shoulder with Zachary, and help Winry through the changes racking her body and mind as we speak. It's time for you to prepare for the dangers to come. Most of all, it's time for you to picture this new world, this world you want instead of the one you live in, and fight for it.

Goodnight, Wren. This world will be waiting for you when you get here. It's waiting for you, and it's beautiful.